# THE SHADOW RUINS

BOOK TWO OF
## THE LAST DRUID TRILOGY

## GLEN L. HALL

G22 PUBLISHING

Published in 2018 by G22 Publishing



ISBN Paperback: 978-0-9957985-4-0
Ebook: 978-0-9957985-5-7



A CIP catalogue copy of this book can be found in the British Library.

Published with the help of Indie Authors World

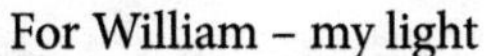

For William – my light

# BY THE SAME AUTHOR

*The Last Druid Trilogy*
The Fall

# ACKNOWLEDGEMENTS

Many people have played a part in helping me write *The Last Druid* and I am grateful for and humbled by each and every one of them.

I must begin by thanking Lizzie Henry, my editor, who has worked with me to make the book the very best it can be. Without Lizzie's guidance and patience, the book would have fallen short in so many ways. Thank you so very much.

To Jill Davidson from Purdy Lodge (they do the best breakfast in the whole of Northumberland), thank you for putting up with my writing schedule. I couldn't have done it without your love and understanding. The view of Bamburgh Castle is simply amazing.

I approached Philip Gray (http://philipgray.com/) with an idea for the front cover. He brought my imagination and words to life in the most powerful way: he produced a painting that now hangs proudly in my living room.

The book would not have seen the light of day without David Hamilton, author of *The Five Side-Effects of Kindness*. When the path to publishing got a little tricky, he threw light into the darkness.

A big thank you to Kim and Sinclair Macleod from Indie Authors World, who made everything seem so easy.

My love affair with books started with my primary school teacher, Mrs Flather, who gave me a copy of *Prince Caspian* when I was seven years old and sparked a lifelong love affair with fantasy. I wrote to her in 1997 and received a reply which I will keep forever. There have been others along the way: David

Bullock, Patricia Curran, Pat Carvis and the remarkable Richard Wilkinson. They must have known the phrase *carpe diem*, for they each taught me to 'seize the day'.

Thank you to Charlotte Ryder for all the little things that made the big things work.

To James Fowler for all his support, in particular his photography skills in making me look respectable.

And last but certainly not least, to Paddy Symons, my iconic head of English. Thank you for letting me have your stunning pictures of Northumberland and for your wonderful review of the book. Diane Arbus must have been talking about you when she said, 'A picture is a secret about a secret, the more it tells you the less you know.'

*'You will be drawn into this war whether you like it or not. When the Fall dies, nowhere will be safe for those who locked the Ruin beyond time. The only option left to us is to defend the Druids with our last breath. The time for hiding has come to an end. The time to stand together has only just begun.'*

# CONTENTS

N
W E
S
MAP OF NORTHUMBERLAND
Bamburgh
Dunstanburgh
Craster
Howick
Alnmouth
Alnwick
Birling Wood
Warkworth

# PROLOGUE

The raging storm was falling away from him, whilst all around the burning bridge hissed and whistled as it plunged into the blackness. He felt the flow leave him as he sank beneath the cold black waters of Crag Lough, barely conscious and unable to move. But still he felt the Shadow searching for him. It knew it had been cheated. He was not the last Druid. Even as the last of the burning bridge fizzled and went out, he could feel its ire, could feel its unbearable malevolence probing the waters. But soon he would be beyond its reach.

Drifting deeper into the silence, his thoughts leaving his body along with the last mouthful of air, he waited for what seemed an eternity, but still the final darkness did not come. A faint light was flickering through the mirk.

Flowing through the darkness, the light was calling him back. Then a hand reached out for his. A pale and beautiful woman was there, her fiery locks flowing behind her as flaming strands. The glimmer seemed to be coming from her and in the faint light he could see others moving through the darkness. Who they were he couldn't tell, for the Faerie was taking him upwards and the pain he had felt was spreading once again across his body. A feeling of suffocation was thick around his throat, and water was rushing into his mouth, stinging his lungs. Then the horror on the bridge flooded his mind and he felt its power engulf him, shattering his body and mind. The Shadow had broken him.

They erupted through water to air. Arms were wrapped around him and he was being carried, for his body and mind were slipping away.

The light of the flow was all but extinguished.

# I

## THE MOUTH OF THE ALN

The faint autumn dawn began to break across the Northumberland hills. But it could neither lift their spirits nor dull their exhaustion. Behind them the orchard was lost in the seemingly impenetrable sweep of Birling Wood, whilst ahead they could now see the river Aln curving down from the hills before being lost to the sea.

Sam walked with his head down whilst the events of the last six days spiralled through his thoughts. He wanted to put as much distance as possible between himself and the horde that had come streaming out of the wood into the trap set by the Forest Reivers.

To his right Eagan walked in silence, his dark eyes fathomless and empty against his pale skin. Sam shot a quick look at him. What tale did he have to tell? He'd only just been brought back from the edge of death by Oscar's shadowy protector Culluhin. Now he was striding on grimly, lost in his own thoughts.

'*Sam!* Can't we stop for a moment?'

Sam turned to his left and looked into Emily's face. Her dark hair was matted, her eyes puffy. How beautiful she was, even now. And how exhausted.

'No – we have to go on.'

'I'm so tired…'

'I know. So am I.'

Emily took his arm and leaned into him as they walked on. Ahead of them, framed by the breaking dawn, Eagan was walking with his head bent almost to his chest.

'I'm sorry, Emily,' Sam whispered, 'but we have to get away from the wood.'

As she pressed his arm, too tired to reply, guilt washed over him. She'd been spending a peaceful summer in her uncle's bookshop until he'd arrived with his Oxford professors in tow and a mysterious Shadow at his heels. And now he knew it had never been coming for him at all. It had been coming for her, and he'd led it straight to her. The thought sent a ripple of pain through him. He didn't know why anyone should be seeking her, but obviously they were. The shapeshifting Grim-were and its crow horde had pursued her from the bookshop to Birling Wood. *I seek the girl.* He shuddered as he remembered.

Now the crow-men were battling the Forest Reivers in the wood, but where was the Shadow? Memories of the night before burned through his mind – Oscar and Culluhin on the bridge in the Garden of Druids, fiery arms outstretched, holding back the towering blackness… What had Culluhin meant by saying 'Our trap is sprung?' Had they trapped the Shadow in Oxford or was it free? The thought of it being close behind him made his blood run cold. What if it caught them here, out in the open, without Oscar and Culluhin to protect them?

There were so many unanswered questions that Sam's mind felt heavy with the weight of them all. No wonder the Keepers had been troubled by the paradox that had been created. He reached into his back pocket and felt the reassuring creases of the tattered envelope containing their letter to him. He had almost got used to the way it kept changing – at least someone was helping him, even if they were writing from the past, and events in the present were out of control to say the least.

Time itself seemed to have come adrift. If Oscar had really died several years earlier, then how had he met him in Oxford? And when he had met him again in the Garden of Druids, why had he acted as if they had never met at all? Was the garden part of the Way that Professor Stuckley had talked of, the in-between places where time could not reach? But now Sam's legs were becoming heavier, as if his swirling thoughts were sucking the last of the energy out of them, and he knew he just had to focus on putting one foot in front of the other.

And yet, looking at the pale and silent Eagan just ahead, still he couldn't prevent his thoughts from running on. The Grimwere had taken the form of Eagan's father, Jarl. Did that mean Jarl was the traitor that Oscar had spoken of? He shuddered, remembering Eagan's wild temper. Who knew how he might cope with that possibility?

Then he realised Eagan was waiting for him.

They had come to the brow of a hill. A mile to the northwest they could clearly see the quaint houses of Alnmouth nestling on the edge of the picture postcard estuary, all bathed in the early morning glow. Though Sam's bones ached and the darkness of the last few hours hung like shackles around his body, the view seemed to anchor his whirling thoughts.

As they began descending the hill, though, he couldn't help but take one last look over his shoulder. Back the way they had come, Birling Wood was dark and foreboding, and for a moment in Sam's tired mind, a twisting shadow seemed to emerge from it and reach out long fingers for him, making him stumble.

'Are you okay?' Emily croaked, her throat dry and parched.

'I'm not sure.'

Bretta's face flashed through his mind and he remembered the chill voices of the horde.

'Are we doing the right thing? Should we have left the Forest Reivers? What if the crow-men overrun them?'

Eagan stopped and lifted his head. His eyes were full of dark musings.

Emily turned to him. 'I know,' she said, 'that we did leave your friends, Eagan. But we had to – I mean, they literally got us away from the battle before it started. Well, *almost* before it started...'

She tailed off, remembering the awkward gait and hideous calls of the crow-men. How could you stand and fight such creatures? Where would such courage come from? She had been frozen with fear, almost unable to move. Then there had been the thing that had looked like her uncle and had turned into a feathered monster. How could Sam have spoken to it, fought with it? What had happened? There had been a light in his hands that had danced with each unknown word, each sound that she could still feel vibrating through her.

'I'm just wondering,' Sam was saying now, 'whether Alnmouth is going to be any safer than Warkworth.'

'Probably not, but where else is there to go?' Eagan's voice was full of weariness. 'We can't go back, and we can't just stumble around the Northumberland hills not knowing what we're doing. At least let's wait in Alnmouth until my father or Brennus and Drust catch up, and then we can hear their news and decide what our next move should be.'

They stood still for a moment, gazing at one another, then Sam nodded. It seemed a logical plan, he thought, and he wasn't about to upset Eagan, not after what he'd seen of him at the old school house.

But now Eagan was showing his engaging side. 'Once we're out of this morning chill,' he said, with a flicker of a smile, 'you can tell me what happened whilst I was busy being poisoned.'

Sam felt guilty as he remembered Eagan's wounds. But Emily was thinking ahead.

'We hardly know anyone in Alnmouth,' she said.

Eagan turned on his heel. 'Yes, we do. Now come on, I don't think we should stay in view of the wood. We should get across the bridge and out of sight.'

* * * * * *

They came down from the hill and crossed a muddy field before climbing over a short fence and finding themselves on a road bridge that spanned the meandering estuary. On either side of the road were hedges that had already felt the long arms of autumn, whilst to the west the river came snaking through the flat land in several rivulets and to the east it opened out into a gaping estuary.

They entered the village quietly, as the pale autumn light washed over its rooftops and chimneys. The sky was a deep blue streaked with wispy clouds. It was as if the night had never been, as if the battle in the wood had never taken place.

The village was still asleep and the roads empty. Eagan led them to the main street, cutting a path through houses and cottages of all shapes and sizes. The village had once been a sea port; its fortunes had waxed and waned over the years, and it was now the gateway to the Northumberland coastal route and full of small hotels and B&Bs brimming with holiday-makers. Its beaches stretched both south and north as far as the eye could see, and as he stumbled along after Eagan, Sam remembered the first time he had ventured here on holiday with his mum. They had stayed at the Dandelion, overlooking sloping sand dunes. The village had become a favourite holiday destination and Sam had once walked for two days, following the Aln from its mouth to its source high in the Cheviots.

Now he was passing the Red Lion, an eighteenth-century coaching inn that was at the very heart of the village. It reminded him of the Eagle and Child in Oxford. He still found it difficult to accept the last seven days. But what had happened at the Eagle and Child had been spellbinding, if not altogether fantastical. If he was right, then he had spoken to three of the best-known and most influential Inklings, the group of Oxford scholars who would read their work to each other there and talk into the early hours of the morning. They were said to have created Cherwell College, the mysterious college he had attended in Oxford. How wished he was back there. The syllabus had been bizarre – quantum metaphysics, quantum uncertainty and Professor Stuckley's now infamous lecture where light existed at both the end and the beginning of the universe, as light, according the professor, did not need time to exist. Sam had been fascinated by it all. If only he was wrestling with those problems now! Life at Cherwell College had brought a lot to ponder, but life now was a scattered jigsaw whose pieces kept changing.

He could feel Emily holding on to him again, almost a dead-weight he was dragging along. Every now and again she would trip and he would have to use the last vestiges of his strength to keep her from falling. Stumbling along in a stupor, he was brought up sharply when he found himself bumping into Eagan, who had come to a sudden stop. Without fully realising it, they had walked the length of the village high street and had come to a place that looked down onto the mouth of the Aln, with its twisting estuary flowing from the west.

The noise of Eagan knocking on a large blue door snapped Sam out of his daze. They were in front of an elegant Georgian house. As Eagan rattled the door knocker again, the noise seemed to ring out across the quiet village. When they finally heard bolts being slid back one by one, for a split-second Sam was back at his own front door in Gosforth, but this time the door swung open to reveal not his anxious mother, but an old lady with glasses and white hair. She was leaning on a walking stick, but a warm and welcoming smile was spreading across her face.

'Eagan, my dear child – a most unexpected pleasure!'

She glanced at Sam and he felt her calm gaze sweep through him.

'Your friends look tired. Bring them inside.'

She turned slowly and led them into a grand hallway with doors leading off to the right and left.

Sam was glad of the warmth that wrapped itself around him. How cold the night had been.

Emily smiled up at him, her face beginning to flush with the heat.

At the end of the hallway was a large kitchen with an open fire. The old lady led them through the cosy room and up several steps into an orangery overlooking the estuary.

Sam couldn't take his eyes from the breathtaking vista. His gaze was drawn to the far horizon, where Birling Wood was a black rim on the edge of the world, almost like the rim of a black hole ready to swallow the autumn light. And here they were in full view of it, with only a river and a short harbour wall between them and the murderous horde.

'Eagan, put the kettle on,' said the old lady, as she seated herself in a high-backed chair.

Eagan disappeared back into the kitchen and she turned to Emily.

'My poor child – you look as though you've spent the night in the open.'

'In a way I have,' answered Emily.

'Blankets, Eagan,' called the old woman firmly, with a kind smile in Emily's direction.

Eagan soon reappeared, carrying two thick woollen blankets. He handed one to Sam and the second to Emily. The old lady pushed herself up from her chair and wrapped Emily up.

It wasn't long before they were sipping tea from delicate cups and eating breakfast. The old woman busied herself making sure the toast and jam kept flowing, and Sam realised how hungry he was. The last meal he and Emily had eaten had been the light supper they'd had at the old school house.

Eagan, however, remained pale and ate little. His face was drawn and his eyes seemed not to reflect the sunlight pouring through the large windows. He no longer looked like the flamboyant young man they had met rowing down the river Coquet only the morning before.

The village was beginning to stir as Sam and Emily finally finished eating. The old woman sat down on the edge of her chair, resting both hands on her walking stick, her white hair shimmering in the morning sun, and smiled at them.

'I can see you have struggled greatly during the night,' she said. Then she turned to Eagan, who was sitting next to her, and her face became troubled. 'I couldn't sleep last night and spent most of it in this chair watching the waves breaking until first light. I didn't expect dawn to bring me such unexpected company. But by the look of you, Eagan, I know now why my sleep was broken. So tell me your friends' names.'

'I'm sorry, Alice.' Eagan seemed to wake from a stupor. 'You've heard of my cousin Emily Pauperhaugh, and this is her friend Sam Wood.'

For a second surprise and amusement flit across the old lady's face, but then she was smiling again and saying, 'Well, it's a real pleasure to meet you both, Sam and Emily. My name's Alice and you are very welcome in my home. Why don't you rest and regain your strength for a while? Then we can have a late lunch together and you can tell me all that has happened to you.'

Sam felt the woman's words take the last of his strength. He was ready to sleep then and there, but Emily was sitting up.

'Can I ask you a question?'

Alice nodded. 'Of course.'

'I think I've been here before, a long time ago – is that right?'

'Yes. You used to come here when you were a small child, with your mother and uncle. I am pleased you remember.' She smiled and sat back in her chair.

'Yes, of course,' Emily said slowly. 'Uncle Jarl came here with me – I must have only been about two or three when we stopped coming. I never understood why.'

'My child, I'm just glad that you are here now and that we can spend a little time together.'

Alice smiled at Emily, then turned back to Eagan, and Sam couldn't help but notice her give him a little wink.

'Take them to the third floor, Eagan. Let them shower and enjoy their sleep.'

Eagan helped Emily up and took the blanket from her.

As Sam stood up, he grimaced at the ache in his legs. He felt as if he had spent all night running. Then he realised he had.. He followed Eagan and Emily out of the garden room, through the kitchen, with its welcoming fire, and out into the large Georgian hallway.

Eagan took them up two flights of stairs onto a landing with the most beautiful ornate banister. There was a large window at one end of the corridor and then a third staircase. Sam noticed this was in a more recent style than the rest of the house. Perhaps this floor had been added on. But this was soon forgotten as Eagan reached a thick oak door with a pattern that was only too familiar.

Emily had seen it too and her hand reached out for Sam's.

Eagan pushed the door open and a stale smell hit their nostrils. They found themselves in a room that looked completely different from the rest of the house. Most of the roof had been replaced by a glass dome, and a beautifully crafted oak floor had several steps in the centre leading down to a circular table.

Even before Sam had fully set foot in the room, he knew where he had seen this before.

'It's like the reading room in the bookshop!' said Emily, amazed.

If the last week had taught Sam anything, it was to expect the unexpected. And yet here he was again, stunned by what lay before him. He was yet to understand who the old lady was, but now he knew why Eagan had brought them here.

As he moved further into the room, he saw that there were several large windows that he guessed gave views across Alnmouth to the south, west and east, and that the round table in the middle of the room had several seats stationed around it. And, just like the one in the Seven Stories, it had a map spread across it.

The hair on the back of Sam's neck began to prickle. Somewhere there was more, he knew it. He could feel its presence before he turned and saw it – another tapestry. Only whereas the one in the bookshop had displayed a map, this one showed five men standing outside the little boathouse on the northern bank of the estuary with their arms round each other. Smiling out into the room were Oscar, Jack, Ronald, Charles and a red-headed man he didn't know.

'It's all true – Oscar was really an Inkling!'

He felt overcome by a flood of emotion, remembering Oscar facing the Shadow and the black fire engulfing him.

'Well, I did tell you that,' said Eagan a little impatiently. 'When he was here in the fifties, the others would often come here to speak to him. They would spend many a happy hour in the Red Lion before walking the coastal route all the way to Holy Island. That tapestry's based on a photo of them taken in 1960.'

'Really…?' Sam found himself gazing at the men's faces. 'Sorry, Eagan, it's all so weird. The more I think about it, the less it makes sense. You told me Oscar was dead, too, but last night in the orchard we met him. And it *was* him, this Oscar – well, a slightly older Oscar.'

'But Oscar *is* dead.'

'He wasn't dead last night,' said Emily flatly. 'I saw him with my own eyes. In fact he probably saved your life, Eagan.'

'Oh, I don't know!' Eagan turned away. 'I'm too tired to argue about it now.'

He walked a short distance to a row of bookcases and ran his hand along one side of the smooth wood. The bookcase swung inwards, just like the one in Sam's room in the Fellows' House, to reveal a narrow corridor.

Eagan walked down it, calling over his shoulder, 'Come this way!'

Emily was beginning to look worried, but Sam gave her an encouraging smile and stepped into the corridor after Eagan. He found it led to a small room with a single window, two single beds and another door.

Eagan was standing in the centre of the room. 'Why don't you get some sleep?' he said. He nodded towards the other door. 'There's a shower through there. I'll come and get you when lunch is ready.'

'Hang on – aren't you going to tell us what's going on?' asked Emily suspiciously. 'I'm guessing there's a reason you've brought us here. Look at that room next door – it's just like the reading room.'

'I'm sorry, Emily,' Eagan yawned. 'I will tell you, but I need some rest myself first. We've all been through the wars a bit.'

'Well, that's true!'

Emily sat down on one of the beds, then lay down and seemed to fall asleep as soon as her head touched the pillow.

Eagan turned to Sam. 'Look, I don't know how long we can stay here. Why don't you get some rest too? Sleep might be difficult to come by over the next few days.'

He left the room.

Sam rubbed a tired hand across his face. That reminder was the last thing he needed to hear. He crossed the small room to stand in front of the narrow window, whilst behind him Emily began to snore gently. They were still effectively on the run. And there was still that immovable paradox that he couldn't see past. If the Shadow was back in Oxford, where it had all begun, shouldn't there be an endless loop of it following him from Oxford to the Garden of Druids and then going back again? Oscar hadn't stopped the Shadow – in many respects Oscar had in fact led it to him. But then again hadn't he led it to Oscar? And round and round it went.

Sam sighed and leaned forwards, pressing his hot forehead against the glass. Looking out, he could see the black rim on the horizon that was Birling Wood. His thoughts again turned to the Forest Reivers. If they had lost the battle, then what? Would the horde come pouring out of the wood? He half expected to see crows scouting for them already, but the skies were empty and the beach spotted only with dog walkers. Sam scrutinised them, but they all looked innocent enough. Perhaps he and Emily were safe here after all. At least for now. And he was too tired to think straight. Exhaustion made the last few days feel like a dream. If the Shadow found him, he knew he didn't have the strength to run.

Sliding down the window, he could see small boats bobbing up and down as the tide began to move against the river's flow and the estuary widened. Then his breathing became heavier, and the autumn sun glistening off the calm waters was the last thing he remembered before he fell asleep.

* * * * * *

Eagan stopped in front of the tapestry, rocking back on his heels for a moment, still feeling weak from the crow-men's poison. He gazed up at the smiling men. What had they written in their letter to Sam? '*We must tell you that Brennus and Drust are journeying to the Dead Water and are pursued relentlessly by our enemy. You cannot expect them to return to you.*'

He knew that could be true. As the crow-men's poison had flowed through his veins, he had dreamed a remarkable dream. At least he preferred to think of it that way, though at moments he believed it to be real. Someone had carried him to a dark place, a place where indistinct figures were reaching out for him, trying to pull him down into cold black waters, into a ghostly sea of the dead. He had felt their hands on him and then he had been falling into their embrace … and had surfaced to find the old man from the Blindburn waiting for him, sitting on the shore.

This time he had not been alone – Brennus had been there. He had been silent, watching, as the old man had placed a gentle and worn hand on Eagan's head. Then the dream had quickly turned into a nightmare. Eagan had found his blood turning to fire, burning open his wounds and then flowing from him, along with the poison, into the still waters.

From those waters, as he had burned there in agony, a woman had arisen, untouched by the grasping hands of the dead. She was carrying an unconscious figure who looked like Drust, but at that moment the old man had withdrawn his hand and Eagan could remember no more.

If the place had been the Dead Water, was Brennus was alive or dead? Was Drust?

How he wished they had told him more. They had been his mentors, but he hadn't even known they were in Oxford, masquerading as professors and protecting Sam. Why Sam? He didn't understand it. Up until this last year Sam had simply been Emily's friend from Gosforth. He had grown big and strong, but was awkward around people; you really had to get to know him before he opened up. Why the sudden interest in him from Brennus, Drust and his own father? But it was obvious that Sam was right in the middle of everything that was going on and that he could use the flow.

And then there was Emily. Half a Reign and half a Pauperhaugh. How his aunt could have married a Pauperhaugh was anyone's guess, Eagan thought. He was fond of his cousin, but she was difficult. Defiant to the last word, and she'd had plenty of them. She was bright and kind and yet stubborn in the same breath. She was full of contradictions, but what else could be expected from combining the blood of two of the oldest families in Northumberland? Feuding families at that. Most people had said it wouldn't last, and after twenty years they had been proven right. Emily's parents were divorcing and both were more interested in trying to gain the upper hand than in the collateral damage or the welfare of their daughter. That was partly why Emily had spent most of the summer with his father, helping to manage the bookshop. He had said she could no longer bear the relentless battle for loyalty.

Eagan sighed. What was he to do with this pair? How could he keep them safe when he didn't really know why they were being hunted? He had brought them to Oscar's home because he really had no idea where else to go. He had visited this place several times with his father over the years. He had only been young when one day he had realised that Oscar was gone and wouldn't be coming back, and then it had been a while, perhaps a few years, before Jarl had been able to bring himself to visit again, but Alice had always made them feel very welcome. They had of course brought her to the old school house and she had visited the bookshop once or twice. But these days she very rarely ventured out – perhaps a short walk to the edge of the estuary or the post office, but nothing more.

The night after being released from prison after the Morcant incident Eagan had come here seeking solace and had found it in a warm meal and a soft bed. He didn't like the idea of leaving now for the wilds of Northumberland, not with the stories he'd heard from the Forest Reivers. There were things moving in the borderland he'd rather not meet, especially since he'd lost his long knives when the crow-men had attacked him. He resolved to borrow some from Alice's kitchen. What then? He could always take refuge in the Hoods' home at Bamburgh, but what if Brennus and Drust weren't coming back?

His thoughts had just taken him in a giant circle. He left them hanging in the sunlit room and closed the door behind him.

* * * * * *

Sam opened his eyes. He was on top of one of the beds, still fully clothed, but somehow with a pillow under his head. When he turned to look at Emily, he realised she was awake and watching him. Her eyes were sparkling, her cheeks were glowing and damp hair was plastered around her face. When she saw he was awake, she smiled at him.

'Have you had a shower?' he asked. 'You look—'

'What? Clean?'

'Well, now you mention it, yes!' Sam laughed.

As Emily joined in, it was almost as though they'd woken from a bad dream and the events of the last six days had never really happened.

'How long have we slept?' asked Sam, slowly pushing himself up into a sitting position.

'I don't know how long, but I think that was the best sleep I've ever had. I feel really rested.'

'So do I. My headache's completely gone. My legs and back – not a thing!' Sam grinned. 'Do you think we can just go home now?'

'What?!'

For a split-second Emily almost smiled, but her expression quickly changed. Looking away from him, she frowned and started twisting her wet hair through her fingers.

'I don't know. I don't think…' She stopped speaking and looked back at Sam. 'Do you remember what happened when we entered the orchard?'

'What – the leafless trees and the cold weather…?'

'No. Well, yes, but not just that.'

She shuffled to the end of her bed and sat hunched over, remembering.

'You were speaking a language I couldn't understand,' she said slowly. 'There was a light coming from your left hand – a light which moved with your voice. It lit up your face and for a moment I didn't even recognise you. You looked so different…' She shivered. 'When that creature dropped Eagan, I didn't know who I was more frightened of, you or it.'

Sam felt his face flush. 'I'm sorry,' he mumbled. He remembered there had been light, colour and voices, but he couldn't remember speaking, or any light coming from his hand.

'Even though I must have been standing twenty feet from you,' Emily continued, 'I could somehow feel your words as vibrations in the air, or in my head, or both.'

She looked up, clearly expecting an explanation, but Sam was silent.

'I think I saw it in your garden, too, the night the Grim-were came. Or rather, I didn't see it, but I felt it. I was behind you, on the other side of the lawn, but I could feel tingling across my face – the same feeling I got when we met Oscar. It was as if the light was reacting to your words.'

'A tingling?' asked Sam. He moved to the edge of his bed, opposite Emily. 'When I met the Keepers at the Eagle and Child, I could feel an electricity. And then when I saw Oscar and the Shadow in the tapestry at the Seven Stories, I felt it again.'

In the small bedroom they looked at each other across a sea of swirling dust caught in a cascade of autumn sun.

'At your house,' Emily went on, 'there could have been someone standing there with you as well, or it could have been a reflection from the light.'

Sam nodded. 'The Fall.'

They were both silent for a moment, lost in their own thoughts.

Then Emily said, 'Oscar told you she was dying… The old man told you as well. That's why these things are getting into this world – she's the barrier that's been keeping them back.'

'Yes.' Sam suddenly felt tears coming into his eyes. He looked away.

Emily frowned, trying to piece it all together. 'But didn't Oscar tell you what needs to be done about it? Didn't he show you that circle with the crumbling statues?'

'No, he didn't show me it exactly, but I came across it after meeting him – when he disappeared in the Fellows' Garden and I was looking for him. But he did say the Circle was broken.'

'Yes, Sam,' said Emily impatiently, 'and didn't he say only the bloodline of the Druids could mend it?'

'Er…'

'Listen, Sam,' Emily took a deep breath and stared straight into his eyes, 'you are related to that bloodline.'

'Oh, I don't know—'

'You don't know anything about your father, right? Or not much? That's *why*. And it's why they've been protecting you. It's why Brennus and Drust have been parading as professors – to keep an eye on you. They made up an entire college to keep you close to them! Think, Sam, when Oscar showed us the stone circle, you said you'd already seen it back in Oxford. *You* – it all revolves around you. Come on, Sam, help me out a little – don't you think it could be true?'

Sam looked away. It was a conclusion that should have pleased him, made him feel special, but it didn't. He didn't believe it. Not after meeting the Grim-were.

'I'm not sure,' he muttered.

'Not sure? I don't understand you at all!' Emily complained. 'When you told me about the Shadow back in Gosforth, I didn't believe you, but now the whole thing's making sense. In fact, Oscar had already given you the answers. That's why he appeared in Oxford in the first place. And why he protected you in the Garden of Druids – why he sent the Shadow back.'

A shudder ran through Sam at the mention of the Shadow. He kept his face turned away from Emily, unable to look her in the eye. When Oscar had sent the Shadow back, he hadn't been protecting him, but *her*. Somehow the Shadow had known he would lead it to her. That's why it had let him get away from the Fellows' House and let him live at the gates of Magdalen.

Looking back, he could see he had played his part to perfection, going from Oxford to Gosforth and then using the Way-curve in the bookshop. After that the crow-men had attacked and later that night the Grim-were had come for her. It all made sense. In the orchard the Grim-were had almost taken her, and the Shadow hadn't been far behind… He shuddered.

What could he say? How could he tell Emily she was in mortal danger? She was still watching him for any signs that what she was saying would click. He couldn't tell her, not yet, but he could give her a hint.

'What if they are wrong?' he said, standing and moving towards the window to avoid her burning gaze. 'What if the bloodline doesn't run through me? What if they have bet on the wrong horse?'

He leaned his head on the glass once more. Outside, the road leading down to the beach was busy with people coming and going. Further south, that thin black border was all that could be seen of Birling Wood.

'Sam! How can you doubt it? A lot of people have gone to a lot of trouble for you,' Emily retorted. 'Remember what the letter said – there's a chance Brennus and Drust may not come back.'

Sam kept his face turned towards the window.

'You said that letter could have been written by anyone. Including the traitor. You said we couldn't rely on anything in it.'

'Well, okay.' Emily drew breath. 'But after last night I think anything's possible. I watched you command light with a language that sounded more like thunder than words. I felt its heat. I saw you save Oscar.'

'No, Emily!' Sam turned back to her. This was too much. 'I didn't—'

She cut him off with a wave of her hand.

'You held back the night! The Shadow! You stopped it! Oscar would have been swept from the bridge if not for you. Don't you remember? When he fell, you stood over him. You faced the Shadow and it didn't touch you.'

'I stopped the Shadow?' Sam couldn't believe it. 'No, Emily, you've got it wrong. I can't remember leaving your side. I was terrified.'

Standing there, totally bewildered, he looked so lost that Emily's exasperation melted into sympathy. With an awkward half-smile, she stood up and put her arms round him.

'Believe me,' she whispered, 'you saved him. The Shadow burned him, didn't it, but left you untouched.'

She pulled back enough to look up at him and give him a smile.

Sam shook his head. 'I just remember seeing Oscar standing on the bridge and then Culluhin joining him. I don't remember going to his aid. I was struck rigid with fear – unable to move.'

'You did move – you put out your hand and shielded Oscar until he regained his feet. Without you, I hate to think what would have happened. I know you're scared, but I don't think you're defence-less – not at all. You threw down the Grim-were at the orchard, didn't you?'

'Oh, *I* don't know. I don't know anything,' Sam said wearily.

With the afternoon sun at his back and Emily's body against his, he closed his eyes and tried to block the memory of Oscar's burning arms raised against the swirling darkness. He really just wanted to go home. And then back to his studies in Oxford. And then have Emily visit him.

But Emily stepped back once more and fixed her dark eyes on his.

'I don't know what's happening either,' she said, 'but I think you have to accept you are key to stopping it.'

* * * * * *

When they found Eagan and Alice, they were in the orangery with its staggering views across the estuary. Eagan was dressed in an old woollen jumper and a pair of corduroy trousers, and his long dark hair was still damp. He was gazing out of the window whilst Alice was sitting knitting, her walking stick resting against a small table. When she saw Sam and Emily, she put her knitting down and gave them a warm smile.

'You look much better – clean and fresh! I'll find you a change of clothes later. But come along now, sit yourselves down at the table and have something to eat.'

No sooner had they sat down than Eagan began placing quiche, potatoes and a selection of salads in front of them. Sam could feel his mouth begin to water. Even though they had already eaten a good breakfast, he was starving. Emily must have felt the same. She was already shovelling food onto her plate and straight into her mouth. When Eagan had poured the tea, they ate almost in silence. The only sounds were the excited voices of children pass-ing by outside on their way to the beach.

Alice sipped her tea and smiled at Sam with a warmth that was both reassuring and uplifting. Sam felt he needed her welcoming presence. Emily's revelation upstairs had complicated things. How could he begin to explain to her that the Shadow and the Grim-were had been coming for her, when she was convinced not only that they were after him, but that he had special powers? He sighed and helped himself to another piece of quiche.

When they had finished their lunch and had washed the dishes and drunk the last of their tea, it was Alice who broke the silence.

'I have to tell you, Sam, that you do remind me of your father. He had blue eyes and red hair too.'

'I didn't know him,' stumbled Sam.

'No, I know. But he would have been very pleased to see you here.'

'Why?'

Alice shifted a little in her chair. 'Alnmouth was one of his favourite places.'

'Really?'

'Oscar's too, of course.'

'Oscar?' Emily broke in. 'Can you tell us if he's really dead?'

'I am afraid he is,' smiled Alice. 'He died fifteen years ago. I am his widow.'

Emily found herself blushing. 'Sorry,' she mumbled.

Eagan glared at her, but Alice hadn't taken offence. 'Oscar was a kind and generous man,' she explained, 'and a cultured one too. He was part of a group which journeyed the length and breadth of the borderland, from the Solway Firth in the west to Bamburgh in the east. He was part of a literary circle that had its roots in Edinburgh, Newcastle and Oxford. They would meet at the Eagle and Child in Oxford, the Seven Stories in Newcastle and the Green Dragon in Edinburgh's New Town.'

'I met some of them in Oxford last week,' interrupted Sam. 'It was really strange...'

Alice showed no surprise at this. 'I heard you in the Way-curve,' she said calmly.

Eagan put down his cup with a thud. 'What? You used the Way-curve to speak to the past? Brennus is the only one who can do that now!'

Sam, too, was staggered by the old lady's words, but for a different reason. 'They all link up? You can listen in?'

Alice smiled. 'What do you think?' Then she looked down. 'Yes, we can listen in, though, as Eagan says, only Brennus can actually make the connection to the past now.'

'I don't mean to be rude,' said Sam, 'but that can't be right, because I made a connection with Oscar at the Seven Stories.'

'*Really*?' Eagan was looking at him curiously.

For a moment Alice was too, but she just smiled and said, 'Oscar – ah yes. Well, of course he used the Way-curves as well.'

'I don't understand how it works at all,' Sam confessed. 'But I met Oscar in person, you know – earlier on, in Oxford. He gave me two letters that this literary circle had given him. One was for me and one was for Professor Stuckley – Brennus, I mean.'

His words hung in the air like the rays of sunlight from the windows. Alice edged forwards on her chair and reached for her stick.

'Can I see your letter? I remember Oscar telling me that Ronald and Jack had written two letters and told him not to touch them. All these years, never knowing what was in those letters – I've often thought of their significance. Oscar never broke his silence, and here we are now – these are strange days indeed. I would love to see your letter.'

'It keeps changing. I can't say what's in it now.' Sam reached into his back pocket and withdrew what was now a brittle, yellowed and battered envelope. He placed it on the table.

'I remember that very letter being on the mantelpiece for years, gathering dust,' said Alice, looking at it with interest. 'It disappeared, along with the other letter, when we lost Oscar. So, Sam, tell me how you came by it – how you met him.'

Sam took a deep breath. Though it had only been a week since Oscar had delivered his message, a lot had happened in a short space of time. He began at the beginning, telling Alice about Oscar turning up in the middle of the Fellows' Garden at Oxford and delivering a message that Sam couldn't make head or tail of.

He explained that he'd then somehow managed to become lost in a garden he knew like the back of his hand, only to come back to where he'd started from and find a crumbling stone circle of terrifying statues.

As he was speaking, Alice rested her chin on her walking stick. Her face remained warm and she wore an encouraging smile.

Sam spoke about the Shadow, and even with the warm light flooding the room, he felt its chill. He explained how the professors, who were apparently Brennus and Drust, had saved him and accompanied him to the Eagle and Child, where he had met Jack, Ronald and Charles, and how he had read their letter outlining their trip to Oscar in Alnmouth and how the letter had become his counsel.

Alice sat smiling as he related how he'd seen both Oscar and the Shadow in the tapestry in the Seven Stories and moved quickly through the appearance of the crow-men and his and Emily's decision to leave Brennus, Drust and Jarl travelling to the Dead Water whilst they went on to Warkworth.

'And there is no news about Brennus, Drust or Jarl?' interrupted Alice, the first signs of worry showing on her face.

'I saw them in a dream,' answered Eagan. Then he paused.

Alice looked at him enquiringly. 'Eagan?'

He hesitated. 'They were at the Dead Water.'

Alice went pale and bowed her head. 'How were they?'

'It was just a dream,' Eagan said.

'*Eagan!*'

There was a pause.

'I don't know,' Eagan whispered.

Sam and Emily looked at each other. 'Do you know them?' asked Sam.

Alice raised her head. 'They are my sons, dear child. And this is grave news indeed.'

## THE RED LION

'I just don't understand why they would have gone there.'

Alice looked round the table. Everyone appeared uncomfortable. Eagan got up and stood with his back to the window, frowning.

'They went to seek counsel,' Emily said quietly.

'From the Dagda? But his daughters are now hostile to mortal men.' It was Alice who now looked surprised.

'They were looking to understand the nature of the Shadow that hunts Sam,' Emily continued. 'They were giving him time to escape Gosforth and reach Oscar.'

'And they were *both* at the Dead Water, Eagan?'

Eagan nodded.

Alice bent her head once more. 'That is no place for the living. Few who venture there ever return. Let us hope the Faeries are kind to them.'

'What do you know about the Faeries?' asked Emily curiously.

Alice drew a long breath. 'Most people in these parts would have you believe they are nothing more than fireside stories told to children in the dark nights of winter,' she said, seeming to pull herself together as she spoke. 'But they are real enough. Some years ago, I travelled with Oscar and the Keepers to the final stronghold of the Druids – Holy Island. The island is protected by a tidal causeway and druidic magic. We reached it having skirted Bamburgh and arrived on the seventh day. Amongst those gathered there were those who would become Oscar's fellowship. We travelled to a garden on the far side of the island, where summer turned to winter, and at last we came to a river.'

Her face softened.

'Though it was many years ago, I dream of it still – it remains as fresh as if I had returned only yesterday. Beside the river we met an old man. Whilst he sat there, one by one they came. One rose from the lake, dressed only in its shimmering waters. Her hair was blood red, her face ageless. When she spoke, her voice broke across those gathered like a waterfall. At times there were those amongst our company who could barely listen. We were all mesmerised.' She smiled. 'A second came riding in on horseback, her mount dressed in moonlight… She had golden hair and a beauty that still takes my breath away. There was a light dancing from her horse's mane the like of which I had never encountered before and never have since. She seemed to be made of the setting sun. These were two of the old man's daughters.'

All eyes were fixed on the old lady remembering the past. The letter lay forgotten on the table.

'Was that the only time you saw the Faeries?' asked Emily.

'No, my dear. But it wasn't long after that meeting that things began to change. I'm sorry to say it, but I can see things are beginning to move again now. I fear for you all.' She paused. 'And for my sons.'

'What are we to do?' It was Emily who had spoken again.

'My father will know to come here,' Eagan said, 'so we should wait for news. I don't think there is anything else we can do. I don't think we can go back, nor can we go blindly forwards. We should stay together and seek strength in numbers.'

'I think that is a sensible idea, Eagan.' Alice sat back in her chair, placed her walking stick across her lap and looked at them in turn.

Sam smiled at her. He liked the idea of staying where they were. He liked the idea of going home even better, but how was he to do that?

'Why not pour everyone another cup of tea, Eagan?' Alice asked.

Biscuits were passed around, whilst outside Alnmouth was beginning to settle down, with small sailing boats returning to the estuary. And always just on the periphery was Birling Wood.

'So, Sam, tell me more of your story,' said Alice. 'You say you met Oscar in person in Oxford?'

'To be honest, I don't think I did actually meet him in Oxford,' Sam explained, 'or at least the Oxford we know. I think I met him in the Otherland. Brennus says it's the in-between places.'

'The Otherland…' said Alice reflectively. 'The Otherland is a strange one. Yes, Brennus is right – it can be seen as the in-between places, but it is everywhere and nowhere all at the same time. I remember Oscar telling me it was the borderland between a number of different worlds. If the Fall begins to weaken, creatures from the Otherland will be able to come into the Mid-land. Without the Fall, the Ruin itself will be able to cross between the worlds.'

'Other beings are able to enter our world now,' Eagan said. 'I saw—'

Sam interrupted him. 'Is the Otherland where the crow-men come from? I thought they were from the Underland.' He was keen to find out whether there had been any truth in the Grimwere's words.

'Yes, it is said they are from the Underland,' Alice said. 'Many creatures were once asleep there, but they are awake now and on the move, and that frightens me greatly.'

'So what happened?' said Emily, but Alice was shaking her head.

'I know I don't have the whole story. But according to Oscar, a war has been raging down the centuries. Two thousand years ago the Druids managed to break the connection between the lands by setting up the Fall, but their magic was not perfect and that is why the Fall is vulnerable to the passage of time. Some say the Fall was once the Dagda's daughter Brigit, but others say Brigit was trapped in the Darkhart and her power was twisted by the darkness.'

Sam shivered. 'And where did the Druids come from?' he asked, trying to change the subject.

'That's a good question, Sam, but I don't know the answer to that either. According to Oscar, no one knows where the original Druids came from. Some say they all perished when they created the Fall. But clearly they didn't all perish. Their bloodline continued. The Ruin's servants have been pursuing that bloodline for what seems an eternity.'

'Was Oscar a Druid?' To Sam it was the obvious question.

Alice looked at him and a smile broke across her face.

'Whether he was at the beginning, I couldn't say. By the time he returned from his journey, there was no longer any doubt that he could command the flow. For a while I didn't recognise him – it was only when he started writing that he was like his old self again.'

She sighed, then pushed herself back in her chair and stretched out her arms.

'Look, you've had a tiring few days. Why don't you two get some fresh air? Then later Eagan could take you to the Red Lion for tea.'

'Yes, let's do that,' said Sam, smiling at Emily.

'But stay this side of the river,' Eagan added.

'Why?' asked Emily at once.

'We're not that far from Birling Wood,' Eagan reminded her.

Emily was silent, suddenly remembering the battle.

'I think Eagan is right,' said Alice. 'A walk north of the river and then tea at the Red Lion is the safest bet.'

* * * * * *

Sam helped Emily clear the plates and cups from the table and stuffed the letter back in his pocket as he did so. They left Alice and Eagan enjoying each other's company and headed down the long hallway to the front door.

Outside, with the sun hidden behind a number of clouds, the temperature had dropped. It was early September and most holiday-makers had gone back to their lives in the cities.

Sam and Emily decided to follow the estuary down to a small beach.Coming through a break in a wall that opened directly onto the beach, they found a man fixing an upturned rowing boat with a black Labrador sitting by his side. Behind him, small boats were anchored, bobbing up and down haphazardly on the afternoon tide.

Sam and Emily sat on a bench with a remarkable view, a light wind brushing their faces.

'Alice talks a lot of sense,' observed Sam. 'Why didn't Professor Stuckley just bring me here in the first place?'

'What? With the Shadow and those things in the wood in hot pursuit? I think he did what was right under the circumstances.'

'Why didn't you know that you'd been coming to his family home as a child?'

'I was so young, Sam! I hardly remembered it at all. And later I was always told Brennus and Drust were from Bamburgh. That's where they live now.'

'Hmmm...' Sam was thinking it through. 'Well, it seems as though now they're at the Dead Water anyway.'

The man was now gently tapping his boat with a small hammer.

'And where does this leave you?' Emily turned to look at Sam.

'Me?'

'There *is* something going on with you, Sam. After all, you stopped the Grim-were, and if you hadn't helped Oscar, we'd all be dead.'

The man working on his boat stopped banging nails into it and turned to look at them.

Sam flushed. 'Keep your voice down, Emily, and stop spooking the locals.'

Emily fell silent and the man turned back to mending his boat.

'I know it does sound very weird,' she muttered.

But Sam wasn't listening. 'Look over there,' he whispered.

Back in the direction they'd come from, several specks were on the horizon. The black dots stood out against the white clouds. Long before they could see any shape to them, Sam and Emily knew what they were. They both stood, straining their eyes to see the crows flying out of the dark rim of Birling Wood.

The man stood too, putting down his hammer and gazing in the same direction. Without warning, his black Labrador began to growl.

'I think we should be getting back to the house,' Sam said, trying to remain calm.

Emily turned to him and he could see the fear in her eyes. 'We *are* close to the wood, aren't we, and I don't know why we're risking it – not after what we saw last night. Do you think the house is protected?'

'If you mean protected like Oxford, or the bookshop, I hope not – look at what happened there. Let's hope Jarl turns up before nightfall and tells us we can all go home.'

Sam gave Emily a reassuring smile, but she wasn't to be comforted. 'You *know* we can't go home.'

Sam felt his stomach knot. Her words brought back the harsh reality of their situation. Only days ago Emily hadn't believed a word about Shadows, Druids and letters that kept changing. And now here she was, determined to persuade him to keep moving forwards, when all he really wanted to do was go home.

'*Why* can't we go home?' he asked, suddenly defiant. 'I'm not Oscar, I'm not a Druid, and I don't want any of this. The Shadow could be caught in a paradox. The Forest Reivers may have sent the crow-men back to their Underland, for all we know. Those crows could be perfectly normal birds.'

Emily turned sharply. 'Didn't you hear what Alice said? The Fall is dying and without her this Otherland joins with ours and then the Ruin comes through and then…'

'And then what?'

Emily opened her mouth to say something, but Sam's question had thrown her. In fact, it had thrown Sam too.

'Let's just get out of here,' said Emily, standing up.

Sam stood too. 'All right, but when we get back to the house, let's at least talk about the possibility of going home. I came to see Oscar and I saw him. He locked the Shadow in the Otherland. So that's it. Brennus, Drust and Jarl will just have to go on without me.'

'And you think that the Shadow is going to forget all about you? And that those things over there won't pay you a visit one night? What about that shapeshifting thing?'

'Come on, let's get moving,' Sam said, anxious not to answer any of those questions. 'There's something not right here. Listen to that dog.'

The dog was now standing on the edge of the small sandbank, hackles raised, barking loudly.

'Jasper, calm down.' The man joined the Labrador beside the estuary.

'I hate this,' Emily whispered, looking across at them.

Just as she spoke, several figures appeared beyond the wide gaping mouth of the river. Even at that distance their stance gave them away.

The dog was now standing rigid next to its owner, who was squinting into the distance, trying to make sense of the figures.

'Come on. It's not safe.'

Sam took Emily by the hand and they moved quickly back onto the paved path and headed back up to the top of the hill.

'Where are they now?' Sam turned to look down on the estuary to see if the figures had started to cross the river, but it was no longer possible to see the stretch of river where the shapes had been.

Back at the house, they both found themselves knocking on the door a little too vigorously. As they stepped back and waited, it seemed to Sam that he noticed the door for the first time.

'Look.'

'What is it?' Emily moved alongside him.

With the sun beginning to wane, there was a vague outline on the door. It was as if the grains in the wood had looped around a knot, a knot that looked oddly like a tree.

'The emblem of Cherwell College,' Emily said wonderingly. 'Although it isn't the emblem of Cherwell College, is it? It's all to do with the Circle from Oscar's message. Even I can see that, Sam.'

Just as they were both staring at the patterned wood, the door opened, revealing the pale face of Eagan, looking sombre in the low afternoon sun.

Sam pushed Emily into the large hallway before following her quickly and heading for the kitchen.

'What's happening?'

'The crow-men from the wood are down by the river,' he answered, moving swiftly to the orangery to look across the estuary.

Emily and Eagan joined him, scouring the southerly banks.

'Are you certain it was them?' Eagan asked.

'We noticed the crows first and then several figures appeared at the water's edge. It had to be them,' Sam replied. Tension was knotting his stomach. The day had been so peaceful, but the appearance of the figures had reminded him just how close danger was.

'Don't worry,' came a voice from behind them. 'They can't easily cross the river or enter the village.'

Alice had returned.

'Are you sure?' Sam turned towards her anxiously. 'I'm sorry,' he added quickly, 'I never meant to bring trouble to your door.'

'I know you didn't, my dear. Now listen. I spoke with Eagan at some length while you were out. We think you should stay here until my sons or Eagan's father returns. They may have news from their journey that will help you decide your next move.'

Alice sat down, holding her walking stick in one hand, her smile never leaving her face.

'You have been through much pain these last few days – the least you should offer yourselves is a little kindness. Why don't you go to the Red Lion? The landlord there will look after you.'

'Those crow-men attacked my uncle's bookshop. They attacked Eagan – poisoned him. Are we really safe here?' asked Emily nervously.

'The river will not let them pass, not if its master is again walking these lands.'

'But what if the Shadow comes here? Are you sure the river can stop it?'

Sam sometimes wondered whether Emily meant to be so rude. But the old woman seemed untroubled. 'Let us hope it is never tested,' she said calmly.

'If we stay here, *will* it be tested?'

'I see your fear, Emily,' Alice replied, 'and I understand that fear. But I don't think you can leave just yet. The road may well be watched. You cannot go back south, and going north or west will become more dangerous in the days ahead. And I can say that Oscar made his home here for many years and nothing ever breached its defences.'

With that, Alice leaned back in her chair and seemed to doze off, making it clear that the talking was finished for the evening.

* * * * * *

The Red Lion had an enviable position in the middle of Alnmouth village. It had been a pub since the eighteenth century, serving the port of Alnmouth until freight moved to the railways, and was now serving villagers and visitors in equal measure.

Sam, Emily and Eagan entered the pub through a side door and walked into its twilight interior almost unnoticed. The atmosphere was friendly and welcoming, and instantly Sam began to feel more relaxed. He sat down and began to wonder what was on the menu.

Emily sat directly across from him and looked around her.

The oak floor groaned beneath Eagan's feet as he crossed to the bar. He came back with pints for himself and Sam and a soft drink for Emily.

She looked at it in disgust. 'Don't you think I deserve something a little stronger after today?'

'No,' came Eagan's short reply. 'Besides, you are only seventeen.'

Emily scowled. 'I feel about ninety after the last few days.' Then a slight smile softened her face. 'Or I did until I fell asleep at Alice's.'

'I wouldn't mind a few more nights there,' Eagan admitted.

'Neither would I,' said Sam, reaching over to a nearby table to grab a menu. 'What do you recommend?'

'Everything!' Eagan laughed. 'And the portions are huge.'

'Let me have a look,' Emily said.

Sam passed her the menu. He was starting to feel very at home here.

Eagan, however, was feeling uneasy. 'You know,' he said, 'I'm beginning to wonder whether it's a good idea after all to wait here.'

'Why?' Emily put down the menu, suddenly alert.

'We're too close to the wood. If what you saw were crow-men, then the road south is being watched. And I'm concerned that no news has come from the Forest Reivers. If Brennus and Drust are really at the Dead Water – and, okay, it probably wasn't a dream – I don't think we can rely on anyone coming here.'

There was silence for a moment. Sam felt a shiver run down his spine. 'The letter said as much.'

Eagan took a long drink from his glass. 'Where is it now?'

'I don't think we should read it.'

'Why not?' Eagan lowered his voice and took a swift look round the interior of the pub.

'It told me that Brennus and Drust wouldn't return and it looks as though it could be right – what if it tells us that one of us will be next?'

'He's got a point,' admitted Emily.

'We don't have an option,' retorted Eagan.

'What do you mean? You've just said the road south is being watched and we can't stay – doesn't that mean we should go north?'

Eagan sat back in his chair. 'I know we have to go north, Emily, but I need to understand what path to take. The letter may help.'

'It might give us information we don't want to know.'

Eagan turned to Sam. 'It has been given to you for a reason. I suggest we use it.'

Sam found himself reaching into his back pocket. Across from him, Emily had stopped sipping her drink and Eagan's eyes were fixed on him. He could sense their apprehension and their excitement. Just like the nights at the Eagle and Child and the old school house, his mouth went dry as he thought about reading the letter.

Taking it from his pocket, he placed it on the table. It was looking more bedraggled than ever.

'If it tells you anything about me,' Emily said nervously, 'I don't want to know.'

Sam nodded. He knew how Emily felt – his own anxiety was building second by second. As he took the letter from the envelope, Emily looked away, but he could feel Eagan's dark eyes burning a hole into the torn and yellow paper. He found himself staring at it, unable to bring himself to unfold it.

His attention was caught by the door opening and the man from the beach entering the pub, dog in tow.

'Go on,' Eagan whispered.

Sam watched the man buy a drink and go and sit in the far corner of the pub, his dog settling close by his side.

'Do you really want me to do this?'

'Like I say, we have no option.'

Without any further hesitation, Sam unfolded the letter.

Instantly he could see that the handwriting was no longer either Jack's or Ronald's. Their elegant calligraphy had been replaced by a scrawl he could barely decipher. He found himself taking a deep breath and starting to read the letter out loud:

*Dear Sam,*

*You are in grave danger.*

'I don't think you should read another word.'

Emily was interrupted by a low growl from the corner of the room. Eagan looked over his shoulder, his eyes taking in the tables where people were quietly talking and drinking, enjoying a night out.

'It's just a dog. Keep going.'

*Dear Sam,*

*You are in grave danger. The Grim-Witch is coming after you. Her crow-men attacked the Forest Reivers in Birling Wood. The Reivers were hard pressed and the wood is lost.*

The enormity of the words didn't sink in at first. Then Eagan said, 'The Reivers … I asked them to come down from their homes. I called them together. I can't bear to think of what has happened to them.'

He sank back into his chair, placing his hands over his face.

'What is this Grim-Witch?' Emily's eyes were growing wider.

'I don't know.'

'She's the leader of the Grim people,' said Eagan in a muffled voice. He dropped his hands and raised his head. 'She's supposed to be asleep in the Underland. Sam, you need to keep reading. We need to know what we must do next.'

Sam turned again to the letter.

> *Make for Bamburgh, for it is the home of the Marcher Lords and they will again protect the heir of the* Druidae. *Go quickly and do not look back. The roads out of Alnmouth are watched...*

He stopped reading and sighed. 'I was hoping the running and hiding would come to an end.'

Eagan was leaning forwards, his face pale, the dark rings under his eyes a touch deeper. 'Does the letter say anything else?'

> *Look to the river for your escape and do not despair.*

> *Charles*

'"Look to the river." Great – the only way out of Alnmouth is by boat,' Emily said, throwing herself back in her chair. 'And does anyone have one?'

'Bamburgh is only twenty-five miles north,' Eagan said slowly. 'We could make it in a day.'

'*Please* don't tell me we have to row all the way to Bamburgh – I don't fancy getting caught out at sea at night.'

'I don't fancy rowing all the way there either, to be fair. I think we come ashore at Craster and make for Bamburgh on foot.'

'What do you think, Sam? Couldn't we wait for news after all?'

'No, Emily, I think we've already delayed too long.' Sam was feeling even more worried now. 'We should pack some provisions and then borrow a boat.'

'Just remember who is at the centre of all this,' Emily muttered, picking up her drink.

'If only she knew the truth,' thought Sam. 'Come on,' he said, 'that dog's spooked and that makes me nervous.'

On the far side of the room, the dog was growling steadily.

'It's the man we saw earlier!' Emily exclaimed, looking round.

Eagan turned too. The man bending down, trying to comfort the dog, but it was having none of it.

'It was like that on the beach earlier,' Sam said. 'When the crowmen were there.'

Eagan and Emily both looked at him.

'Right,' said Emily, quickly draining her drink. 'Eagan, is there another way out of here?'

'Yes, follow me.'

Eagan took them through a back room and out into the pub's long beer garden, where one or two people were still sitting in the twilight. They quickly passed through the garden and then went down some stone steps that led to a narrow street.

'Wait!' called Sam, pushing himself and Emily back against a stone wall.

'What is it?' Eagan's voice was strained, almost desperate. He placed himself on the opposite wall and Sam watched as he reached behind him and half drew what looked like a horrible long carving knife.

Then Sam felt a slight wind brushing his face, although the night was still. There was a taste in his mouth and his hands felt strangely warm.

'Something is here,' he said.

'In Alnmouth?'

'No – *here.*'

'Sam, you're scaring me!' Emily's eyes were wild. She jumped as Eagan drew another long knife. Standing in the gathering gloom, he looked a frightening figure, capable of striking anything down at will.

'Where?' he asked.

'I don't know exactly,' answered Sam. 'In the air – or it could be everywhere.'

'Focus. Tell me what you see.'

'I don't know *what* I see. It's more a kind of feeling. I just know something bad is coming and we need to get out of here.'

'Then let's go!'

Without another word, Eagan took them down the long alley, looking around him as they ran. Now and again he would signal for Sam and Emily to push themselves against the wall and wait before running on.

The alley quickly came to an end and they were soon running through the back streets of Alnmouth, catching glimpses of the darkening estuary as the last of the sunlight sent a crimson wave against the horizon's black edge.

As they approached a steep hill leading up to the back of Alice's house, Eagan made them crouch beneath a hedge.

'We warn Alice, we pack as quickly as possible and then we borrow a boat, okay?'

'I really hate this,' whispered Emily. 'It feels as though we're about to go from the frying pan into the fire.'

Eagan didn't stop to answer, just leaped from the hedge to several stone steps that led into a narrow alleyway. Reaching the house in a matter of seconds, he produced a key and slipped it gently into the lock. With a click, he opened the door.

The house was in near darkness.

'Alice! Alice!' Eagan called softly, but there was no answer.

He went into the kitchen, then through into the garden room. With the house in darkness, he could see right across the estuary. He scoured the south bank, but it was too far away to see movement in this light; the sea and river had melded into one. He hoped it would be difficult for anything coming down from Birling Wood to cross.

Behind him in the kitchen, Emily exclaimed, 'The fire's out. The ashes are cold.'

'Can't be,' Eagan called back, 'they stay warm for ages.'

'Well, this whole place is stone cold. What's going on?'

'I don't know. But I suggest you get a few things together and we leave whilst the tide is with us. There are some spare clothes in the drawers in your room – you get those and I'll pack some food.'

Sam and Emily quickly went back into the hallway, leaving Eagan opening kitchen cupboards. They went up one flight of stairs, then another, past the large Georgian window, and then turned to go up the final flight.

'It looks as though the house hasn't been lived in for ages,' said Emily, puzzled. 'Look at all this dust!'

Sam stopped in midstride. 'I know. These are strange times and they are getter stranger by the day.'

They went quickly up the stairs, into the first room and through the bookcase into the small room where they'd had the best sleep ever, but now their minds were again filled with panic.

'Emily, hurry up. This feels like Oxford all over again.'

'All right – I'm coming.' Emily was shoving clothes almost at random into a rucksack.

They were half running back across the reading room when Sam stopped.

'The tapestry!'

'What?' Emily turned back.

In the room's soft glow, they looked at it with renewed wonder.

'It's the man with the dog!' said Emily.

'I know,' replied Sam in disbelief, 'the man who came into the Red Lion.'

They had now seen the fifth man for themselves, looking no different than he had in 1960.

'Sam! Emily! Come on, we haven't got time to mess around!'

Eagan calling up the stairs startled them both. Without further delay, they left the picture of the five men, pipes in hands, smiling gently into the quiet room.

They found Eagan back in the garden room, watching the now unlit southern bank of the estuary.

'Can you see them yet?' asked Sam.

'I don't know. I can't make out the beach,' he replied anxiously.

Sam felt Emily's hand touch his arm. They stood almost shoulder to shoulder.

'I watched them come down from the hills northwest of the wood.' Eagan's voice was taut. 'I'm sure if we stay here one more night, they'll find a way to cross the river.'

Sam looked out across the estuary. 'Where are they now?'

'There – look!'

Sam stared into the distance, his eyes adjusting to the new night until at last he could see a movement, a blurred ripple.

'Is that really them?'

Eagan nodded.

'Why don't they just cross the bridge a mile north of here?'

'The village is protected. You heard Alice. They won't cross until there is one amongst them who can break its spell.'

'The Grim-Witch from the letter,' Sam breathed.

He felt Emily's sharp intake of breath. 'Can she break the spell?'

'I think so. She's on her way – I can feel it. I think I've already stopped her from finding us.'

'Stopped?' Eagan's eyebrows arched.

'Yes – don't ask me how, but listen, the red-headed man from the tapestry upstairs is here in Alnmouth.'

'What? This is all just crazy, just crazy, you hear?' Eagan's face flushed with anger.

'I know, but it's true.'

Then Sam felt it again – a tremble, an electric current that passed across his face. Beside him Emily flicked her hand as if to brush something away, and he knew she had felt it too, and Eagan was shaking his head.

'If we don't go now, Eagan, the estuary will be closed to us.'

Eagan looked at him and then his anger faded, leaving the pale, almost frail Eagan they had seen that morning.

'You're right, Sam. Let's go.'

Sam reached out for the bag of food and slung it over his shoulder.

'There's a boat down by the river,' he said. 'I know it's crazy, but the man from the tapestry really was fixing it this afternoon.'

'Then it's meant for us.'

* * * * * *

With Sam leading, they quietly opened the back door, which couldn't easily be seen from the estuary banks. Eagan took one final look over his shoulder and then closed the door behind them.

As Sam left the safety of the house, he felt a great sense of foreboding passing through his mind and down into his body. With the Shadow, there had never been a sense of awareness, just a cold and mindless pursuit. This was different – it was as if part of him was linked to something he could almost feel moving around him, one minute in his deepest thoughts and then the next passing through him until he could feel its presence in his hands.

Now Eagan led the way, taking them down through the village until they were standing just across from a gated entrance to the estuary's north bank. The tide had come in with the night and there was a hush right across Alnmouth.

They huddled together, trying to be certain that the danger had yet to cross the river.

'The boat is just down there,' Sam whispered. 'It can't be more than ten feet from the water.'

Eagan crossed the narrow street, signalling for Sam and Emily to wait for him. Just like Sam, he could sense something. He had always naturally felt the flow and Drust Hood had taught him well. Bent double so as not to be seen from the opposite beach, he moved slowly through the darkness, his long knives again in his hands.

When he saw the boat, his eyes widened in surprise. How had the *Celtic Flow* turned up in Alnmouth? When he had last seen it, it had been tied up in its usual place by the old school house in Warkworth. And he had been surrounded by crow-men, he reminded himself ruefully. Anything could have happened to the boat since then. The fact that it was here was reassuring, though. It really was meant for them.

Lying flat against the cold wet sand, Eagan edged forwards so that he could look out onto the estuary. The waters were still, but beyond them he knew the horde was waiting. Remembering their poison, he shivered. He had to get Sam and Emily out of there.

He would need Sam's strength to dislodge the *Celtic Flow*. He turned back to fetch him and Emily.

When he took them to the boat, they were as astonished as he had been, but there was no time for questions. The three of them had to put their backs into getting the *Celtic Flow* seaborne.

It took them several long minutes of pushing before anything happened. Then, painstakingly slowly, the boat began to inch towards the water, the bow catching in the wet sand.

Then Sam stopped pushing.

Eagan looked over his shoulder. 'What's wrong?' He had felt a trembling in the air, but Sam was standing there shaking.

'We don't have much time!' he managed to croak before feeling a second huge shudder pass through his body.

'Your nose is bleeding, Sam.' Emily leaned forwards and wiped the droplets of blood from Sam's nose with her sleeve.

Sam felt his strength had been momentarily knocked out of him. Unable to speak, he fell to his knees.

'Emily! We need the boat in the water!' called Eagan.

Emily left Sam kneeling in the sand and threw her weight against the boat, but without Sam's strength, it wouldn't move.

'Sam! We can't do this without you!' Eagan cried out.

But Sam didn't hear him. He was listening to another sound, one that was echoing in his head. A disembodied voice calling to him, urging him to stand and show himself. It was soft and full of kindness – something he hadn't felt for what seemed such a long time…

'She is coming!' he cried, overjoyed. 'And means us no harm. Her people are already here. They are waiting for us.'

Eagan stopped pushing. 'What are you saying? Now come on, we need your help.'

The *Celtic Flow* was now inches from the water, but Eagan could feel his legs shaking and Emily's face was a mask of pain and frustration.

'You don't understand! She is coming to help!' Sam cried.

Just as he finished speaking, the *Celtic Flow* slipped from the shore into the still waters of the estuary. Eagan held onto its side, looking back at Emily, who was regaining her feet, whilst Sam continued to kneel on the sandbank.

'Sam, quickly! Stop this nonsense. Get in the boat!'

Eagan's voice died in his throat as a noise came rushing across the estuary and he saw flashes of light on the far shore. He helped

Emily into the boat and waded as fast as he could back to the shore, where Sam was struggling to stand.

'What are you doing? Sam!'

Sam looked dazed. Blood was still oozing from his nostrils. 'Eagan…?' he muttered.

Across the estuary tiny flames were flickering and falling to the ground and Eagan knew the attack was underway. He grabbed Sam by the shoulders, half lifting him from the sand and propelling him through the waves.

Emily was already sitting hunched in the boat and jumped as Sam was dumped alongside her.

'Get down!' Eagan shouted as he quickly found his rowing seat. His eyes blazed as he placed the oars in the still waters and began to haul the *Celtic Flow* out into the river.

To his left he could see fluttering flames and it was clear they had been seen. A hiss out broke across the entire southern bank and hundreds of tiny sparks were suddenly falling into the waters.

'The Fall protects Alnmouth, but she is weak,' cried Sam from the bottom of the boat. He tried to stand, but Emily pushed him back down.

'Emily, whoah…'

'Just stop it this minute and pull yourself—' Emily broke off as the boat suddenly lurched as if had struck a sandbank. '*Eagan!*'

'It's all right,' Eagan replied through gritted teeth. Then he was pulling the boat back on course. They could hear his grunts of exertion as the *Celtic Flow* hung almost unmoving in the middle of the estuary.

The flames had been all but extinguished, throwing the south bank into complete darkness.

It was Emily who saw them first – a sea of dark shapes breaking the surface of the waters no more than a hundred feet from them.

'*Look!*' she screamed.

Sam lay in the boat, totally unmoved by her cry, unable to break the spell that was slowly suffocating him.

Eagan looked towards the south bank and saw the horror that was wading into the still waters. Whatever protection Alnmouth had offered them had been broken and the horde from Birling Wood was no longer hiding, but was breaking from the long grass in endless droves.

From the prow Emily watched in horror as the southern estuary became a writhing mass of crow-men desperately throwing themselves into the deep waters. It was clear that most could not swim, and they disappeared beneath the waters, drowning, whilst those behind clambered over their fallen brethren.

'Eagan, get us out of here before they reach us!'

But the *Celtic Flow* had now stopped and was being pulled inch by inch towards the south shore, irrespective of Eagan's efforts to wrest it back. He heaved on the oars and still the boat would not move.

The first claw appearing over the side made Emily recoil in horror, but Eagan was quick. In one swift movement one of his long knives took the claw clean off and the creature fell back into the dark waters. But others were already reaching the marooned boat.

Emily turned to Sam, who was still in the bottom of the boat, a dazed look in his eyes, his T-shirt now covered in blood.

'Sam, you've got to help us!' She grabbed hold of him, trying to shake him from his stupor. 'Sam!'

Without warning a thin feathered arm burst out of the water and seized her.

Eagan leaped over Sam in a desperate attempt to save her, his hand outstretched towards hers, but several hooked claws wrapped themselves tightly around her body and dragged her down into the murky waters.

Eagan turned to Sam, horror-stricken. The boat was now being attacked from all sides and he knew it wouldn't be long before they were both poisoned and helpless. He was putting his hands together, ready to dive in after Emily, when a fiery boom threw him forwards into the bottom of the boat.

'*Emily!*' Sam was standing in the middle of the boat with his left arm ablaze. The first crow-men were slithering over the edge of the boat, their beaked and feathered faces snapping and their clawed hands reaching for him, but they never touched him.

Eagan scrambled to his feet and seized his long knives, ready for one final battle. A voice was bellowing, or it could have been a surging vibration in his head. All around him the crow-men were falling, flapping, then turning into giant black crows, their murderous cries becoming squawks of fear as many drowned, whilst others burst into flames then became nothing more than a wisp of black mist that swirled and disappeared into the night.

Eagan watched as Sam raised his hands and sent the last of those clinging to the boat burning into the darkness. He could feel heat surging around him and for a second thought he heard a chorus of voices rising up across the estuary. Sam's voice grew ever louder until Eagan thought it echoed in his soul, and the boat lurched forwards, set free from whatever had been holding it.

The waters around the boat began to stir and it was all Eagan could do to hold himself steady. He looked down into the darkness where Emily had disappeared and prepared to dive in once more.

'Get back!'

Sam's words seemed to churn through Eagan's mind and he found himself unable to defy him. He watched dumbstruck as Sam stood at the bow of the *Celtic Flow* uttering words he did not understand with fire in his hands that reminded him of Drust Hood. Whatever Sam was doing, the river was answering him. Sprays of water were erupting around the boat like hot geysers, soaking him, and still Sam was speakingwords that he could feel pulsing through his veins…

* * * * * *

Emily never even saw the feathered arm that pulled her from the boat. It happened so quickly that she didn't have time to call out before she hit the cold waters. The last thing she saw was Eagan's grasping hand. She closed her eyes, unable to look at the dark forms closing in on all sides.

Then their iron grip lessened, a searing pain erupted along the length of her arm and a sudden tug span her around and out of her assailants' grasp. She opened her eyes to find herself breaking the surface of the water. The hideous forms of the crow-men were erupting into fire and Sam was standing atop the boat with his arms arching above his head and flaming arrows raining down on the estuary's churning water.

* * * * * *

There was a force running through the boat that Eagan had never felt before. His eyes were streaming from a hot wind that made his eyes and throat dry, a vibration that made his head hurt. There were hundreds of crows floating dead on the river's surface, when without warning Emily broke through the surging water and he dived in and was beside her in an instant.

A sudden and intense silence rang in his ears and the vibration, fire, light and energy were replaced by a sweeping emptiness that threw the blazing figure of Sam into complete darkness.

* * * * * *

Sam stood there, drained and shaking. He had moved the light and colour from his mind to his hands and then he had battled something huge that had propelled the crow-men into the waters. There had been voices and light and this time he had been able to direct them more easily. But now he was spent.

'Sam!' Emily called as Eagan pushed her into the boat and then pulled himself up behind her.

Sam was shaking his head, then sitting down suddenly. 'Eagan, we can't stay here. The danger has only been delayed. The Grim-Witch – I felt her in the flow. She is coming. The Fall can no longer help. She was protecting the village – I heard her voice – but now she is weak and cannot come to me.'

Eagan and Emily watched as he lowered his head, seemingly grief-stricken.

'And if we stay,' he whispered, his voice cracking, 'then Alice and those who have chosen to remain here will be put in danger.'

As if on cue, he felt the trembling begin again. Whatever he had faced was gathering itself once more.

'Eagan, help me. You need to get us out of here.'

Eagan sat back on his rowing seat and started pulling on the oars. The *Celtic Flow* immediately responded, cutting through the sea of dead birds.

Emily was sitting next to Sam, shivering from the damp clothes against her skin. She took a dry jumper from her rucksack, and when she had put it on, Sam placed his arm around her shoulders.

Eagan was rowing as never before, almost snarling with the effort, his legs and arms pushing and pulling, his wet hair flying, his jaw set. Every now and then he would let out a growl of pain. He was trying to steer the boat into the deepest part of the estuary, where the river and sea came together in twisting currents. He knew the north and south banks of the river's mouth drifted back together and soon they would be at the south bank's closest point.

Sam kept his arm around Emily, who was watching the tall grasses along the bank. Then he realised what was happening.

'They're going to try and stop us at the head of the estuary!' he called.

He turned to Eagan, who seemed oblivious to anything other than striking the oars into the murky waters.

'Eagan!'

Eagan began to feel the boat slowing down once more. He could see Sam standing and facing the south bank, which was cloaked in darkness. He felt the hot wind again and the strange feeling of electricity sending subtle vibrations through his body. Whatever had attacked them a few moments ago was going to strike again.

The boat came to a complete stop and Eagan could no longer set the oars against the current. It felt as if they had hit a sandbank. The boat was now still and Eagan was sliding his long knives out into the night and moving to stand beside Sam and Emily.

'What is it, Sam?'

Sam didn't take his eyes from the south shore as he replied, 'They are there waiting. And I can no longer hear the voice of the Fall. We are alone.'

High above them came a short caw that sounded like a command.

On the south shore a roar answered the call, and only then did the companions understand the scale of the horde that was hiding in the grassland over a mile in length.

Eagan thought of the Forest Reivers who had faced this horde in the confines of Birling Wood and his heart sank.

Emily's voice died in her throat as she caught sight of a winged fiend, scaled and feathered. Eagan had seen it too, circling the boat just on the edge of his vision like a giant vulture.

But the first attack came against Sam. The beast hurled itself out of the sky, missing him by inches as he twisted away from its claws, and went hissing away over the dark waters. It would only be moments until it came again, and he knew if he fell, it would attack Eagan, and then only Emily would be left. Didn't that prove this was all about her?

Then the creature was back, flying lower this time. Once again Sam swerved, but he wasn't quick enough A wing caught him and he fell backwards, with all his strength knocked out of him, and hit his head on the wooden bottom of the boat.

Out of the night came the feathered beast once more, this time aiming for Eagan. He raised his knives. It flew low, trying to rake his face with its long grasping claws, but he twisted and rolled across the floor of the boat, slashing the fiend with all his fear and might combined. It swung out across the estuary and met the jeers of the crow-men, who were now entering the waters a second time, desperate to reach the boat. A poisonous reek burned Eagan's nostrils.

The beast wheeled round and continued its attack. A low claw wrenched one of Eagan's knives from his grasp and hurled it into the water. Steadying himself, he gripped the remaining knife with both hands. As it turned again, he drove the knife up into its chest with all his strength.

There was a horrifying wail that for a second silenced the horde. Then the creature fell, landing on the prow of the boat, a hideous abhorrence that should not have been amongst the living. But it was still amongst the living. As Eagan stood staring at it in horror, a claw reached out to the knife protruding from its scaled and feathered chest, and with a sickening movement, pulled it out and tossed it almost contemptuously into the sea.

'I seek the girl.' It was the chill voice that Eagan had heard in his father's garden.

'Why do you seek the girl?'

Eagan was standing between the creature and Sam and Emily. He did not want to feel the poison in his blood, but neither would he run. Emily kept her face turned away, huddled down in the boat and holding on to Sam, who was floating in and out of consciousness.

'She is in danger,' came the surprising response. 'The Ruin has sent its servants into your world and you cannot hope to stop them. My mistress is her only hope. The Otherland is coming and winter will come to the Fall in her last days. They are not far off now. My mistress is not your enemy, as the Keepers would have you believe. She will be here soon.'

Sam's head swam. He could hear a voice that sounded like the one he had heard beneath the Fellows' House. Was this real? His head was pounding and he was finding it difficult to think straight.

'The girl isn't going anywhere,' Eagan said flatly.

The beast looked straight through him. 'Say what you like, Eagan Reign, the Ruin's servants are coming. Even the Druids cannot stand in their way.'

'How do you—?'

There was a horrible thud and suddenly a white-feathered arrow was protruding from the creature's throat.

It staggered back, stunned, its long hooked claws grasping at the arrow. Then a second arrow took it though the heart. Its wings began to flap, but it was lifeless as it crashed into the water.

Instantly the *Celtic Flow* sprang back into life, and Eagan didn't waste any time grabbing the oars and putting his back into escaping from the estuary. Cutting through the waters, he found the mouth of the Aln blocked by thrashing crow-men, but there were deadly arrows coming in now from both the left and the right. It was as if they were opening up a path through the horde, and Eagan seized his chance.

Emily was sitting holding Sam's head, pale with fright. They were now approaching the closest point to the southern shore and both she and Eagan could see the horde gathered there. More were crashing into the water, desperate to reach them.

'There are so many of them!' Emily wailed.

Then a single horn blast sounded somewhere in the night.

'Over there!' Emily twisted round, pointing.

Eagan raised his eyes for a split-second. A line of ghostly figures, bows held against their faces, was still firing arrows back towards the estuary. Even in the darkness, their skin shone silver.

'Who are they?' Emily cried.

Wordlessly, Eagan shrugged.

Emily watched the archers for long moments as the boat was jostled by the incoming waves, but Eagan didn't stop rowing until the small boat was through the last of the dying crow-men and moving beyond the estuary and out onto the dark sea.

# 3

# THE DEAD WOOD

Brennus knelt on the edge of the Dead Water, stunned and unable to stand. He held his hand out as the old man approached, stepping gently through the now calm waters.

As the old man took him in his arms, he found himself brought to tears. The old man tenderly took him by the arm and led him from the chill waters back to the stony beach.

Brennus could barely speak for the burning poison that was moving through his body.

The old man placed his hand on Brennus's head. He began to hum, then speak words that Brennus did not understand. The words changed and became vibrations coursing through his body. He couldn't help but weep as a burning pain took hold of him, but the old man held him close until the agony left his body and his head fell forwards, sinking into the warmth of the old man's robes.

'Brennus, Brennus, my child, forgive me, but such poison cannot be left in a man's body.'

'I remember you,' whispered Brennus. 'All those years ago, you and Oscar brought a child to me. But now I have betrayed your trust and come on a fool's errand. I have let my brother sacrifice himself. And for what?'

He looked into the old man's eyes and was overcome by their kindness and understanding.

'All is well. I met that child only yesterday.'

Brennus looked up, his grey hair and beard dishevelled, but a look of hope in his eyes.

'Where?'

'On the outskirts of the Otherland searching for the Garden of Druids. I could not stay too long, because I needed to be here. There is another who will come through this place before the day's end and you must be gone when she does. She is fully awake now and I have not felt such energy for a very long time.'

'I don't understand…'

'You will understand soon enough. But first there are others who are approaching these waters.'

He stood, leaving Brennus kneeling on the short beach, and turned back to the lake, striding into it until it was almost to his waist. He raised his hands and called out. Brennus could not make out the words, but he knew the voice was no longer that of an old man. He knelt there, taken aback by the voice that thundered across the lake and out into the boundless Northumberland night.

It wasn't long before the Dead Water answered the call. The water around the old man began to tremble, then light flickered from its surface and merged with the spray of geysers shooting up into the air. Brennus could feel and taste the energy as the old man directed the light and water until a figure appeared, silhouetted against the shimmering light. He was a giant, dressed in what looked to Brennus like armour. He seemed strangely out of place as he emerged from the swirling clouds of rainbow light and towered above the old man. His skin was black, as if charred by fire, his head bald, his face hidden behind a singed beard that had once been neatly trimmed.

In his arms he was holding an unmoving figure.

'Fer Benn.'

When he spoke, his voice seemed to rumble from the depths of a bottomless cavern.

'The Rower is wounded.'

Brennus couldn't help but edge into the lake, trying to get a closer look at the unmoving figure, but the light and water obscured his view.

'Bring him to me, friend,' said the old man.

The knight walked towards him.

Once more the old man lifted his hands high into the air, the brown sleeves of his tunic falling back to reveal thin and wrinkled arms, but Brennus could see and feel energy coursing through the frail figure. The waters began to tremble again and then shoot high into the night. Soon the Dead Water was roaring back into life, sending up great spouts of frothing water until the man and his unmoving charge were veiled in fizzing energy with a magic that seemed to run through every molecule.

When the water fell back, they were gone.

The old man stood for long moments looking out across the dark waters, then turned again to Brennus.

'Make haste to leave this place. The Ruin's servants are again in the world of men. In the end you cannot hope to outrun them. You must prepare to make your stand. There is a talisman that was taken from the unknown tree and given to Oscar by the Elves. It is known as the Staff of the Druids. You will find it in the last house of the Druids on Holy Island. That staff is your only way into the Darkhart. The Druids used it to create the Dead Wood – there is no way in without it.'

'The Staff of the Druids,' Brennus repeated.

'Yes,' continued the old man. 'The last of the Druids will need it to unlock the energy, the magic, of our beloved First Light in the heart of darkness. If this is not done, then the Fall will perish and the Ruin will come again into the Three Kingdoms.'

'Where exactly is it?' asked Brennus eagerly.

But the old man did not answer, as the calm of the Dead Water was broken by a flow of light and water that came sharply together. A woman was emerging slowly from the dark waters, her face pale and her hair blood red.

'The Morrigan,' Brennus said to himself. He was entranced, his weariness forgotten.

As she rose from the waters, he saw she was cradling a form against her bosom, and this time he saw it clearly.

'*Drust!*'

He tried to move forwards, but the old man held out a hand to stop him.

'Be still.'

The old man turned back to the woman.

'Father, I could not leave him.'

Her voice was musical, yet strong and forceful. The sound echoed through Brennus, yet she seemed not to notice him as he stood there waist-deep in the water.

'Daughter, bring this child to me, for I must at least free him from his journey.'

Brennus watched as the form dressed in light approached the frail elderly figure. He could see Drust clearly now. His clothes were torn and bloodstained, and he was pale and still.

Gazing at his brother, Brennus felt the strength run out of his own body. Remembering how he had asked Drust to act as a decoy, drawing the Shadow to him on Hadrian's Wall, he bent his head and sobbed.

As the woman reached the old man, with great strength she held Drust out before her. In reply, the old man reached out and placed a slender hand on his forehead. Instantly a surge of electricity skipped across the waters. The old man then lowered his head as he spoke words that cascaded through Brennus, unfamiliar sounds that seemed to sting his face and leave him almost breathless.

A rumble across the Dead Water answered the old man's words. This time the water around him, Drust and the woman seemed to spin, then spiral upwards, shooting high into the night. Brennus stared, open-mouthed, entranced by the sparkling show of light and water as it turned on itself in the air and fell twisting back to earth.

Then he heard a sharp intake of breath.

'Drust!'

Stumbling through the water, he made his way to the woman. Shuddering at the intrusion, she turned her gaze on him and he felt it pass right through him. But his brother was coughing. Without a word, he took him from the Faerie's arms and turned back to the shore.

Breathing heavily, he reached the stony beach and placed Drust gently on the damp ground.

'Drust, Drust, I'm so sorry… I never meant for you to come to harm. I know I asked you…' He could say no more as his tears fell on Drust's pale face.

Drust was breathing more easily now, but he was still unconscious.

The old man came to the edge of the water and stood there watching them.

Behind him the woman had turned to look out across the lake. 'Father,' she called, 'I don't think we can stay here much longer, for the Otherland is in the water and in the air.'

'I feel it too.'

The old man turned to Brennus. 'Watch your brother closely.'

Brennus was only half listening, stroking Drust's face. The colour was coming back into his cheeks.

'Father, we have no time – they are coming!'

The old man nodded.

'Now remember, you must find the Druids' staff. Without it, the way to the Darkhart will be closed. So, form a new fellowship. In seven days' time you must be ready – the fellowship must be ready.'

He turned away and started walking out to his daughter, who was standing waiting for him.

Then Brennus felt hands grabbing hold of him.

'Brennus! Where am I?'

'Drust, wait—'

Brennus put an arm round his brother, but his eyes were following the old man, who had now reached his daughter. They stood there together, reflected in the still water.

The old man looked back at him. 'You must go. Go!'

Without another word, Brennus pulled Drust to his feet and led him up the short beach.

* * * * * *

Brennus stopped before the wall of twisted trunks, remembering his journey through the suffocating wood that bordered the lake and wondering how he would get himself and Drust over the steep mountain pass that he had come down only hours before. That had been bad enough and then he'd been fit and without his injured brother. Whichever route they took, there would be no easy paths from here. They were high up in the borderland and the journey to Holy Island would be tortuous.

'Brother, where am I?'

'You are at the Dead Water, but you are safe. The Faeries saved you.'

'Ah yes, I remember. The Morrigan saved me.'

'How do you feel? Can you travel?'

'Yes.'

'Then we should go,' said Brennus, but even as he said the words he couldn't help but take one final look back at the old man.

What he saw terrified him. On the dark horizon, shadows were rising from the lake's surface, turning the water to ice. Then they took form. They were taller than any man, dark and heavy-set. He was horrified to think what the old man and his daughter were about to face, alone and without help.

'Shadow Ruins.' The words came from Drust.

'What are they?' asked Brennus. 'Are they from the Underland?'

'No. Come, we must go, brother.'

Brennus's eyes were fixed on the old man and his daughter. They were standing together, motionless, as both the figures and the ice moved inexorably towards them.

'Is there nothing we can do?'

'We cannot achieve anything here. We must find another way.'

But Brennus was still staring at the spectacle unfolding before him. 'Look at those numbers! The Faeries will never survive. They saved us both, Drust. Don't we owe it to them to at least stand with them?'

'Don't underestimate them. Come now,' Drust took his brother's arm, 'it's time to reunite with Sam and discuss our next step.'

With one final look, Brennus allowed himself to be led into the dense wood.

* * * * * *

A suffocating wind was choking him and roots were beginning to coil around his legs. His eyes were watering, his throat starting to sting.

'Let's get moving,' he managed to say.

'There is a magic in this wood,' gasped Drust, leaning heavily against him. 'We are not welcome here, brother. This place is weary of the living. The trees are fearful. They can sense the changes already taking place. Things are beginning to move – nothing can stop it. We must have some purpose as yet unrealised, or we would not be leaving this place.'

'I am just pleased we are together again and can still help Sam. I have much to tell you, Drust, but let's get out of here first. I can't bear it a moment longer.'

Brennus took them what he guessed to be north, but the wood was confusing. Its dark interior spread out before them like an impossible maze.

'I really dislike this wood!'

'It is an unnatural place,' Drust agreed. 'The wood and valley protect the Dead Water and the flow cannot reach here. Those who tried to use it would be helpless. I have never known anything like it.'

The wind was burning their throats and clinging to their faces, but the further they went, the more it was clear to Brennus that Drust was somehow regaining his strength. He was still leaning on him, but he could feel his weight less and less. Reassured, he pressed on.

Finally they were breaking out of the dark wood with its choking mist and clinging roots, and ahead of them Brennus could see the mountain pass. In the gloom the mountain appeared like a threatening giant waiting to snare the weary traveller, but they found the broad ledge without incident and then the narrower one leading over the pass.

They began to ascend in single file, watching every step. The path grew steeper as they moved further up the mountainside and a steep drop opened up beside them.

Drust knew this place belonged to no one. And down below he could still feel it watching and listening to their echoing footfalls. It reminded him of the wall. These places not only existed in different moments in time, but also in different locations.

At the highest and narrowest point of the pass they suddenly saw flashes of light shooting through the dark valley far below. Then seconds later a deep rumble filled the pass. The very ground seemed to shake and they flattened themselves against the reassuring black rock face.

'What's going on down there?' Brennus gasped.

'I don't know, but I do know that if the Faeries lose, you can expect the beginning of the end.'

They stood there for long moments, pressed against the dark rock, whilst below the lights continued to dance. The rumbles turned to booms that reverberated through the darkness, seeming to burst in their ears and making them clutch at the sheer rock face.

Then silence fell.

'What now?' Brennus whispered.

They waited.

'Listen, Drust, the old man says there is a talisman that will get us into the Darkhart, a staff that was taken from the unknown tree and placed in Oscar's keeping. It's on Holy Island. I think we should press on there as quickly as we can.'

'A staff? Really? And Oscar never mentioned it to Sam?'

Though he could barely see his brother's face in the darkness, Brennus shook his head.

'It would have been a lot easier if we'd known about it earlier,' Drust commented.

'I know. I don't understand either. Oscar never said anything to me.'

Brennus could sense his brother's eyes searching for his in the dark.

'Oscar never said enough, in my opinion,' Drust said bitterly.

'I know. I think he was just traumatised by what happened on the shores of the Dead Water.'

'Ha!' Drust laughed. 'As well he might be! No, he never said much, but Braden's father did, didn't he? His memory was never as short as Oscar's, or as scrambled. And *he* said Culluhin left James on the shores of the Dead Water, at the gates of the Darkhart. And *I* have never heard of the Staff of the Druids.'

He turned away.

'Well, we must just make the best of things now,' said Brennus soothingly.

Drust did not answer. He was staring blindly into the chasm.

'What is it?' Brennus could barely see his brother's face.

'The Fall is gone from this place.'

The words sent a chill through Brennus. 'Are you sure?' he faltered.

'*Yes*! The Dead Water is lost. It won't be long before the spirits of those who fought against the Druids find a way into the Mid-land. What hope do we have? There is no Fellowship of *Druidae* to be had.'

'We have to warn the others.'

'Then what? Wait until every last one of us is dead? I felt the Shadow's potency. There is nothing that can stop it.'

'We have to resurrect the fellowship and go into the Otherland.'

Drust laughed. 'You can't get any sort of fellowship going in the *Mid*-land. Look at the families in Warkworth – it's civil war all over again. And you're thinking of going to the *Other*land?! You aren't Oscar, brother! And would you want to be? Remember what happened to his fellowship.'

He paused and pressed his cheek against the dark wall.

'And if Sam isn't the last Druid, then what? The Shadow won't be fooled a second time.'

Brennus took a deep breath.

'Then what would you have us do?'

Drust turned and looked down into the abyss.

'Nothing can stop what is unfolding before our very eyes. There is an inevitability about all that you do and say. Don't you know it? But history doesn't have to repeat itself. The Shadow is not without awareness.'

'What are you saying?' began Brennus. He was stopped by the sudden flash of cards in his brother's hands.

'The Shadow spoke to me.'

'*Spoke to you?*'

'Words I did not understand at first, but they are becoming clearer in my mind.'

Brennus watched as his brother began flicking the cards from hand to hand, slithers of light in the darkness.

'I think we have to keep our hearts and minds open,' Drust continued. 'We know a little of Oscar's story. But what do we know about the doomed Fellowship of *Druidae*? We don't even know the names of all those who went. We only know that few returned.'

Brennus shivered. 'There's no time to talk about it now. We have to get off this mountain pass and away from this place.'

'All is not what it seems, brother. I think we have held the Druids in high regard without questioning who they were, where they came from and what part they had to play in the creation of the Fall.'

'They stopped the Ruin from finding its way into the Mid-land, didn't they? They sacrificed themselves. What more could you have asked of them?'

Brennus didn't like the look in his brother's eyes. The cards were moving from hand to hand more quickly.

'We don't really know what happened – we only have fragments of the story. Let's hope those fragments do not come back to bite us,' Drust warned.

Down in the dark valley, lights were flashing again and there were further rumbles.

'I'm just glad we're back together to fight another day,' Brennus said firmly. 'Now we should move on from this place and stand against the enemy. We owe it to the memory of the earlier Keepers and to Sam.'

Drust didn't move. 'And if we are wrong?'

'Without the Fall, the servants of the Ruin will be unstoppable. We are all vulnerable. We must stand together.'

'But we aren't asking why – why this is all happening!' Drust eyes flashed as he held his brother's gaze.

'Why—?'

With a rush of wings, a vague and fast-moving outline swept out of the night. Drust reeled, feeling a penetrating power surge through him. For a moment he thought he would fall. Then he felt his brother's arm holding him against the wall.

The chasm became a thousand beating wings as a vast murder of crows poured out of the Dead Water.

Brennus and Drust pressed themselves against the rock once more, clinging on as the noise grew fainter. Behind them the lights had gone out and silence was again falling across the valley.

Brennus let go of his brother. 'What was that?'

'The Grim-Witch and her horde.'

'No! I thought she was a myth.'

'That wasn't a myth, was it?! I didn't see her fully, but I saw her resonance in the flow. A powerful Faerie – though she has been under a spell in the Underland for many long years.'

'A *dark* Faerie,' Brennus corrected.

'*Dark*? If you think there's a difference between her and the old man, think—'

A deafening roar came from the night-filled valley.

'Let us leave arguments for better times,' said Brennus, shuddering. 'It serves no purpose to be caught on this ledge with whatever made that noise.'

And with that he edged past Drust and began the last bit of the climb.

* * * * * *

They arrived at the top of the valley breathless and thirsty. Brennus paused for a moment, looking down into the darkness, hoping that he would never set foot in the Dead Water again. Resolutely, he turned his back on it. Ahead the hills of Northumberland rolled out like giant waves, but something was wrong. He was trying to put his finger on it when he felt Drust move alongside him.

'Where is the storm?' Drust asked, looking round him.

'I don't know – how long have we been at the Dead Water? But Kielder Forest should be to the east and we need food and water before making our way to Holy Island, so we should go and seek Braden's clan and see whether we can borrow horses. We need to travel with all speed.'

'The Scaup Burn will take us to Catcleugh Reservoir and from there it is only a short walk to Ravens Knowe.'

'No, we will take the horses through the Blind and Barrow burns.'

'Those are strange places at the best of times, Brennus. You will be going through the heart of the Underland.'

'But to circumnavigate the Cheviots would take days – days we no longer have.'

Drust didn't look convinced.

* * * * * *

They left the valley wrapped in a weary darkness. Brennus was feeling the strain of the last few days and couldn't go as quickly as he would have liked. As they left the fell and followed the rocky ground down a steep incline, he felt his thoughts scatter. Relief at seeing Drust alive had quickly been replaced by new streams of apprehension. What did losing the Dead Water mean? Remembering the Grim-Witch and her horde, he was filled with fear. What else might come through? The Shadow Ruins? He dreaded to think what would happen when they reached the shore. How had Drust known what they were?

As he walked on, his legs aching, he couldn't help but feel inadequate. Drust was right. Where would he find a fellowship able to combat those beings if the Faeries couldn't stand against them? Who would be part of the fellowship? He could of course guess, but how could they be assembled? He suspected that it would be only a shadow of the fellowship Oscar had assembled anyway. And as for Sam, they had watched over him for years, and yet when it really mattered they had let him down.

Remembering Sam's eager face back in Oxford, waiting for his exam results, Brennus regretted he hadn't told him more about his history then. But who could have guessed they would find themselves in such a situation? It almost seemed like a dream. Were they really expecting a teenager to travel into the Otherland in search of the Darkhart? How were they supposed to get there? Why had he never heard of the Staff of the Druids?

Brennus sighed. If only he could talk to Oscar. Or the Keepers. He guessed the Way-curves were still closed. Who knew where the Shadow was?

Drust cut across his thoughts: 'We are being followed.'

'The Shadow?'

'No.'

'The creatures from the Dead Water?'

'Perhaps. We cannot stay in the open – we need cover. We need to reach the forest.'

They went as quickly as their tired bodies could go. The ground rose again and soon they were walking across an open hilltop.

Brennus kept looking south. 'We should be able to see the lights of Yarrow or Kielder by now,' he said. 'I have never known a night as black as this.'

'There is more to this night than meets the eye,' Drust replied thoughtfully. 'That storm that came from the north couldn't have come and gone as quickly as this. And does this feel like an autumn night to you?'

'There is definitely a wintry chill in the air,' Brennus agreed.

They walked on for an hour in anxious silence. Every so often there would be a call in the night that brought light flickering through Drust's fingers and made Brennus wish he still had his short sword, but whatever was following them never showed itself.

'They have been sent to track us,' Drust concluded, 'or they would have attacked by now.'

They arrived at the Scaup Burn without incident. Its frothy waters flashed white as they tumbled towards Kielder, hugging a steep hill that ascended sharply towards the Northumberland sky. With the rush of the Scaup in their ears, they stood surveying the way they had come, but there was nothing to see but the rolling emptiness of hills and mounds.

Drust turned to Brennus. 'The river runs north and then sweeps northeast. We'll be going into the wilds, brother. There is an easier path that runs south. I don't understand your insistence that we go through the Blindburn. It's a foul and treacherous place.'

'The Shadow will be far ahead of us,' Brennus explained. 'We don't know if Jarl has taken my message to Braden, or whether Sam is safe. The old man said that when he met him he was searching for the Garden of Druids. He will need our help if we are ever to establish this fellowship.'

'Fellowship?!' Drust laughed. 'Brennus, it's a fool's errand!'

'The old man—' Then Brennus stopped. 'I think we no longer have a choice,' he finished simply.

'And if Sam *isn't* safe?' Drust smiled and raised an enquiring eyebrow. 'Besides, I thought the Garden of Druids was now hidden to all *but* the Druids.'

'Well,' Brennus said uneasily, 'he *is* the heir of the *Druidae*, after all.'

'Is he? Are you convinced of that? Still?'

'Of course. Why?'

'And where does Emily come into all this?'

'Emily? I don't understand.'

'She looks nothing like her mother or father,' Drust reminded him with an impish smile, 'and she's been chased all over the place as well. I could be wrong, but don't be surprised if the Shadow is searching for her and not Sam.'

'No!' Trying to think it through, Brennus felt confused, and for a second he thought the burning poison was back in his body. Then he pushed the problem out of his mind. 'Either way, we need to catch up with them. That's why we're going through the Blindburn. It cuts right through the Cheviots and will be the quickest way to Holy Island.'

'It will also bring us within a stone's throw of the Underland.'

'That's a chance I'm willing to take,' said Brennus, walking on and leaving his brother to catch up.

# 4

## EZRU

They marched on, keeping the Scaup on their right, Brennus taking the lead. Once or twice a sudden guttural bark would rise above the surge of the stream's fizzing water, but whatever was following them never showed itself. Still they could not shake off the sense of pursuit. Silently, they pressed on.

Soon the stream turned east again and the hills on either side became more jagged. The landscape turned from green to grey, with flecks of brown. The burn was beginning to wind its way through a stark and wild place and to narrow as it cut through the rocks.

Brennus could feel the tiredness in his legs. Looking up, he couldn't distinguish where the tops of the hills met the sky. He had never known such darkness. At his side, Drust was struggling now, grunting and stopping every so often so he could get his breath. Brennus felt guilty, but he knew the urgency of their mission and that behind them the Dead Water was now an open door.

They came to a place where the Scaup broke up into a number of forks. Some disappeared underground, whilst others became nothing more than dried-up scars. Brennus knelt beside the now gentle stream, scooping several cold handfuls of water, and Drust sat down, looking back the way they had come.

'Tell me what happened, Drust.'

'You know. We needed to be sure the Shadow followed us. Followed *me*. It did. The plan worked perfectly.'

Brennus was silenced.

Then Drust laughed – an open, friendly laugh. 'Don't look so stricken! I agreed to it, remember?'

'I remember all too well. I should never have asked it of you. I know that now. I'm so relieved you've come through it all. That's why I want to know what happened. I want to know how you survived the Shadow.'

'I don't think I did.'

'What?! What do you mean?' Brennus was shocked.

'I won't lie to you, brother. I feel its touch on my soul. If the Faerie hadn't come for me, it would have searched those cold dark waters until it found me.'

Brennus shivered.

'But even as it sought to extinguish my life,' Drust went on with sudden intensity, 'there was an anguish there – an awareness that only flickered for a second, but it was there, and I felt it. I think it was once one of us – that it was once human.'

'Can that be true?' Brennus breathed.

Drust nodded. 'I'm sure of it.'

'How could it have happened?' Brennus's mind was spinning. 'Could it have been one of the fellowship? Was that why Oscar barely spoke about it? Why we don't even know the names of half of them, let alone what they actually did in the Darkhart?'

He let his hand trail in the cold waters. When he looked up, his eyes were troubled.

'Drust, is it safe to take you back with me?'

This time it was Drust who looked surprised. Then he seemed to recover himself, but there was still a glint of pain in his eyes as he replied, 'I cannot answer that, not yet, it is too early, but you are right to fear it, for I fear it.'

Suddenly Brennus felt very alone. 'When we get to Bamburgh, we should use its Way-curve and speak to the Keepers.'

'I thought we'd agreed the Way-curves were no longer safe. Isn't there a traitor in our midst – one who may be listening to our conversations?'

Brennus stood and stretched before helping Drust to his feet.

'I'm not sure. I'm just keen to get to Bamburgh.'

* * * * * *

Brennus decided to choose a path through the myriad forks of the stream that was every bit as difficult as the way they had come. He knew just beyond the ridge of hills would be the Catcleugh Reservoir and after perhaps a couple of hours they would be in the Forest Reivers' homeland. But when they reached the ridge, they were stunned by what they saw.

'Where are the waters?' gasped Brennus.

Where the Catcleugh Reservoir should have been was a small valley with leafless woods on either side. Brennus looked north and could see they were still between Carter Bar in the north and Castle Crag Forest in the south.

'I don't understand—'

Drust interrupted him. 'Look at Crag Forest – it covers the whole of the valley! It was only a wood when I came this way last year.'

'I see what you mean – it stretches off in every direction.'

'At least it will give us some cover.'

They quickly walked the mile to the edge of the forest. The naked trees now towered over them, imposing and still.

'What are these?' enquired Drust, reaching out a hand to stroke the bark of the nearest tree. 'I thought Crag Forest was mostly native woodland. I've never seen trees like these in Northumberland.'

'Neither have I. And when did autumn turn to winter?'

The cold air they had felt since leaving the Dead Water now fell into place.

'*How* long were we at the Dead Water?' asked Brennus.

Drust shrugged. 'I don't know. But the real question is what do we do now?'

'Yes, you're right. Do we go through and see whether we can get to Ravens Knowe or do we track back?'

'If we go back, we're likely to meet whatever's been trailing us. And from what I've heard of it so far, that could be a very bad idea. Carter Bar is to our north, though, so I'm guessing we're still within Northumberland.'

Brennus found himself looking back the way they had come, but he could barely make out anything in the dark night.

'Are you also guessing that this is the…'

'…Otherland?' They said it together, their eyes growing wide in the night.

'Is this what we can expect with the Fall fading?' Brennus asked.

'What other explanation can there be?'

Brennus turned to the trees. 'This is so strange,' he said wonderingly. 'It's unlike any wood I've ever seen. Look at these trees – their trunks, their branches, their roots… It could be my eyes playing tricks in the dark, but they look strangely twisted.'

'The wood is expectant,' Drust replied.

'We might not find Ravens Knowe on the other side,' mused Brennus. 'What then?'

'What now? We either go back and find out what's following, or we go through and hope it brings us out in the shadow of the Cheviots.'

Without another word, Drust walked past Brennus and into the wood.

Brennus was about to follow when he felt the hair on the back of his neck prickle. Quickly he looked over his shoulder. There were shapes coming up from the direction of Scaup Burn. At first he thought they were men bent over, but he quickly realised they were moving on all fours.

'Drust!'

His brother took a couple of steps back towards him.

'What are they?'

'Grim-wolves from the Underland. There's no going back, brother.'

Drust turned and stepped back into the twisted wood. Brennus followed. Ahead of him, his brother was weaving swiftly between the alien trunks, whilst above the giant branches hung like broken arms and below the forest floor was bare, stripped of all cover apart from a sea of coiling roots entwined around one another.

At first they made good time, but soon the trees were becoming closer together and the branches were hanging almost to the ground.

'Do you have a sword?' Brennus asked.

As he spoke a sigh seemed to run through the forest, yet there was no breeze. Startled, he looked around him.

Drust caught his arm, leaning into him so he could whisper, 'Don't touch the trees. We are being watched.'

'By whom?'

'I'm not sure.'

Brennus found himself looking into his brother's eyes and for a split-second did not recognise them. Unnerved, he stepped back and let Drust lead the way deeper into the forest.

Progress became painstakingly slow as the gaps between the trees continued to close whilst the roots pushed through the ground in ever greater numbers. Behind, a series of muffled snarls broke out, then silence descended again. There was obviously no alternative but to keep winding their way through the maze of trees.

At first Brennus hadn't noticed the cold, but soon he could no longer ignore the biting chill. It found its way through his clothes and into his bones, and it wasn't long before he could feel himself beginning to shake.

'This place is unnatural,' he whispered. 'How can it be so cold?'

Ahead, Drust turned. 'The flow is strong here. Though I cannot feel the cold.'

Brennus watched his brother turn back and continue picking his way through the snaking roots. He couldn't help feeling uneasy. It wasn't humanly possible not to feel the chill.

Setting off again, he stumbled over a root and felt a sharp pain against his cheek. When he touched his face, he realised blood was running down it. He stood slowly, shaking off a momentary dizziness.

Drust was waiting for him, all signs of exhaustion gone.

'Quickly, we can't afford to lose our way in here. The wood is waking. It will soon be aware of us.'

Brennus was trying to wrap his collar around his cheek to keep the raw air from the wound. 'What are you saying?'

A hint of a smile twisted his brother's lips. 'Look at the root that caught your foot – see the fresh earth around it. It seems the trees don't take kindly to trespassers.'

Brennus looked down. It was true – the root looked as though it had only recently pushed through the ground. He liked this wood less than the one surrounding the Dead Water. There was now a clear sense of something watching and waiting.

'Should we go back?'

'You know we can't – there are Grim-wolves back there. Let's see what this place makes of them and us. I've never known the flow so strong before. It's in the trees, in the air and in the earth. This place is protecting something or someone. I've felt that before in the Fellows' Garden and at the wall. Let's keep moving.'

'I think it was unwise to set foot in this place,' Brennus grumbled.

The trees were hanging over them now and as he walked on, bending and weaving, Brennus was caught by branch after branch until his cheeks and neck were covered in painful scratches. There were several occasions when he stumbled over looping roots, too, and it took him all his skill not to fall.

'This is deliberate,' he muttered to himself, as from the corner of his eye he saw a root twitch and a branch reach out.

The wood was alive and hostile, and yet the darkness was lifting. At first he barely noticed, then it slowly dawned on him that he shouldn't have been able to see Drust so clearly ahead. Eventually he realised the wood had its own light – an indefinite haze. But the trees were now so impossibly close together that their knotted roots and entangled branches were beginning to form an impenetrable wall.

The chill was also deepening and Brennus felt himself beginning to shiver uncontrollably. Soon his eyes were watering and his hands and face were almost numb.

'I cannot bear this cold!'

Drust turned and looked back at his brother, clearly baffled and untouched by the chill air.

'We need to keep going.' He leaned a little closer. 'The wood is alive. It is shepherding us. We have no choice in the path we are taking. Every time I have tried to turn south or north, the road simply moves from west to east.'

'I thought I saw the branches moving.'

'Yes. I don't think we should stop.'

'And what of the cold?' asked Brennus.

He watched a flicker of a smile cross Drust's face, one he wasn't sure he liked.

'I think it's meant to slow you down. I can already tell that you would struggle if we were attacked. Let's hope the wood offers safe passage back into Northumberland before that happens.'

Just as his brother had said, Brennus could feel the chill beginning to affect his movements. Even worse, there came a sudden bark that made him jump and then several answering calls. They seemed to have come from different directions. Brennus looked around, but could see nothing.

The calls appeared to have gone unnoticed by Drust, who was still slowly making his way between the giant trunks and twisting roots. It wasn't long, though, before shadows were moving off to the left. Were these what had been following them from the Dead Water?

Brennus counted three figures, one standing upright and two moving on all fours. Whatever they were, they sent a shiver down his spine that didn't come from the freezing air.

To their right stood an impenetrable wall of grasping roots and branches, but ahead the path was clearer. Brennus slowly caught up with Drust, who had come to a complete stop.

'What is it?'

'I am no longer sure. The flow runs like a river through this place, but stops at the line of trees. I've never felt or seen anything like this.'

In the darkness the line of trees was like the walls of a castle and their roots looked like figures carved from wood. Brennus couldn't keep his eyes off their intricate shapes.

'What are they? This looks like some form of barrier. Do you think the trees are keeping us out or keeping something else in?'

He didn't like the sound of his own question. Neither did Drust apparently, as he didn't answer it, saying only, 'I've never seen roots thrust so far from the earth. Look, there are faces amongst them.'

Brennus had already noticed them. The more he stared at them, the more he could pick out knotted features. There was an eye, there a cheekbone, there a wide-open mouth. There was a whole face, seemingly frozen in time… The more he looked, the more he saw. It wasn't just faces, but entwined bodies. In the darkness, beneath the giant trees, an army was staring back at him.

'Brennus!' Drust was shaking him gently by the arm. 'Don't look at them!' His voice was low and urgent.

'But who are they? What are they?'

Drust shook his head. 'It is not our concern. Let us be gone from this place.'

They passed by the towering trees, but Brennus couldn't help but keep glancing at what he could only describe as people carved from twisted roots and earth. When he had first seen them, they had only loosely resembled human form, but the further he and Drust travelled along the mysterious boundary, the more intricate they became, until there was no mistaking their human shape. He was haunted by their contorted faces. There was a horror about them. Had they once been alive? What had happened to them? A dark and freezing fog was beginning to drift into his mind, pulling him back into the distant past. What had they been running from? Who had done this?

Snarls echoed through the silent wood, breaking the spell of Brennus's thoughts. With a jolt, he was back in the present.

'Behind you!' Drust shouted.

Brennus wheeled round, reaching for the sword that was no longer there.

Back the way they had come, a single figure was emerging from the trees. Its stooping frame was bigger than that of the crow-men. Instead of black feathers, this creature had scales across its chest, and rather than a beak, it seemed to have more human features. It too was looking at the frozen army woven into the giant roots of the trees.

Brennus felt Drust move alongside him and was surprised to see his hands glowing as if he had dipped them in fairy dust.

'What do you want?' Drust called out.

The creature turned slowly towards them. It lifted its head and seemed to be smelling the air. Through the trees to their right, two further figures were moving, seemingly on all fours, just on the edge of their vision.

'Why are you following us?' Drust called, his voice steady.

'We mean you no harm,' came a guttural reply.

'We will be the judge of that – why are you following us?'

The creature seemed not to hear the question. Instead it was looking again in the direction of the frosted shapes beneath the trees. Brennus could tell it was unsettled. Every now and then it raised its nose into the air and its breath streamed out in icy clouds.

The creatures to their right were beginning to growl, their pacing becoming exaggerated. Even though Brennus couldn't see them fully, he could tell that they too were finding this place unbearable. Only Drust seemed to be calm, sending the light from hand to hand. Brennus marvelled at his composure.

Keeping its face turned towards the fortress of trees, the creature growled, 'My mistress seeks your counsel.'

'And who is your mistress?' Drust's tone was cool.

'She is known to you as the Grim-Witch, but to our people she is the Bodika.'

The creature turned its head and seemed to look at Brennus for the first time. He was glad he could not fully see its face.

'There is a war coming.' Its words were slow and deliberate.

To his right Brennus heard a number of low growls from the pacing creatures.

'That may be true,' Drust commented. 'And why does your mistress seek our counsel?'

'Not *yours*.' Surprisingly, the creature looked at him contemptuously and turned its attention back to Brennus. 'She seeks the counsel of the Keepers of the Druids.'

'And what business does she have with these so-called Keepers of the Druids?' asked Drust.

The creature gave an angry growl that reverberated in Brennus's chest. 'We are not here to be mocked! Our mistress knows that the Fall is perishing. She wishes to speak to the one who will lead the fellowship into the Darkhart. She must speak to those who know the way to the Sea of Souls.'

Brennus was surprised. He had only ever heard Oscar and the Keepers mention the Sea of Souls before. Where had this creature come from? What did it know?

Drust, too, seemed perturbed. He shot his brother a quizzical glance before turning back to the creature and saying, 'We know of the Keepers of the Druids. But tell us about this Sea of Souls.'

The creature was clearly becoming irritated. 'No, we do not wish to speak to you.'

As it spoke, further growls sent torrents of frozen air into the night.

'And this is no place to stop. We must keep going. These places are not for the living.'

'Tell us about the Sea of Souls first.'

The creature stepped forwards, showing a long line of sharp teeth.

'Well then, I will tell you that it is said that only the Three may find the way to its shores.'

'The Three from Oscar's message,' thought Brennus, then jumped as he saw a giant black wolf, its eyes almost white in the darkness, pass between two tree trunks and fade back into the darkness as quickly as it had emerged.

'Why would your mistress have an interest in the Three?' questioned Drust, ignoring the now almost continuous growls.

'The Three must be protected. Without them, there is no way across the Sea of Souls. Now enough, let us move on.'

'The Three? The Dagda's daughters?'

There was a sneering half-laugh as the creature again edged forwards. 'The *Druidae*! You should have been protecting and watching *them*,' it snarled, glaring at Brennus, 'but instead you have wasted your time seeking out the Ruad Roshessa, who serves only himself.'

Brennus was reeling, but Drust instantly suspicious. 'Why should we trust you and your mistress?'

The reply was long growl. 'The Bodika knows the way through the Otherland to the Darkhart. You will need her before this is over. The Ruin's servant will no longer be denied by your tricks. It will arrive at the Otherland first to reclaim its own servants.'

'And who are these servants?' asked Drust.

'This is no place to talk of such things. We have to go whilst the wood sleeps. There is much danger here. We have already talked too long.'

With another low growl, the creature moved past them, quickly joined by the two beasts who had been hiding behind the trees.

Drust began to follow, but Brennus caught his arm. 'It could be a trap.'

'We don't need to trust them, brother. If they can find a way out, great. We can worry about what we do with them later. We know there's at least some truth in what they say. I don't think we should test our luck in this place. He's right – we have to leave before the wood wakes.'

Drust dropped in behind the three figures, who moved through the ill-lit wood with ease. Brennus tried his best to keep up, but he was almost delirious with cold. Oscar's message to Sam kept running through his mind: '*Seek the help of the Three.*' He had been certain the Three had been the old man's daughters. Oscar couldn't have meant Sam, Emily and Eagan, could he? Anyway, who could believe the words of a creature from the Underland? He had been led to believe that the Underland was the enemy and that the Grim-Witch had been responsible for the death of Sam's father. For many years the Underland had been sleeping, and he couldn't help but wish it wasn't awake now.

Slowly the space between the tree trunks was widening. The wall of trees was falling away and the twisted roots with the frozen bodies were fading away into the darkness. Lost in his thoughts, Brennus was no longer sure how far they had walked or what direction they were going in, and it was some time before he realised how much the wood had changed. Looking around him, he saw that the giant trees had all but gone and in their place were the familiar shapes of conifers, while the bare forest floor was softening with bracken, woodrush and trails of honeysuckle and ivy. As the last of the chill left the wood, the smells of autumn returned and the hazy half-light that had accompanied the sterile coldness vanished, to be replaced by the familiar soft darkness of an autumn night.

Warmth was returning to Brennus's feet and hands, and he was glad he could feel his feet again, for he could now increase his pace and get a better look at the creature that had spoken to them. It was tall and sinewy, and naked save for long grey feathers that covered a hideous hide. It was different from the crow-men who had attacked the bookshop and Brennus couldn't help but wonder what it was. He couldn't tell whether it was man or beast. Could it be a Grim-were? He had heard of such things, but never expected to see one.

The wolves also were unlike any he had seen before. For the most part they travelled on four legs, but now and then they would walk on two, presenting a surreal and frightening spectacle. They perhaps weren't entirely wolves either, as they didn't have fur, but short black feathers. Every now and then one would turn and look at Brennus and he found he couldn't bear to look at its eyes gleaming in the darkness.

Drust was moving on, seemingly untouched by both the wood and the strangeness of their companions. The glow of his hands had dulled, and Brennus felt strangely relieved by this.

Suddenly the wood ended and they both came to a stop, looking out at the view before them. To the east, dawn was gently breaking over what Brennus hoped was the huge hill of Ravens Knowe. Just beyond the giant hill was the home of the Forest Reivers. They would find food and shelter there. Although the creatures who were already making their way down the short slope would need explaining.

Drust seemed to be thinking the same. 'It would be foolish to take these creatures into the homes of the Forest Reivers.'

Watching the wolves spreading out behind the feathered man, Brennus could only nod in agreement. 'Perhaps it's time to part company,' he suggested.

'Yes, although they have been of assistance,' Drust admitted. 'I think that without the help of those wolves we wouldn't have found our way out of the wood so easily. What do you think of your journey through a little of the Otherland?'

'I'm not that impressed,' Brennus shivered. 'And I suppose we're going to be seeing a lot more of these places before this is over.'

'Yes, we are. But it is now fully clear to me what the Otherland is.'

'And what is that?'

'It is the fracture between worlds. Look at those tortured souls back there. It is the same with the Dead Water. These places are all connected through the Otherland.'

'There is no time to talk.' The feathered creature had stolen back up the hill and was now standing ten feet from them. 'The Vargr say we are hunted.'

Brennus and Drust looked at each other and this time Brennus saw a brief flash of fear in his brother's eyes. Oddly, he took comfort from it. It made him seem more human.

'Hunted…?' Drust asked.

'The more powerful of the Ruin's servants have broken through the Fall. We did what we could, but even we cannot do anything against the unliving.'

'*Unliving*?' asked Brennus, feeling a sudden chill.

'The Shadow Ruins.' The creature seemed to snarl as it said it. 'We must go. Even the wood will not be able to stop them.'

It turned and moved towards the wolves, who were back on all fours.

Brennus hesitated. 'I really don't like any of this, Drust. There's no way of knowing what path to take. But I think for the moment we have no choice but to go on with them. If the Dead Water is lost, I don't think we want to meet whoever has taken it from the Faeries, whether they are living or unliving.'

He set off down the hill, leaving the wood behind, whilst in the distance the dawn was gathering pace across Ravens Knowe. He sighed. He'd never heard of Shadow Ruins. He'd been hoping they wouldn't have to face the Shadow again, let alone several new and possibly worse enemies. He needed more information. Though the Keepers had warned against using the Way-curves, he was going to do just that. He wanted to know what the Staff of the Druids was and why that had never been mentioned either. For a moment he felt angry as he thought of all that Oscar hadn't told him. Now he and Drust were reduced to relying on creatures from the Underland! And could *they* be trusted?

Once again Brennus couldn't help but feel inadequate and lost. Oscar had said the Underland was awake, but he hadn't expected to meet the Grim-Witch herself at the Dead Water. She had been unwilling to help then. Why had she now sent a Grim-were and its wolves to search for him – even to help him?

How he wished her magic had not charmed out of him exactly where Sam and Emily were heading. Whatever her motives, he had to get to them first.

* * * * * *

In the half-light of a new morning they came to a stream that cut deeply through a short vale locked between two hills. On either side were plantations of conifers, but they couldn't hide the rawness of the land. The stream was shallow but fast, winding its way down from the heights above. The Grim-were waded into its waters, clearly trying to throw their pursuers off their scent. The two wolves separated and headed off in opposite directions. Brennus watched them go, one choosing to run all fours whilst the second balanced on its hind legs, looking half-human in the light. They had soon reached the tops of the hills almost effortlessly and disappeared. Brennus couldn't help but wonder whether this was an elaborate trap or whether their intentions were honourable. Was it all an attempt to get close to Sam? The sooner he could speak to the Keepers, the better.

He too waded into the stream. The water's icy touch made him gasp. But he knew this was the only way to make their trail disappear, whilst whatever was following would have to break up and follow both wolves. Whatever the Grim-were might be, it was clever. This would make it a useful ally, but also a cunning enemy.

Standing in the stream's fast-flowing waters, Brennus looked down the length of the short valley and out towards the dark fringes of Kielder Forest. In the morning glow there was no sign of the wood with its giant trees and their alien roots, but he was glad when the Grim-were left the stream's icy fingers and started to climb the side of the valley and he and Drust followed.

The Grim-were seemed to be able to climb without ever stopping for rest and quickly pulled ahead, leaving Brennus and Drust clinging to the side of the hill and looking down at the thin line of the stream below.

'Any more thoughts on when we try and leave these creatures?' Brennus asked.

'We need to know the nature of those that follow,' Drust replied, scanning the valley. 'These creatures are afraid of them, and we should pay heed to that. If I were you, I would get through the Blindburn, perhaps wait until we are through the Cheviots.'

They looked at each other and smiled briefly before they turned and began to climb the hill together. It was steep, and they literally had to climb the last few feet bent in two, grabbing the coarse grass and hauling themselves over a flat ridge. They came to the top of the hill with both legs and lungs burning.

The creature was standing with its feathered back to them, looking towards the east, towards the sunrise, towards the threatening Blindburn. To the south lay High Green and to the north the unmistakable rolling edge of the borderland. Even from here Brennus could make out the dark formations of Mozie Law, Beefstand

Hill and Windy Gyle, where northern England embraced southern Scotland in a dramatic line of hills and valleys. To the west, Kielder Forest had become a haze of green in the morning sun.

'If there is a way back for the Vargr, they will meet us at the gate to the Underland,' the creature announced.

Brennus didn't like the idea of going anywhere near the gate to the Underland. 'Our path lies to the east,' he said quickly.

The creature turned to face him. It was now silhouetted against the rising sun and Brennus was glad he couldn't see the details of its scaly neck and mouth.

'My brethren are risking their lives for us,' it said indignantly. 'If the Shadow Ruins catch them, they will have a life far worse than death.'

'What are these Shadow Ruins?' Brennus asked.

'They are the unliving – fragments of a darkness before the First Light. They are servants of the Ruin. And they cannot be stopped by mere mortals.'

The words had been said without emotion. They had not been meant to shock, but they did.

The creature continued with more cold facts. 'That is who you will face when the Fall dies – an enemy from before the First Light and the dawn of time. The most powerful of their kind has already passed through. Its purpose is to find the *Druidae* and make sure the Fall's death is final.'

How did this creature know so much? Could they really trust it? Was it simply trying to persuade them that they needed it?

'Why are you telling us so much?' asked Drust, his voice showing no signs of the fizzing shock that Brennus felt.

The creature seemed to be nettled by the words. 'All those who are connected by the Otherland are in peril,' it said stiffly.

Drust fell silent.

The creature went on, 'The Bodika is the wisest of all the Faeries, the most powerful of them all. She seeks the counsel of the Keepers of the *Druidae*. I understand your mistrust, but if we separate now, you won't make it back without our help.'

'How can you be sure?' Drust demanded.

'No one can defeat the Shadow Ruins other than the Druids carrying the flames of the First Light.'

Brennus caught a quick glance from his brother. 'Which Druids are these?' he asked, but the creature was shaking its head.

'That is a question our mistress would like to ask the Keepers. Our paths must cross again. We *must* stand together against the enemy of the living.'

Brennus was taken aback. Weren't these creatures the enemies of the Forest Reivers? Hadn't the Dagda kept them asleep beneath the Cheviot Hills?

'If we do not stand together, we will fall one by one.'

Brennus could only agree with the creature. It stood bathed in the morning sun, looking grotesque, and yet its words had an eloquence and a truth that could not be denied.

'Now is not the time for talk. The Otherland will only have delayed them.'

They set off again under white clouds moving with a stiff wind, following a Roman path that allowed them to quicken their pace. In the far distance Brennus could see that the land was beginning to weave up and down as if they were moving towards stormy seas. On the tip of the horizon, bathed in a new morning, was the Blindburn. He knew they would have to have their wits about them there, for it was full of ancient roads crumbling into unseen gorges. The Forest Reivers travelled that way only rarely, for they believed ghosts haunted the passes. Now he and Drust were heading straight there, to the very gate of the Underland, in the company of a creature so strange it could only have come out of such a place. Brennus shook his head in wonder. Then he had to twist sharply to avoid Drust, who had stopped suddenly just in front of him.

'What is it?'

'I'm not sure. There is a peculiar resonance in the flow, a vibration I've never felt before.'

'My brethren are being hunted,' the creature said.

Drust turned to it, recoiling slightly from its twisted features. 'Do the Shadow Ruins use the flow?' he asked.

'The flow touches only the souls of the living. The Shadow Ruins are filled only with the darkness of the Ruin – the Dark Light.'

'Dark Light?' repeated Drust.

'The Ruin's flow.'

'That's what it is! I can see it!' Drust exclaimed. 'They are dead. That explains it.'

He seemed to be looking within, almost excited. Brennus stared at him and did not like what he saw.

'How do you know they are dead?' Even as he asked the question, he thought the answer would be hard to bear.

'I told you – I can feel it, this Dark Light. Do not ask me any more.' Drust turned away.

A flicker of something like pain crossed the creature's face. 'My people have long suffered. There has to be a day when it stops.'

Brennus could only nod in agreement.

* * * * * *

Both Brennus and Drust kept close behind the feathered creature as it followed the remains of the Roman road, whose purpose was long forgotten. Ravens Knowe was now behind them, whilst ahead the menacing gateway to the Cheviots began to rise steeply towards the blue autumn sky with wisps of white cloud still throwing shadows across the hills and valleys.

It wasn't long before the creature found another stream. Without breaking its stride, it left the road and ploughed through the clear and icy waters. Brennus followed, gasping once more as the cold flow spiralled through his burning legs. The Grim-were was clearly determined to cover their trail and keep them moving as quickly as both he and Drust could manage, but he knew he couldn't keep this up for long.

Even in the morning glow, there was nothing welcoming about this landscape. There was a savage look to these hills that made Brennus feel insignificant. They were soon approaching the first one. The stream hugged its craggy side, thrown into shadow now by the rising sun. Brennus knew he would have to rest soon. The relentless flow of the water against his legs had brought him to the edge of exhaustion. Just ahead, he could tell Drust was also beginning to suffer. More than once he had fallen forwards into the stream's chilling flow and each time he had taken longer to get back on his feet. If the creature's intention had been to make them helpless with exhaustion, thought Brennus, then it had succeeded.

'We need to rest for a while,' he managed to say.

The creature turned. It seemed to be frowning and he knew instantly that it did not agree.

'There is no time for rest. We must make the Underland gate. There is a magic there that will protect us from the Shadow Ruins, at least for a while.'

'He is right, brother,' added Drust. 'If they catch us in this place, we would not survive the encounter. Whatever the wolves were, they are no more. I can see them now – they are different. Unliving. They are searching for us.'

The thought of those giant wolves being dispatched so easily sent a fearful shudder through Brennus.

'Yes, okay, we'll carry on.'

He grit his teeth, and, with the thought of his pursuers firmly at the forefront of his mind, began putting one foot after the other. But the last few days had taken so much out of him. He had not slept properly for over a week, not since the night in the Eagle and Child, and even the icy stream could not keep fatigue from closing its fingers around his body.

Fortunately, as the stream began to flow more freely, the creature brought them up its steepening banks. A moment later they rounded a sharp turn and the Blindburn was revealed in all its dark glory – a vista of threatening beauty, its hills and valleys sweeping down to meet the shimmering horizon; an empty wilderness, devoid of people and animals. But, if the tales were true, full of ghosts, trolls and giants. Brennus did not believe in such things, yet until the last few days he hadn't really believed in crow-men either, let alone creatures such as the one walking before them, its strange body thankfully once more in shadow.

Almost without noticing, they had entered a deep valley with sheer drops to their left whilst to their right the gentle hills had been replaced by a rock face. They could no longer see back the way they had come and ahead the hills were becoming desolate. There were coarse grasses there, touched with heather, but there was a hostility to the place that Brennus could almost feel. His legs buckled and he found himself falling forwards, grimacing as he scraped his knees and a sharp pain passed across his back. He lay still for a moment, glad just to rest. Then he saw Drust turn and quickly make his way back.

'Are you okay?' Drust leaned over him.

Brennus shook his head. 'Just give me a moment.'

'There is no time. They are coming.'

'What's important is that one of us makes it back to Jarl and tells him about this staff. Go on – I can't.'

Drust shook his head and unexpectedly pulled Brennus to his feet. 'I know what is following and there is no way I am leaving you behind. Okay? Then let's go.'

Brennus again was surprised at the resilience his brother had shown since being pulled from the Dead Water. But he was becoming conflicted about what this actually meant. Why exactly had the old man asked him to watch his brother?

On he went, but his legs were burning with the effort. Ahead the hills of the Blindburn beckoned, looking like an impenetrable fortress. He could not possibly scale its walls. His legs were heavy and his whole body felt numb with fatigue. Only the frightening thought of his pursuers made him set his teeth against his pain and start the climb out of the valley.

A bleak and startling landscape closed in all around him. The narrow path began to crumble, clinging desperately to foundations that had been built by ancient hands. In places it was nothing more than bits of stone.

In the distance a steep, wooded hill rose higher than any other. Brennus felt his eyes being drawn to it. Again, the trees there seemed unlike any he had seen before.

A moment later, as they traversed a sharp bend, a second valley opened up before them, split by a shimmering river that emerged from the hills and wove its way through the coarse grass. A small wooden bridge crossed the fast-flowing waters. The creature was waiting for them beside it, the full horror of its form now lit by the morning sun.

'The gate to the Underland is beyond that wooded ridge. Beware now, for not all creatures from the Grim-scape are ruled by my mistress, and these valleys are the home of the Trow-Hulda. In the old days they lived side by side with the Forest Reivers and a long time ago fought alongside the *Druidae* with my mistress. But that was before the Forest Reivers began to be influenced by men. Now they are a secret people who are mistrustful of the outside world. They will be unhappy when they discover I have brought men to their lands, and unhappier still when they know what pursues us. We must move quickly and cannot stop until we are through.'

Finishing its small speech, the creature turned towards the wooden bridge. It did not cross, but stood beside it without moving, then without warning it leaped across the span, almost without touching the wooden boards.

From the other side, it beckoned Drust and Brennus across, but Drust put his arm out, stopping Brennus from setting foot on the bridge.

'There's magic at work here.'

'It is safe,' said the creature impatiently. 'That's why I tested it. The Faeries' magic has gone from this place. You must hurry.'

It turned its back on them and set off across a grassy meadow.

'What is it, Drust? Has the Faeries' magic gone?' Brennus asked anxiously.

'Not entirely.' Drust was standing with a hand on the bridge. 'It still resides in the wood, and perhaps the water, but it is only a hint of what it once was. I fear for them.'

They stepped onto the bridge together and could feel a gentle vibration pass through them, but it was weak. The river's waters momentarily twisted and raised a gentle spray, but it did nothing other than cover them in a fine mist.

They entered a valley of tall grasses moving slightly in the breeze. Here the raw wildness was replaced by something far gentler. On either side of them the hills were no longer bald, but full of trees, bushes and autumn flowers. There was a freshness to the air and even the river's flow seemed to soften as it wound its way towards the distant hill with its strange wooded cloak. Brennus felt his legs regain some of their strength, as the valley's floor was flat.

They followed the river's course until the creature stopped in the shade of some trees.

'You must stay close to me. We need to go through this wood.'

'Shouldn't we go round it?'

The creature shook its feathered head. 'There is no other way to reach the Underland.'

'I still don't see why we need to go there,' Brennus said. 'Our path is to Bamburgh and then on to Holy Island. Can't we just continue?'

'You cannot outrun the Shadow Ruins,' the creature explained, with a slightly exasperated air. 'They have been sent to kill each and every one of you. The most powerful of the Ruin's servants came through the Dead Water eight days ago. It broke the Dagda's spell and our mistress awoke. Be glad that she did, or the *Druidae* would be no more. Now follow me!'

Without waiting for a response, it plunged into the trees, leaving Brennus and Drust standing beside the river staring at each other.

'I know you don't want to go to the Underland,' said Drust softly, 'and neither do I, but we have no option but to follow. We are hunted, and I know what by.'

Seeing the fear in his eyes, Brennus shuddered. He took a final look back the way they had just come, but it seemed that the hills themselves had closed the path. He could no longer see Ravens Knowe and wondered whether they were back in the Otherland.

Then two dark specks appeared on the horizon. Brennus rubbed his eyes, but when he opened them again, they were still there. It seemed the Shadow Ruins had found them.

## FALLING LEAVES

Darkness was all around them. Only a thin line separated the sea from the sky. The estuary had dropped over the horizon and the *Celtic Flow* was rising and falling with the incoming tide. Eagan fell forwards, exhausted, his legs burning and his arms heavy with fatigue. It seemed hours since they had left the crow-men and silver-haired archers behind. They sat in the heaving boat, traumatised, wondering when the madness would end.

Emily was cold and the boat's motion was making her feel sick. 'You can't just stop rowing and leave us in the middle of nowhere.'

She suddenly felt very small and very afraid. In the darkness she couldn't even be certain which way was the shoreline and which way was the open sea. The sooner they were on dry land, the better.

Eagan sat up, nodding, but it was clear he was spent.

'What happened back there?' asked Sam. His T-shirt was still covered in blood, although his dazed look had finally left him.

'What *happened* back there?' Emily repeated through clenched teeth. 'Well, we went to the Red Lion and the letter said we were in grave danger and warned you about a Grim-Witch and said we could only escape Alnmouth by boat. So then somehow the *Celtic Flow* turned up with the man in the tapestry with Oscar. You know, Sam, Oscar, the man who visited you in Oxford who happens to be dead.'

Emily's voice was getting louder and was now echoing across the empty sea.

'Now don't get me wrong, Sam, I was your biggest critic. I thought you were stark raving bonkers last week. But I've seen a few things since then. I saw you save Oscar and now I've seen you save me.'

Sam found himself swallowing down his shock and embarrassment. It would appear that Emily was intent on winding herself up.

'Now don't look like that,' she went on. 'You won't admit to it, will you, but I saw it all for myself.'

She stood up in the middle of the boat.

'Emily! Sit down!' said Eagan irritably. 'Can't you be quiet?'

'*No*! Listen, Sam, you said you could see this Grim-Witch coming. You said you could see her in this flow that everyone keeps going on about.'

Sam gazed at her, his heart thudding. Even in her dirty and damp clothes with her hair sticking up in all directions, she still looked stunning.

'Is the flow like light?' she demanded. 'Because I saw light in your hands outside the Garden of Druids, and when you saved Oscar, and then you turned light into fire to save me from those crow-men.'

Sam was silent. He simply didn't know what to say.

Emily took a step forwards.

'Emily! Stop rocking—'

'Shut up, Eagan! Whether you like it or not, Sam, Oscar came to you that night in Oxford because he thinks you are the heir of the Druids. The Shadow didn't stop you in Magdalen because it couldn't, just like it couldn't stop you in the Garden of Druids.'

Sam felt heat rising from his toes to his head. In the middle of the night, in the middle of the sea, Emily's voice was ringing out, and she'd still got it all wrong. And he still couldn't bring himself to tell her the truth.

But Eagan had no such reservations. 'Emily! Sit down and listen to me! The Grim people aren't searching for Sam!'

His voice cut through the darkness like a knife.

'Who are they looking for then?!'

Emily sat back down on the boat's wooden seat.

'The girl,' said Eagan flatly.

'What? Sam…?'

Emily was looking at him again and he knew the game was up.

'Eagan's right – we can't say for certain, but the Grim-were was asking about you the other night and not me.'

'*And* just now,' Eagan added.

'Thanks a lot, Eagan!' Emily glared at him before turning back to Sam. 'But *you're* the one with the magic. *You're* the one who got into Cherwell and who Oscar came to deliver his message to.'

'I know,' he admitted. 'But they're looking for you.'

The silence was broken by the *Celtic Flow* grinding against its oars whilst the sea splashed against its bow.

'Why me?' Emily complained.

'I don't know,' confessed Sam, 'but when Oscar delivered his message, he told me to tell the professors that the girl was safe. Then the Grim-were in the tree-house asked about you and the one outside the Garden of Druids asked about you too. It might have been the same one, actually. I don't know, but the question was the same.'

'But I'm just caught up in this because of *you*!' Emily was half exasperated, half pleading with Sam to agree.

'I did think they were after me to begin with,' he admitted, 'then I thought perhaps they were searching for Oscar, but when you look at the jigsaw pieces, you have to be in there somewhere.'

'No! You have to be wrong! Oscar pretty much said you were the heir of the *Druidae*.'

'I don't think it's as simple as that.'

They both turned to look at Eagan, who was slumped back over his oars.

'Why not?' asked Emily.

'I think it has to do with all of us.'

'All of us?' she repeated.

'You just have to remember what Alice said. Oscar formed the Fellowship of *Druidae*. It was a fellowship – they all played their part. Perhaps without knowing it, we're all part of another fellowship.'

In the darkness, with the *Celtic Flow* beginning to move with the tide, they looked at each other in silence.

'What if we don't like the part we have to play?' Emily asked grumpily.

'Do you *always* have to ask the difficult questions?' implored Sam.

'Of course. And I don't like any of your answers so far. I was minding my own business just over a week ago. Fair enough, I'd not had the easiest summer, but there'd been no shadows, no crow-men, no Forest Reivers, no colleges that didn't exist and certainly no mad professors until you came to the bookshop, Sam. I thought Brennus and Drust were musicians! Ha, ha!'

She stood up again in the middle of the boat, adjusting her balance as the *Celtic Flow* gently rocked backwards and forwards. She pulled her jumper round her and looked forlorn, and Sam just wanted to stand up too and take her in his arms. Instead he had to tell her the whole truth.

'You were with me the night in Warkworth when the Shadow turned up. Have you ever thought that I might have led it to you?'

His words skimmed across the boat and were quickly swallowed by the dark sea.

Emily continued standing where she was, staring towards the invisible shore. But Eagan sat up.

'That is a thought,' he said. He paused. 'There's just no knowing whether the Shadow was first in Oxford or in the Garden of Druids,' he added.

'It came for you in Oxford, Sam, so it must have started there,' Emily said. 'It can't be anything to do with me.' She shivered.

'No,' replied Sam, 'it was in Warkworth before that – do you remember that night down by the Coquet? I think Eagan is right – there's no knowing what came first. And we're all caught up in this, whether we like it or not. Though I think some more than others.' His gaze rested on Emily. 'I don't know what's happening, though, because answering one question just seems to open up a dozen more.'

He looked out over the dark waves and hunched down a bit more in the boat.

'I thought it strange how Oscar said he'd never met me,' he went on, 'but now I've been thinking and I've realised it tells me something about the nature of the Garden of Druids.'

'Does it?' exclaimed Emily, still looking bewildered in the middle of the boat.

'Yes. Professor Stuckley gave a lecture on space and time and what would happen if you removed time. He suggested places without time could exist and that they would exist in more than one place. If time's arrow didn't work in these places, then they would never change, only the worlds they were connected to would. I think the Circle of *Druidae* is in such a place. I think the Druids purposefully sought out such a place to create the Fall – to make the barrier holding back the Ruin an eternal one.'

Eagan was sitting up listening, his exhaustion forgotten. 'I've never thought of it like that. But if that's the case, then why is the Fall dying? If there is no time where she is, she should live forever.'

'There are a lot of things I don't understand,' admitted Sam, 'and that's one of them. Oscar told us that the Fall was created two thousand years ago. And yet it can only have been about twenty years ago that he embarked on his quest with his fellowship. Why? I've been thinking about this ever since he delivered his message to me. Was the Fall dying twenty years ago? And if she was, why hasn't anyone told us what they did to revive her? No one seems to know.'

'Perhaps the Fall just naturally needs replenishing every so often?' Emily offered.

'But why, if there's no time where she is?' Eagan persisted.

'Because that Circle was broken?' Emily sounded doubtful. 'That's what Oscar said, anyway.'

'But then how was it broken?'

'*I* don't know, Eagan!'

'I still don't understand,' Sam said slowly, 'why the Faeries and Grim people were at war. That's how Oscar said the Ruin got in in the first place. From what Alice said, we can presume their lands are connected through the Otherland...'

'Is one of them the Darkhart?' asked Emily.

'I don't know, but Oscar said that where the Circle was, so I think so,' said Sam.

'*I* think,' said Eagan wearily, 'that all this will have to wait until we get ourselves safely ashore.'

He picked up the oars and with a grimace starting slowly pulling the *Celtic Flow* through the murky waters.

'Where are we going from here?' asked Emily.

'Howick Hall.'

'Howick Hall?' Emily looked puzzled. Then, to Sam's surprise, she smiled. 'Of course – your Uncle Kenrick.'

Eagan nodded.

'He's a steward there,' Emily explained to Sam. 'He looks after it when Lord Grey's away.'

Eagan stopped rowing, then stood and looked around him. He was glad the sea was calm, though it was a bit unsettling not being able to see the shoreline.

'Do you know which direction we should be going in?' Sam asked anxiously.

'I'm trying to navigate using the constellations,' Eagan explained. 'It's a trick Braden Bow taught me many years ago. It's a shame the night's so dark and cloudy, though. I can't see half of them.'

'Can you see enough?' Emily didn't like the idea of being lost at sea. She wished she hadn't lost her compass somewhere along the way, but then she remembered it had been no use in Birling Wood anyway.

'I think we'll be okay.' Eagan sat down and resumed rowing.

'You know we won't be able to stay in Howick long?' Emily was always good at getting to the point.

'We don't need to – we just need a bed for the rest of the night. We can bring the boat inshore and then there's a tree-lined path that follows the burn all the way to the house. We'll get some food, perhaps a bath. It's only a day's walk from Howick to Bamburgh.'

'And once we're at Bamburgh, is that where the journey ends?'

'You know I can't answer that question, Emily.'

Eagan was starting to get into his stroke and the *Celtic Flow* was beginning to cut through the dim waters, but his expression was grim.

'I didn't really expect to have to get out of Alnmouth quite so fast,' he muttered. 'And we seem to have forgotten that we haven't a clue where the Shadow is.'

'Let's hope Oscar has it trapped in Oxford,' said Sam, but he didn't sound convinced.

Emily sighed. 'Hasn't it escaped from there once already?'

The question brought Sam back to the possibility that the Shadow had simply been delayed by all that had happened the night before. Ever since they'd arrived in Alnmouth, he'd been dreading feeling its presence, and not just in his thoughts.

'It will come again.' Eagan sounded resigned to the fact.

Emily and Sam turned to him. The sweat was back on his brow as he pulled on the oars.

'We don't know that for sure,' said Sam uncertainly.

'Yes, we do, Sam, and we have to make sure that when it does come again we are prepared. If there's a way for my father to meet up with the Forest Reivers, then they will. They'll know to make for Bamburgh and the Marcher Lords. So—'

There was a loud crunch that threw Emily from her seat and brought the boat almost to a halt.

'We've hit something!' cried Eagan, leaping to his feet.

There was a terrifying grating noise as the *Celtic Flow* came to a stop.

For a second no one spoke. Then Sam felt something chilly seep through his shoes. 'We're sinking!' he shouted. Panic took hold of him as the freezing water began inching its way over his ankles.

Eagan was staring down into the waves, trying to figure out what had happened. Then he realised – in the darkness they had hit a ridge of rock that could only be seen when the waves turned white as they passed over it.

Fear washed over Sam as he remembered surfacing in the Cherwell in complete blackness. What would it be like to be at sea with no light for company, not knowing how far you were from the shore and how much water was beneath you?

'Sam, you're going to have to help!' Eagan shouted at him. He had clambered over the side and was standing there. 'Get out and help me push!'

It took at moment before Sam realised Eagan was in no more than three feet of water. Taking a deep shuddering breath, he climbed over the other side of the boat and slowly eased himself into the freezing waves, gasping as the cold hit him. He held on tightly to the boat, looking worriedly at the waters moving around him and wondering what strange creatures were swimming beneath their surface.

'Be careful,' called Emily.

'Ready?' shouted Eagan.

Sam grit his teeth.

He and Eagan set their shoulders against the boat and heaved. There was a horrible grinding noise as the *Celtic Flow* inched across the shelf.

'You need to hurry – the water's still rising!'

Sam could hear the panic in Emily's voice and feel his legs turning numb in the icy water. He wanted more than anything to feel dry ground beneath his feet. Instead he had to put his weight against the hard wood of the boat and push with Eagan while trying to ignore the grinding noise beneath the boat reaching a crescendo.

'Are you sure we aren't damaging the boat?' he shouted.

'Just push!' Eagan shouted back.

A second later the boat was free and Sam was losing his footing and plunging, gasping, into the dark sea. He surfaced, spluttering, and found Eagan, with iron-like hands, grabbing hold of the back of his jacket and pulling him back into the boat.

'Quick,' Eagan called out, 'find the breach and do something about it!'

The *Celtic Flow* was taking in water. There were already several inches swashing around the bottom of the boat. Sam and Emily looked helplessly at each other.

Eagan was quickly back at the oars, but he could tell the boat was sluggish. He was just grateful it was cloudless now and he could use the stars to navigate. Now and then the sea would turn white as a jagged rock churned the waters and he hoped they could make the mainland without further incident.

Suddenly there was a sickening crack as the boat rammed against a barely visible rock, quickly followed by a second thwack that propelled Eagan from his seat. As he picked himself back up, he heard Emily say, 'We're sinking.'

'Not yet,' he replied grimly.

Back in his seat, though, he could feel the icy water begin to slowly inch its way past his legs and could feel the boat becoming less and less responsive.

The shoreline broke above the waves perhaps several hundred yards away, but all around them jagged rocks were beginning to rise through the churning waters. Eagan was finding it almost impossible to steer and now and then there would be a deafening crack as the boat hit another rock.

'Can't you row harder?' Emily demanded.

'What do you think I'm doing?!' Eagan yelled back.

Sam looked down at the water swirling around his ankles and then watched in horror as the boat rammed against yet another sharp rock and bits of wood sprayed up into the air. In the darkness the rocks reminded him of the stone statues in Oxford – silent, unmoving and yet watchful. He couldn't help but shiver at the sight of them.

The *Celtic Flow* skimmed past several more and suddenly they were in open water with waves crashing around them.

'Get ready!' Eagan shouted.

Water was now gushing around their knees and waves were breaking over the prow. Sam grabbed Emily as a huge wave almost engulfed them. He was frightened, but held on to her waist just as another wave submerged the front of the boat. Then they were plunged into the black waters and instantly felt the currents wrapping themselves around them.

Panic and memories of the night in Oxford made Sam break the surface, gasping, terrified, and heaving Emily behind him. But the waves kept coming, crashing over their heads. Salt water was stinging their eyes and the back of their throats, but as they struggled to keep above the waves, they each felt Eagan's powerful arms around them. He propelled them safely through the waters, having spent a lifetime swimming the rivers of Northumberland.

They stumbled onto the shore, wet and coughing but grateful to be out of the churning sea. Sam lay on the shingle, looking up at the night sky and seeing the sparkling stars staring back. At that moment, he felt overwhelmed – overwhelmed by the sea, by the night sky in all its vast blackness, by the endless riddles that seemed never to be answered and by what people were expecting of him. He didn't feel much of a hero lying there shivering and coughing. Emily might be convinced he'd saved them in Oxford, but he knew he'd spent the last few days being scared out of his wits.

Eagan's voice brought him sharply back to the present – back to the crashing waves and the freezing wind.

'Damn you!'

When he sat up, he found Eagan trying to pull the *Celtic Flow* from the clutches of the lashing waves. Its bow was splintered and half-sunk and the boat was rolling helplessly just on the edge of the shore.

Emily was also sitting up shivering, looking at the forlorn figure trying to wrest the boat from the sea's clutches. She turned to Sam.

'Isn't this just awful?'

Somehow Sam found himself wading back into the waves, but the boat was now submerged and he found it impossible to get a grip on it. He drew back, not wanting to walk too far into the black sea and lose the firm ground beneath his feet.

Then Eagan looked up at him. 'Help me – I can't lose the boat.'

There was a look of such anguish on his face that Sam took a deep breath and waded further into the freezing sea. Chest-deep in the waves, he used the last of his strength to get a firmer grip on the wet planks, and together he and Eagan pulled the broken boat slowly from the sea.

Once it was firmly wedged in the wet sand, Eagan buried his face in it and threw his arms round it as if holding a fallen companion. Sam and Emily stood watching him, unsure what to say or do. Above the sound of the waves they could hear Eagan sobbing.

Emily walked slowly to her cousin and placed her hand gently on his shoulder. It was still several long moments, though, before he raised his head, put his hands over his face and turned away from the *Celtic Flow.*

Without saying a word, they left the boat where it lay ruined.

* * * * * *

They walked along the shore for a while in silence. It was Emily's voice that finally cut across their thoughts.

'I know this place.'

'Of course you do. It's Howick Haven,' replied Eagan, without taking his eyes from the floor. 'Just above those rocks will be Howick Burn and then it's a two-mile walk to Howick Hall.'

'How did you manage to navigate your way here by sea?'

'We did have a lot of luck back there. Before the actual shipwreck.' Eagan fell silent.

'Luck? We should have been smashed to pieces!' Emily cried. 'It's a notorious stretch of coastline.'

'You're right,' Eagan sighed. 'There are some foul currents in those waters, but the *Celtic Flow* was a wonderful boat. You see how she brought us safely ashore.'

He turned away.

'Can we be certain that it was the *Celtic Flow*?'

Eagan stopped walking and turned to Sam with a glint of anger. 'What do you mean?'

'Have you forgotten that you left the *Celtic Flow* on the Coquet two nights ago? How did it turn up in Alnmouth?'

'I don't know. But anyone could have rowed it there.'

'You both seem to be missing something.' Emily was already clambering up a small rocky hill. She turned to look back down at them. 'Have you really forgotten the man from the estuary? You know, the one with the black Labrador. Why was he fixing your boat?

Eagan pushed back his wet hair. 'I really don't know, Emily.'

'He was the man with Oscar in the tapestry! What was he doing in Alnmouth, looking not a day older?'

'How should I know? I'm freezing – can't we discuss this when we are sitting in front of a fire?' Eagan asked, looking irritated.

'There's something else that's been bothering me since we first arrived in Alnmouth,' Emily persisted.

'What?' asked Sam, beginning to be irritated too.

'The Alnmouth we arrived at looked different from the one we left.'

'Well, we arrived at dawn and left in the evening, so you wouldn't be wrong there.'

'That's not very funny, Sam, and it's not what I meant. When we left, all the boats on the estuary were rowing boats. I didn't see a single motor boat. But when we arrived, there were definitely boats with motors. And the doors in the village were also different, now I come to think of it.'

'You know, Warkworth was a pretty mundane place until you two turned up,' Eagan remarked. 'Now nothing surprises me. I mean, people are summoning fire from nowhere.'

'I *didn't* summon fire, Eagan.' There was a touch of anger in Sam's voice. 'It wasn't me, but the woman – the one who saved me at Magdalen, and then again at Mum's. The Fall. I heard her voice back in Alnmouth too. She was protecting it.'

'*No,*' Emily broke in, '*you* can summon fire, I know you can! I saw fire in your hands when you confronted the creature outside the orchard. I was terrified, but you didn't seem to care at all. It was all fire and words and you throwing that thing down as if it was a rag doll.'

'But—'

'Whatever excuse you're about to come out with, save it!' Eagan yelled. 'Brennus and Drust have seen something in you, and that's why they're risking their lives for you. Right now. So just get on with it.'

His words hit a nerve.

'What if I don't want it?' Sam cried. 'All it's done is put us all in danger. Look at us now – shipwrecked!'

Emily shifted uneasily as Sam's voice rose higher.

'I didn't *ask* for any of this! Why won't you listen to me? You're both in danger whilst you are with me. It doesn't take a genius to understand the Shadow will come again.'

'You were a match for it in Oxford,' Emily reminded him.

'*No! Oscar* and *Culluhin* were its match! Why won't you listen to me?!'

'It was *you!*' This time it was Emily's turn to shout. 'You saved us! I was there! I know you did!'

'Don't be so sure,' Sam growled. 'And don't rely on me. The Shadow *will* come again and next time there might not be any Oscar around.'

'Forgive me for interrupting,' Eagan said wearily, 'but I'm *really tired*. Can't we just get to Howick Hall and wait until Brennus or Drust or my father can bring news?'

'And what news do you expect them to bring?' Emily muttered.

'How should I know? That's why we need to wait for news!' Eagan rolled his eyes, then grinned suddenly.

Emily wasn't impressed. 'It seems every time we wait, we run into trouble.'

'We're *always* running into trouble!' Eagan laughed bitterly. 'It doesn't matter *where* we are! We can't even go to the pub without being attacked! What do you want us to do?'

Emily stamped her foot in frustration and placed her hands on her hips. Her wet clothes were pressed tight against her body and Sam couldn't help but forget the argument and stare at her.

'Look,' she said, 'Oscar says the Circle of *Druidae* needs to be re-made. So we just find this Otherland and then…'

'Then what?' asked Eagan. 'Face it – we haven't a clue. And if we keep moving, it's going to make it impossible for anyone to find us.'

'If you ask me, that's a good thing.'

'Ha! I see being half drowned has had no lasting impact on you, Emily. Same as ever.'

Emily scowled.

'Let's at least try to stay in one place for more than a couple of days.'

Eagan started climbing up the craggy rock face, signalling the conversation was over.

Sam quickly followed, anxious not to be left alone on the dark beach. As he scrambled over the sharp rocks, he realised just how tired he was. His legs were quickly burning against his damp clothes. Emily reached out a hand and pulled him up.

They found Eagan waiting for them at the end of a line of trees. 'These trees follow Howick Burn, which runs from the main house to the sea,' he explained. 'They'll give us cover from the skies.'

They moved beneath the trees and found a path following the trickling burn. Towering oaks on either side formed a giant archway offering some shelter from the elements.

Sam felt it almost immediately – a gentle current that pricked his senses and made the hairs on the back of his neck stand to attention.

Suddenly Emily's hand was in his. He took a quick glance at her and could tell she could feel it too.

Eagan was passing a hand over his face and looking around him.

Sam stood still. 'You know,' he said softly, 'I think we were always going to come here. Whether we wanted to or not.'

Eagan and Emily stared at him. 'Why would you say that?' Emily asked.

'When I look back, although I didn't realise it at the time, I've had this feeling before – at the Fellows' Garden, the Eagle and Child, the Garden of Druids, even the Seven Stories.'

'There *is* a strange feeling in the air,' Emily admitted. 'It's almost as if this whole place is alive.'

Eagan nodded. 'It's in the wind and in the water – it's everywhere.'

'Is this the flow that you all speak about?' Emily wondered.

Eagan shook his head.

'I think it's different,' Sam agreed, looking back the way they had come. 'It's a feeling of familiarity, of things having to be a certain way, of everything conspiring to make them so. I think from the moment I left Oxford with Professor Stuckley and Professor Whitehart, we were always going to end up at the Garden of Druids. And now I think we are being led somewhere and we no longer have a choice in the matter.'

Emily was nodding in agreement. 'The letter is part of it.'

'Yes.' Sam was still staring back through domed canopy of trees. 'But not the full story.'

He turned to look at Eagan, who was standing motionless, the strain of the last few days clearly visible on his face.

'There's something I haven't got right, though. It's been on my mind for the last few days. Now I think I've worked it out. I don't think it was the Shadow that was after me beneath the Fellows' House. I was just terrified and so I thought that was what it was, but now I think it was the Grim-were – in fact I'm certain of it. When I look back, I think it had been in Oxford for a while. I think it had been watching me.'

Sam looked from Eagan to Emily.

'Think back to Gosforth. The Shadow had found me in the Way-curve. It was then that the crow-men came. The Grim-were was the thing I saw through the window at the Seven Stories. It looked really ugly and frightening, but I think it was trying to help.'

'*Help*?!' Eagan exploded. 'Grim-were are servants of the Bodika!'

'Who?'

'The Grim-Witch. That's what the Grim people call her. Though some say she had another name once – I don't know what.'

'Well, it was the Grim-were that saved me in Gosforth.'

'It was the Grim-were that tried to *kill you* in Gosforth!' challenged Emily.

'No, no. I'm figuring it out now. Emily, listen, the Shadow was waiting for us at the house.'

'The house?!' Emily's mouth dropped open.

'That's why the Grim-were and its crow-men were out there in the garden. If they hadn't been there, the Shadow could have overcome the Fall. And I don't even want to think about what could have happened then.'

'I didn't see any Shadow…' Emily sounded unsure.

'The crow-men sacrificed themselves to stop it. Back in Oxford I remember seeing a murder of crows over the Fellows' House. They were protecting me then – they gave me enough time to escape to Magdalen. They've always been there. In the background.'

'They would have killed me in Warkworth,' said Eagan flatly.

'But they didn't.'

'They poisoned me! I'd have died if Oscar's servant hadn't helped me!'

'They needed to know where we were, Eagan, and you wouldn't tell them. They knew we'd been in Warkworth – you said it yourself. They'd been watching us. Grim-weres are shape-changers. You must recall the grey heron.'

'Yes, of course. I misled it. I was waiting for the Forest Reivers to come…'

Eagan paused. Was it possible he had never given the Grim-were a chance to explain? Had there been a huge misunderstanding?

Sam turned again to Emily. 'Believe me, the crows in Warkworth were protecting us.'

'But what about the crow-men in the wood?' she asked. 'They weren't exactly flying white flags. They meant to do the Forest Reivers great harm.'

'But you saw the Forest Reivers, Emily. They've fought the Underland for ages. Literally. According to them, anything from the Underland is trouble. They'd murder anything that came from there before they'd even asked its name.'

Eagan drew breath, but it was Emily who spoke first. 'Are you sure they haven't used their poison on your mind?'

'I'm not sure. But I can tell you that without the Grim-were's help, we might not be here now.'

'But,' said Eagan, his eyes flashing, 'the Forest Reivers would say they had just cause to fight. What good *has* ever come from the Underland? And what does this say about Brennus, Drust and Father? They fought the crow-men at the bookshop, didn't they?'

Sam paused, uncertain how to answer.

'I think Sam's right,' said Emily quickly. 'We have to keep an open mind.'

'Well, you've changed *yours* quickly enough!' Eagan said, turning sharply towards her.

Sam found himself stepping forwards. For a second the tension between them all bubbled precariously to the surface.

'Remember,' continued Eagan grimly, 'that if that letter is to be believed, a lot of Reivers lost their lives in Birling Wood. And it was the crow-men who pulled you into the water, Emily.'

Emily shivered. 'Okay, you have a point.'

'I know it all sounds confusing, Eagan,' Sam said soothingly, 'but it's important that we don't forget that there is a traitor amongst us. Oscar said they had already done much mischief. They might have told all sorts of lies about anybody.'

'And who do you think the traitor is then?' Eagan pressed.

Sam dropped his gaze. 'I don't know,' he said awkwardly. 'It might even be the letters that shouldn't be trusted.'

'We've already had that conversation!' interrupted Emily. 'Come on, Eagan, let's get moving.'

Eagan ignored her. 'You *are* relying on a letter that could have been written by people who are no longer alive. Have you ever considered *how* it could change so frequently?'

'It's changing because I keep communicating with the past,' said Sam, shifting awkwardly from one foot to the other.

'Right. Well, as I said, we'll just wait here until my father brings news of Brennus and Drust.'

Eagan turned and made his way through the trees.

'We will, will we?' Emily flared.

A tense silence fell as she and Sam followed Eagan along the path.

* * * * * *

As the archway turned north, following the course of the burn, Sam was turning his mind back yet again to Oscar's words. Why had he been so certain of himself the first time they'd met and so confused the second time? He knew he needed to speak to him again.

Emily raised her face to the sky as the path became a broken one made of stone and the giant tree-lined avenue opened out to show the stars. Cobwebs were on her face, there was a strange taste in her mouth and her nostrils were tingling just as they had done in the Garden of Druids. She half-expected the landscape around her to start melting into the darkness, but it held steady.

Walking on, she found herself looking at the back of Sam's head. Over the last few days she had been amazed by her friend from Gosforth. Who was he? He repelled attacks with fire in his hands and Oscar had as good as said that he was from the line of the Druids. In her view, there was no denying that he had some druidic power. She'd heard of the flow, which only the Druids could control. Was that what Sam was using and would he have to use it to heal the Fall?

Eagan was tired, but his blood was boiling. He felt stung by Sam's words. How could anybody sympathise with such ghastly creatures as those from the Underland? *Helping*?! What was Sam thinking? He recalled their poison and shuddered. But more than anything else, the loss of the *Celtic Flow* dominated his thoughts. Sadness and anger were spiralling in his mind as he walked forwards, trying not to think of the broken boat on the beach behind him.

He was so wrapped up in his own world that he barely saw the movement out of the corner of his eye, but then he was dropping to one knee and signalling to Sam and Emily to stop.

Sam had been practically asleep on his feet. He almost fell over Eagan and then he felt Emily bump into the back of him.

'What is it?' she called out.

Eagan did not reply.

In an instant they were all alert, crouching with their backs to one another, staring into the quiet darkness.

Then Emily spoke. 'There's something in the trees.'

Sam was scouring the branches, but there was nothing there but falling leaves. He closed his eyes, but could still see nothing. There was no light and there was no darkness, only silence. Whatever it was, it was well hidden.

The leaves were beginning to swirl around them until they could see nothing but a wall of falling leaves.

'It's a trap,' said Eagan. He put out a hand to stop Sam moving forwards.

'Wait!' Sam brushed off Eagan's hand.

Emily watched in horror as he stepped through the wall of leaves and was gone.

* * * * * *

The wall of leaves whipped around Sam in ever tighter circles and then it was like stepping from a tornado into a cloudless day. He was still on the tree-lined path and it was still night-time, but behind him he could see a wall of leaves ten feet high, and, locked behind it, the unmoving shadows of his two companions.

Ahead, a woman was waiting for him. She was tall and beautiful and Sam knew who she was before she spoke. He stood there exhausted, but there was no fear in him, only peace. He felt the tears long before they welled and slipped down his cheeks.

When she spoke, it was like being touched by the summer sun.

'Sam.'

The word passed through his mind in long ribbons of light and colour. It was a music that filled him with sadness and joy, a voice he had heard only in his dreams.

'I know who you are,' he said, trying to stop the tears, but he might as well have tried to stop the flow of the Cherwell.

'I have long watched you and longed to speak to you,' she replied, 'but you would not have understood. I should not have shown myself to you now, but great danger comes to the Mid-land. Tonight my father and sister are in great peril.'

Her words should have brought unimaginable terror to his heart, but instead he was filled with courage.

'You must bring together the fellowship who will protect the

Three. There is no time to lose, for the Ruin's servants are again in the Mid-land.'

'Isn't there any other way?' Sam asked. He wanted the peace he was feeling now to go on forever.

The woman shook her head.

'It is such a great burden,' Sam sighed.

'It is the burden of the Druids. The First Light chose them a long time ago. Only the heir of the *Druidae* can carry its flame into the Darkhart.'

'Who—?'

But before Sam could finish his question, she answered, 'Go quickly to Holy Island and in the garden there you will find the Staff of the Druids.'

A giant red kite flew out of the night and landed on a tree stump within touching distance. It gave Sam a sharp look before turning to its mistress and giving a number of shrill calls.

'I must go. There is a war coming and I must prepare my followers.'

She turned again to Sam and he felt almost overcome.

'There is much about you that gives me hope. Do not despair. You will make the right choices and help will not be far away.'

She made as if to go, then stopped. As the giant bird of prey took to the air and quickly disappeared, she turned to Sam one final time.

'You remind me so much of your father. Believe in yourself and you could be even greater than he was.'

He blinked and she was gone. In her place he saw a lithe red mare melting into the shadows.

* * * * * *

Eagan and Emily found Sam a few hundred yards from where the leaves had suddenly dropped from the trees.

'Sam, you look as though you've seen a ghost! Sam! Are you listening to me?'

'I'm sorry – what was that?'

Eagan was looking into the trees, from which several giant birds of prey were taking flight. On the soft ground beside the Howick Burn he could see hoof marks.

'What's just happened here?' he mumbled.

Sam could still see the woman, tall, with hair as golden as the leaves that had fallen around her. He wanted to speak to her again, he wanted to reach out and touch her fair skin. He had almost been overcome by her love for him and his love for her. She reminded him of the woman at the gates of Magdalen, but this woman had been real. All his self-doubt and fear had dropped away in her presence. He had a burden to carry and a mission to accomplish, but now he felt ready.

'One of Three came to me,' he said.

'One of the Dagda's daughters?' Eagan was surprised.

They stood looking at each other, whilst leaves again started gently raining down on them.

'What does that mean? Did she tell you anything?' Emily was pushing her damp hair back from her face.

'There is a war coming,' Sam said.

'I think it's already here,' replied Eagan, 'but did she say anything else?'

'I have to gather together a fellowship. The flame of the First Light has to be carried into the Darkhart,' Sam answered.

Eagan seemed to recoil. 'And how do you propose to do that?'

'She said I had to go to Holy Island and find a talisman.'

'What are you supposed to do with it?'

'She didn't say. She didn't have much time. She was preparing for this war.'

'Great!' said Emily. 'Just what I needed to hear.'

'I have to speak to Oscar,' declared Sam. 'He'll be able to tell me—'

'No!' Eagan was shaking his head. 'We wait for Father and then decide what to do.'

'But she said I had to go quickly. That the Ruin's servants were in the Mid-land. What if there isn't just one Shadow next time, but others as well?'

Emily let out a whimper of fear.

'What about the letter?' Eagan asked. 'What does that say?'

Sam felt in his back pocket, but the familiar creases of the envelope had now become a soggy mess. As he withdrew it, he saw that the ink had run and both letter and envelope had all but disintegrated.

For a moment they all stared at it in silence.

'That's that, then,' said Emily.

Sam felt suddenly bereft. Then he remembered there was another way.

'We have to find a Way-curve,' he said, 'and speak to the Keepers of the Druids. I think they were part of Oscar's fellowship. I'd like to speak to Oscar himself.'

'Oh, yes, it's a brilliant plan,' Emily said with a sarcastic grimace. 'We form another fellowship! We set off into the Otherland! We don't even know where it is. And if we do get there, then what?'

'I think if the Shadow hadn't attacked the Garden of Druids, then Oscar would have been prepared to lay out exactly what we needed to do.'

'Yes, but it did attack. And now he's back in Oxford with you.' Emily shook her head in exasperation.

'Well, he's back in Oxford with the Shadow.'

'So you say. But you can't break the paradox so easily! For all we know, the Shadow could be anywhere. Could be stalking us right this second.'

'Okay, enough!' Eagan had heard it all before. 'It's pointless going round in circles. We can't go further into Northumberland without understanding what we're facing. Brennus and Drust went to the Dead Water seeking answers. When they return, we'll know more.'

'But they *won't* return. Remember what the letter said.'

'Can we just leave the letter out of this?'

Eagan and Emily glared at each other.

Sam broke the tension by saying wearily, 'You do what you want, Eagan, but I'm going to find a way to finish the conversation I started with Oscar. He led a fellowship to the Darkhart. And it looks as though I might need to do the same.'

Eagan ran an exasperated hand through his hair, turned and

walked on. Emily stomped along behind him. Sam brought up the rear, wondering how he could ever form a fellowship when he couldn't even get two people to agree with him.

They walked through the avenue with only the babble of the burn for company. As the trees thinned out, they saw that a slight blue tint was edging ever westward. Dawn was breaking when the trees came to an abrupt end and they arrived at Howick Hall.

* * * * * *

They stood on a small rise looking down on the hall and its gardens. Sam was convinced that each place they had travelled through had been connected and this felt no different. He only had to look at Emily once more trying to brush the invisible cobwebs from her face to know that the Fall's power was not yet broken here.

Eagan was already making his way down into an autumn garden fit for a king. They followed him over a short wooden bridge across the burn and into a profusion of trees and shrubs of all shapes, sizes and colours. Their senses were lit up by a thousand earthly smells as they walked through the gardens and climbed a steep bank, and when they came to its summit, the house was waiting for them, its imposing Georgian architecture framed by the dark blue light of dawn.

The stillness, the silence and the smells reminded Sam of the Fellows' Garden in Oxford. Even in the dawn light he could see the Fellows' House reflected in the Georgian style of Howick Hall. There was the same symmetrical flow he had seen in the Seven Stories and the old school house. They were being led from place to place, and whether they had any choice in the matter or not, he could see and feel the connections between each one clearly now. From the emblem of Cherwell College to the successive reading rooms, the Keepers of the Druids had left their mark. Were they there too, willing them on, or was it the Fall herself?

Then they were passing a circular pond and benches, and for a moment Sam thought he was back in the Fellows' Garden, or was it the Garden of Druids? He wondered whether Oscar would come back from the dead and deliver a different message to him there.

As he climbed the steps leading out of the gardens, he couldn't help but turn and look back at them. And all the while he could feel it – an energy, a strange happiness that brushed his cheek. It was as if the darkness of the last few days could not penetrate this place. As if he was looking out of his window at Cherwell before Oscar had turned up with the letter and the Shadow had arrived in Oxford. As if all his fears had simply melted away, as if he was a boy again, looking out from his tree house towards Elgy Green in the late summer sun, waiting for his friends so they could play beneath the shelter of the trees, a time before he had started to see the dancing lights and hear the faraway voices, a time of innocence before he had been drawn into the desperate dance between the hunter and the hunted. And yet, whether he liked admitting it or not, he knew that really the storm clouds had been gathering long before he had gone to Oxford, long before the Shadow had turned up in Warkworth.

He also knew the day would come when he would have to face his fears and confront the unseen enemies that were stalking him in the edgelands of his mind. But there were unseen allies too. He was opening his eyes to a new world. It was as if his first encounter with the Fall had set him free. And every step he had taken into the unknown had brought a deeper understanding of the power that flowed around him. At Magdalen, it had been nothing more than a chorus of voices willing him to awaken to its potential. At Warkworth Castle, the Garden of Druids had called to him because he had started to believe in himself. The more he asked for help and the more he gave of himself, the more help would turn up. Just as Ronald's letter had foretold.

* * * * * *

They finally arrived on the main terrace of the hall. Sam stood between Eagan and Emily, looking up at the building's stately lines.

'Most of the hall is closed and the family are away,' Eagan explained. 'Uncle Kenrick will be in his home in the annexe.'

He started skirting the hall, Sam and Emily following.

Sam looked at the building curiously as he passed by. The

windows were large and dark and he could see nothing of the rooms from outside. They walked under a small archway that led into a garden courtyard with magnificent borders, then Eagan took them down a small footpath that led from the main hall across a manicured lawn to an iron gate that was slightly ajar.

'Look!' Emily said.

Sam and Eagan turned, and there in the gate was a circle with a tree at its centre, crafted perfectly from the metal.

'The emblem of Cherwell College.'

'Another safe house in the wilderness,' Sam said with a smile.

'By the looks of things the *Celtic Flow* knew where she was taking us,' Eagan said. 'Come on, let's have something to eat and drink and go to bed.'

He clapped Sam on the back and the three of them passed through the gate and walked along a stone path to an oak door with a slightly rusty knocker. Eagan tapped it gently and stood back.

There was a pause. Sam could feel his legs beginning to shake, he was so tired. Whoever they were trying to rouse from their sleep was taking an age. He was just about to ask Eagan to knock harder when there was a loud creak as the door slowly opened and a soft light escaped into the night.

'Eagan!' came a stunned but gentle voice. 'Good grief – have you been chasing Forest Reivers?'

A figure stepped from behind the door dressed head to foot in stripy pyjamas. It was an older gentleman with a long handlebar moustache that was almost white and small-rimmed glasses that were sitting on a long thin nose. When he took in Sam and Emily, his eyes grew wide.

'Good grief – Sam!'

'You know Sam?' Eagan asked.

'Know him? We've been looking for him the length and breadth of Northumberland.'

Without further ado, the man ushered them through the door. Once he had bolted it firmly shut, he turned to them.

'I'm very glad to see you. You've had us all worried.'

'Uncle, I don't understand.'

'Well, you should, Eagan. Everyone goes missing for days after Sam returns from Oxford. Not a word from your mother or your father. Even the Hoods have disappeared. There are rumours that all sorts of strange beings have been seen. Then a company of Forest Reivers passes through these lands prepared for battle. Do you expect me and your aunt to remain calm?'

Sam, Emily and Eagan stood in the large hallway feeling slightly guilty.

'And by the looks of you, your journey has not been without incident,' the man continued, looking at them curiously. 'Forgive me, I am a poor host,' he added. 'I have let my excitement get the better of me. Come, dry yourselves off.'

'Some food and dry clothes would be good.' Eagan smiled at his uncle.

'Yes, of course. Come along. Hello, Emily. I'm Kenrick, by the way, Sam. Very pleased to meet you.'

He led them all through a doorway into a living area based around a beautifully decorated fireplace. In it, embers were still glowing red. With a little kindling, within minutes the fire was springing back into life. Then Kenrick disappeared back through the doorway, leaving the others by themselves.

Sam sat down on a leather couch and felt the heat from the fire beginning to thaw out his legs. Emily dumped herself in an armchair and without another word was asleep. Eagan stood with his back to the fire, facing the door they had come through. Sam could tell there was something bothering him.

'What's wrong?'

Eagan shrugged his shoulders. 'I didn't think he knew anything about you. It looks as though more people are aware of you than we think. And I've never seen him look so startled.'

'If someone knocked on your door at 4 a.m., I think you would look startled.'

To Sam's relief, Eagan smiled. 'That's probably it, Sam. These last few days have put me on edge, that's all.'

He sat down by the fire, stretched out and closed his eyes.

It wasn't long before Kenrick returned, carrying a tray full of sandwiches and a large pot of tea. He set everything down on a large round coffee table and sat down in a leather chair opposite Emily, who remained fast asleep.

'Come along,' he said stirring the tea and pouring everyone a cup. 'I am so glad you have found your way to my home. I have heard a lot about you, Sam, this past year.'

'Really?' Eagan sounded irritated again.

Kenrick sat back on his haunches. 'Yes, Eagan, I sat with your father and mother not a week ago at the bookshop and listened to Sam's words – and they fair turned my blood to ice.'

Sam felt his cheeks burn a little as he sipped his tea. Alice had said the same thing. It seemed there had been more people listening to that conversation than he knew.

Eagan scowled. 'I just don't understand why my father would keep such news away from me.'

'Didn't he send you to seek help from the Forest Reivers?' Kenrick asked. 'There isn't one amongst us who could have found them so quickly. No one knows those rivers and valleys the way you do.'

He patted Eagan lovingly on the arm.

'And who else was listening to Sam's words?' asked Eagan.

But his uncle waved his hand in the air. 'That's not important. What is important,' he turned to Sam, 'is that you are safe and sound. You are very welcome to stay here as long as you need. We'll wait for Eagan's father to arrive before we discuss what to do now, but before you retire to bed, do tell me a little of what has happened since you left Oxford.'

'Don't you already know Sam's every move?!'

'No, Eagan, though we have had some news from two visitors this week. Carl Lawrence—'

'Professor Lawrence!' Sam broke in excitedly. 'He was at Cherwell College with Professor Stuckley and Professor Whitehart! He helped me to escape.'

Kenrick smiled. 'Ah yes, Professor Stuckley and Professor

Whitehart, alias Brennus and Drust! I bet Brennus has been loving the chance to lecture on physics!'

Sam smiled back. How long ago that seemed…

'Well, as I was saying,' Kenrick was continuing, 'Carl called in here on his way north. I wouldn't like to be going that way myself. Some very strange things have been happening in the borderland.'

'Where was Professor Lawrence going?' asked Sam, a little perturbed by the man's words.

'To Edinburgh. To make sure that Angus was safe.'

Sam almost dropped his cup. 'Angus? The Angus who was at Cherwell College with me?'

'Yes, we wanted to keep you both together.'

'Why would you keep us together?'

But this time Kenrick rubbed his chin, unwilling to give a quick answer.

'I've perhaps told you too much in my excitement.'

'I wouldn't worry. He has met Oscar in the Garden of Druids,' Eagan yawned.

'The Garden of Druids now!' Kenrick looked at Sam. 'Well, I *am* staggered. Though I admit my view of reality has been challenged this week, you must be mistaken. There has to be a different explanation. It can only have been a representation of the real place. Perhaps even a reflection.'

'Why is that?' Eagan asked.

'Because there is only one way into the Darkhart and one way out.'

'And the garden's there?' Eagan was puzzled.

Kenrick ignored him and kept his eyes on Sam. 'Well, that's what Oscar said. But his fellowship never made it to the Darkhart anyway.'

'Really?' said Sam. 'But they can't have failed, because the Fall survived and the Shadow was locked away…' He found his voice trailing off in confusion.

'Oscar never went to rescue the Fall, but a child.'

'A child?' Sam felt himself sinking back into the couch.

'Yes. Oscar kept it all very quiet, of course, but I had it from Braden's father, and he was one of the few who came back.'

'Who was the child?' Sam could barely get the words out.

'Ah, that I can't tell you. It seems there was some confusion and I don't know whether Oscar told anyone the full story. But I heard that it had to be brought to the Mid-land for safekeeping.'

'*Did* they bring it to the Mid-land?' Eagan was leaning forwards in his chair, his dark eyes fixed on his uncle.

'Apparently. But I don't know what arrangements Oscar made after that. He went back to Alnmouth and very rarely said anything to anyone about what he'd done, as far as I understand it. I think he was embarrassed because most of his fellowship perished at the Dead Water. I don't think they exactly covered themselves in glory.'

Sam's mind was whirling. 'Who knows where this child is now? It will be grown up... *Who is it?*'

'I really can't tell you, I'm afraid,' Kenrick said, picking up his cup of tea.

'Why didn't Alice tell us about this?' Sam wondered.

Eagan shrugged. 'Wait until my father gets here, or Brennus and Drust. If anyone knows more, they will.'

'Anyway,' said Kenrick, 'we're all tired and I think I've said enough for one night. I can only guess what trials and hardships you have faced these last few days. Now is not the time for more questions. I will show you to your rooms. A good night's sleep will clear your minds and then we can think about what to do next.'

It was as if Kenrick's words had reminded Sam of just how tired he was. He found himself taking deep breaths as he got shakily to his feet. Emily was still slumped in her chair fast asleep. Sam could not wake her, so he and Eagan lifted her between them, then Sam carried her in his arms.

Kenrick took them back through the doorway into a short corridor that led to a staircase that had perhaps seen better times. As they climbed the creaking stairs, Emily opened her eyes and gave Sam a faint smile, then she was asleep again.

At last they came to a number of doors leading off a corridor.

Kenrick opened the first one. 'You can leave Emily here.'

Sam walked into the room. Through the long windows he could see the darkness was quickly receding west and a deep blue sky was rushing in to fill the void. He laid Emily down on the bed, threw a cover over her and gently closed the door.

Back in the hallway, he caught sight of Eagan scowling as he opened a door directly across the hall. Kenrick was standing there, looking at Eagan with an expression Sam could not decipher. Then Eagan closed his door with a thud and Kenrick turned back to Sam.

'These are strange days for all of us,' he said. 'But I hope you know how glad I am that you have made it to my home. This is your room.' He opened another door. 'You will be safe here.'

Sam felt his eyes growing heavy and the only reply he could offer was a nod before he too fell into bed and was quickly asleep.

## AN UNEXPECTED VISITOR

How long he had been staring at the pattern on the bedroom ceiling he couldn't say. Light was streaming through the large window. He sat up slowly and realised every part of his body ached.

Kenrick's words quickly came back into his mind. He'd only just met him, but had discovered more in those few minutes than he had in the week or more of running from place to place. And the woman. The Faerie. He would not easily forget meeting her. She had filled him with joy, hope and sadness. Sadness that he had never seen her before and might never see her again. But he knew she was there, supporting him, and somehow she always had been.

He took a deep breath and sat on the edge of the bed, looking out over the neatly manicured lawns where a sprinkler was in full flow. He couldn't tell how long he had slept, but he knew it hadn't been long enough. He stood, stretching and yawning at the same time, and went in search of clean clothes and a shower.

A little while later, dressed in some rather ill-fitting clothes, he found his way out to a small patio area overlooking the well-tended private gardens. To one side of the lawn he saw a table with a single figure sitting reading beneath a large umbrella.

'Feeling better?' asked Emily.

Sam took the seat across from her and looked around the empty garden. Emily was looking refreshed. Her long hair was tied up, showing off her long neck, and she was also wearing clean if slightly ill-fitting clothes.

'What time is it?' asked Sam.

'It's early afternoon. I've been awake for a few hours. I've met Eagan's auntie, who has kindly fed and watered me. Hey, I've got something for you.'

She stood up and came to sit beside Sam. Then, without saying another word, she kissed him on the lips.

'A little thank-you for saving me last night.'

She stroked his face.

Sam flushed. He didn't know what to say. Emily always had the knack of surprising him.

'When you go to Holy Island, I want to come with you,' she continued.

He turned away, unable to meet her eyes. The intensity was a little too much.

'I don't understand—'

But Emily didn't let him finish. 'I don't want you getting any ideas in the middle of the night and coming to the conclusion you're better off without me – you aren't. You might be getting it into your head that the road ahead is too dangerous for me, and it isn't. Eagan was right in what he said back in the boat – we're all already part of this fellowship.'

She kept her eyes firmly on him and the space between them was full of ribbons of sunlight that only seemed to make her beauty stand out even more.

'So you must take me and Eagan with you.'

'Okay, okay!' Sam felt almost panic-stricken. She was so beautiful and so close to him. 'Where *is* Eagan anyway?' he asked hurriedly.

'Where do you think? He's gone to see whether he can recover the *Celtic Flow*.'

'I've never seen anyone so upset about a boat!'

'Well, that boat *is* special. It's been in the family for generations. Eagan spends half his life in it. And now he's the one who's lost it. I suppose it's no wonder he's feeling terrible about it.'

Sam sighed. 'Where's Kenrick?'

'He said he had business to attend to in Craster.'

'But his wife has food in the kitchen?'

Emily nodded.

'Right, I'm hungry. No, really I'm *starving*.'

Emily laughed. 'I'll come with you.'

She reached out to pick up the book she had been reading and the loose sleeve of her blouse fell back from her arm.

'Emily! How did you get those cuts?'

'The crow men did it.'

'What?'

Sam took hold of Emily's arm and turned it over, examining it. 'You didn't feel it?'

Emily looked irritated. 'Not really, but they *were* pulling me into the water at the time, if you remember. It's no big deal, Sam. Stop fussing.'

'You should have been poisoned, just like Eagan.'

'But I wasn't.'

Sam couldn't take his eyes off the long livid wounds. 'Why didn't you mention in the boat that you were injured?'

'I didn't know I *was* injured until I took a shower this morning. Why are you looking at me like that?'

'Aren't you surprised that their poison hasn't had any effect on you?'

'Well, perhaps they decide who gets the poison and who doesn't.'

Sam shook his head. 'I don't know.'

He dropped Emily's arm. The sight of the cuts had unnerved him.

'Look, let's just go in and have some lunch. We might as well enjoy being here whilst we can. You never know when we might have to leave suddenly.'

Emily smiled. 'Does that mean you're taking me with you?'

'Possibly,' answered Sam a little awkwardly.

'Come on, you know we make a good team. Who knows what would have happened last night without me protecting you?!'

Emily grinned, stood, stretched and took off across the lawn, leaving Sam running to catch up.

* * * * * *

After lunch, they had coffee in the private garden and then decided to go for a walk in the grounds. The hall was well known for its gardens and arboretum. Neither Eagan nor Kenrick had returned and for once there seemed to be a small oasis of calm.

'Let's make the most of the peace and quiet while we can,' said Emily, slipping her hand into Sam's.

They left the private garden the way they had arrived the night before and crossed a small pasture whose grass was wild and knee-high. The sun was high in the sky, and for the first week in September, it was warm. Sam drew a deep breath and allowed himself to relax.

They came out of the tall grass and found a small dirt track that cut the field in two. Walking north, they found the entrance to the Bog Garden, which had grass paths surrounding a central pond. To give it structure, a number of trees and shrubs had also been planted in and around it.

As they walked, they felt the familiar buzz in their ears, the gentle ripple in a distant corner of their minds. Sam knew even before he fully surveyed the pond that it had the look of the one in Oxford. The Keepers of the Druids were connected through the emblem of Cherwell College and these garden and ponds in a way that he was only just beginning to understand.

They passed through the Bog Garden to a long narrow lawn adjoining the Wild Garden, a little touch of wilderness in the middle of the ordered serenity. For the first time since arriving in Warkworth, for long moments they felt totally carefree. It was as if the tranquillity of the gardens could not be broken.

When they came to the Walled Garden and found a gate there, they were no longer surprised to find the circle with the unknown tree crafted in its twisted iron. When they pushed against it, though, it was unmoving, even though there were no bolts holding it shut. They could see into the garden, and it was full of trees and shrubs, but they could not penetrate its depths.

Instead, they turned and continued walking down the narrow lawn until they reached the end, where they sat down on a single wooden bench looking back the way they had walked. At first they did not speak. In the warm sun their hands were moist with sweat and Sam couldn't help but feel a little flustered.

It was Emily who broke the silence.

'It's so lovely here, but the Faerie woman said you had to go to Holy Island quickly to find this talisman. So how long are you planning on staying? Until Uncle Jarl gets here?'

Sam shook his head. 'Who knows when that will be? But I do want to question Kenrick a little more. He seems to be willing to tell me more than anyone else so far. Up to now I've just been stumbling around in the dark.'

'Yes, that's true,' Emily replied slowly, 'although I think people have just been trying to protect you, Sam. But what has Kenrick said so far? I don't remember anything after we sat down by the fire.'

Sam laughed. 'That's because you were asleep!' Becoming more serious, he took his hand from Emily's and shifted on the bench so he could look straight at her. 'Whilst you were asleep, Kenrick told me a few things that I found hard to believe, but there is no reason not to believe him.'

Emily was looking at him intently. 'Like what?'

'Oscar never went to rescue the Fall. By all accounts, he went to rescue a child.'

'A child?' repeated Emily.

'That's what he said. Apparently Braden's father knew. He was with him. It's probable that Brennus, Drust and Jarl all knew as well.'

'Is that why they have been protecting you?'

'I don't know. Kenrick says he doesn't know who the child is. They did bring it back, but Oscar was very secretive about it and I'm not sure whether they even know where it is now. They seem to have been covering a few options. Apparently Professor Lawrence is up in Edinburgh keeping an eye on Angus.'

'Angus!' said Emily. She frowned. 'Well, it does make sense,' she added slowly. 'He was the only other person with you at Cherwell College and he was attacked by crows.'

'But were they attacking or protecting?'

'I don't know, Sam. But he was with us the night the Shadow first appeared, remember? At the old school house?'

'I remember only too well.' Sam grimaced.

'Where is he now? Is he still in Edinburgh?'

'I suppose so.'

'And presumably Professor Lawrence isn't a real professor either?'

'No, I suppose not…'

'So what's the significance of this child? Why did Oscar go and get it?'

'Because it had to be brought here for safekeeping.'

Emily frowned again. "Well, somebody had better find out who it is then. Though if you ask me, I know already. Did Kenrick tell you any more about it?'

'No, but he did say that Oscar had never been to the Darkhart. That his fellowship came unstuck at the Dead Water.'

Emily leaned back on the bench and crossed her arms. 'So Oscar doesn't know the way to the Darkhart?'

'I don't know. That's one of the reasons why I need to speak to him.'

Emily sighed. 'So let me get this straight. According to this Faerie woman, you have to gather together a fellowship because this – what is it? – First Light has to be carried into the Darkhart.'

'Yes.'

'Which will presumably stop the Shadow, or the Ruin, which sounds even worse?'

'Yes, as far as I understand it.'

'So you need to go to the Darkhart, which is on the other side of the Dead Water – is it?'

Sam shrugged. 'Oscar needed to get past the Dead Water, so yes, I suppose so.'

'And Brennus and Drust have already gone to the Dead Water, and if that letter's right, they aren't coming back.'

Sam shifted on the bench, looking very uncomfortable. 'Please don't remind me about that.'

He got up and started pacing about on the lawn.

'Oscar said the Dead Water was lost right back at the beginning,' he added.

Emily shivered. 'Oh, it's making my head spin! I just wish it would all stop and you could go back to Oxford and I could visit you.'

Sam looked up and smiled suddenly. 'I'd love that too. But in the meantime,' he went on, frowning again, 'I'm supposed to create a fellowship out of thin air and go to Holy Island for this talisman. That much I do know. So that's what I'll have to do. But the main thing is to speak to Oscar and find out who the child was.'

'Aren't the professors already onto that? Shouldn't you just concentrate on the fellowship and getting to Holy Island?'

Sam stopped beneath the gate with the iron circle and tree. 'I want to know whether that child was you or me.'

Emily looked up in bewilderment. 'Need it be either of us?'

'Well, look what's happened to us!' Sam exploded. 'What's *still happening*! Doesn't that tell you anything? And remember the Grim-were. Who is it looking for? I think that child was you.'

Emily instinctively shrank away from him. 'Don't shout like that! I think it was you. But it might be Angus. It might be someone else entirely.'

'That's *why* I need to speak to Oscar. To find out who that child was.'

'What if you don't like what he tells you? What if it *is* you? What if it's someone we don't even know? Will we have to track them down and take them to the Darkhart with us?'

'We might have to.'

The tranquillity of the gardens had been shattered after all. Walking separately, Sam and Emily went back the way they had come, cutting through the Wild Garden and across the Bog Garden, not speaking except when they said hello to a solitary gardener who was on his hands and knees trimming the edges of the lawn.

They eventually made it back to the private garden, which was still deserted save for darting blackbirds and sparrows.

'Come with me,' said Sam as he opened the large oak door and went back into the house.

He started opening doors until he found the way to the main hall. They stood before an elegant staircase that split in two, leading to a landing of dark polished oak.

'I don't know the exact way there,' said Sam, 'but last night when we were on the hill looking down at the hall, I noticed a glass dome. And where there's a glass dome, there's a reading room, and where there's a reading room, there's a Way-curve, and where there's a...'

'I get it,' interrupted Emily. 'You're going to try and communicate with Oscar. But I thought it was dangerous to use the Way-curves. I thought it could potentially draw the Shadow to you. And you may not like what Oscar says anyway.'

'Whatever it is, I need to know.' Sam took hold of the smooth banister and looked out across the hallway. 'And now we no longer have the letter, the Way-curve is the only way.'

'Be careful,' Emily warned.

'I will. Come on.'

The staircase joined the west wing with the main hall. Sam came to two large doors and first tried to push and then pull, but nothing happened. There was no sign of a lock, so he placed his shoulder against the door and gave it a little shove, but again nothing happened.

'Let me try.'

Sam looked at Emily. 'What?'

'Don't look at me like that – move over.'

Sam stepped aside and Emily placed her hand on the hard wood and gently pushed. The doors swung inward and they were met with warm but stale air.

'How strange—' began Sam.

Emily did not wait for him to finish, but pressed on through the doors. He quickly followed her into a second musty corridor with painted oak panels that were peeling in places.

'You don't have any idea where this reading room is?'

'No,' came the short answer.

'It's probably on the opposite side from Kenrick's living quarters.'

They met another set of double doors that would only open for Emily. Sam reflected on this as they moved across an open landing and looked down into the great hall, which was lit by several immense Georgian windows. Even from here he could feel the warmth of the sunlight coursing through them.

Not stopping to admire the architecture or the paintings hanging from their dusty perches, they went on. A third set of double doors was open, revealing the high ceiling of a short corridor, and just after those the door to a room also stood open.

Sam put his finger to his lips, warning Emily not to say a word as they approached.

Walking as softly as possible, they entered a room that could easily have been the reading room of the Seven Stories. High above them was a glass dome, with the afternoon sun streaming through and glinting off the dark oak floor, whilst in the middle of the room was a circular table with number of chairs.

They jumped as the doors behind them softly clicked shut. No one had entered. But then Sam felt the hair on the back of his neck rise. Someone was here already. At the far side of the room was a solitary figure silhouetted against the light from one of the large windows.

'Please tell me it's not…' Emily whispered.

Sam almost turned back to the door, but it was too late. The figure had seen them and was making its way across the room. Sam felt his stomach knot as a thin smile crossed Morcant Pauperhaugh's face.

'Well, well, Sam, Emily, we finally meet again. Kenrick tells me you've been on quite a journey.'

'What are you doing here?' Sam asked nervously. This time there was no locked gate between them, and Morcant, for all his smiles, looked every bit the villain.

'I was sent here to seek help from Kenrick.'

'Of course,' thought Sam, 'Kenrick mentioned that he had had two visitors. He just didn't say that one of them was still here.'

'Come on,' Morcant raised both hands in the air in mock submission. 'You both look as though you are about to faint. Sit down. I'm just relieved that you're both fine.' He smiled again, showing yellow and broken teeth.

Sam couldn't help but feel Morcant was enjoying catching them both off-guard. He could feel his dislike for the man surging with every passing second.

'How—?'

'Before you ask, I was sent here by Brennus.'

'Why?'

'Sam,' Morcant smiled his thin smile, 'you know that in the coming days we will need all our friends if we are to get through this war in one piece.'

'Then why did you attack Eagan?' Emily almost hissed. It seemed her shock had already reverted to hostility.

Morcant turned his unsettling pale blue eyes on her. 'Whatever you have been told, dear cousin, just remember, there are always two sides to every story. And remember you are as much of a Pauperhaugh as I am.'

'No, I'm not!'

Morcant seemed unruffled. 'As I said before, we ought to stick together. I have the confidence of Brennus, Drust and Jarl. Surely I deserve a little of *your* respect too.'

'Then why did you disagree with everything they said in the bookshop?' Emily asked bluntly.

'Of course, it had been Morcant who had disagreed with Brennus going to the Dead Water,' thought Sam. With a sinking feeling, he wondered whether he had been right after all.

'I was concerned that they would be taking Sam to the very place the enemy would expect him to go,' Morcant explained, 'and that he would walk into a trap. Being a true Pauperhaugh,' he glanced at Emily, 'I am naturally suspicious of the motives of others.'

Emily scowled.

'I am just glad you have found your way to Kenrick,' Morcant continued. 'He is a good man and does not suffer fools gladly. Nor is he interested in the politics of the foolish.'

'The foolish?' Sam thought. 'Does he mean the professors?'

'You seem to be full of answers,' Emily snarled.

Finally she seemed to have got beneath Morcant's skin. 'Sometimes, Emily,' he hissed, 'just like your mother, you have too much to say!'

But then he seemed to recover his poise.

'Look, this is all unhelpful,' he went on more smoothly. 'If you wish, I will tell you what *I* would have wanted. *I* would have wanted everyone to come here, in the present, to discuss matters, rather than listen to the voices of the past.'

It sounded reasonable, but Sam still felt uneasy. Why not learn from the past? What had Morcant learned? How much did he know?

'You know Eagan is here?' It would seem Emily had changed her mode of attack.

A flicker of fear passed across Morcant's face, but it was gone in an instant. 'Yes, Kenrick mentioned that Eagan had nearly drowned you both in the sea.'

His swift response hit home and Sam saw Emily's cheeks turn slightly redder.

'If wasn't for Eagan, we would never have made it ashore,' she retorted. 'My mother hasn't a bad word to say about him.'

'I bet she hasn't. You can't say the same about your father, though, can you?'

Sam didn't like how the conversation was turning tribal. 'Emily's right. If it wasn't for Eagan, we would never have got here in the first place.'

Morcant turned away. 'Eagan Reign is a man whose temper will end up getting him into big trouble. I just hope you aren't with him when it happens.'

Remembering the old school house, Sam could not disagree.

Meanwhile Emily was determined to push home her advantage. 'He will be here soon,' she said brightly, 'and you can tell him that to his face.'

'I can't wait,' said Morcant drily.

For a moment silence fell. Sam couldn't help wishing Eagan would walk through the door at that very moment, but he didn't. Instead Morcant crossed his arms and fixed his pale blue gaze on him and Emily.

'Don't you think that I'm a little obvious to be your traitor, Sam?'

Sam flushed. 'I don't know what you mean.'

'I'm sure you do. Brennus mentioned in our little meeting that there was a traitor amongst us, remember? And I always say you can't judge a book by its cover.'

'I'm not in the mood for word games,' Sam growled.

He took a step towards Morcant, who instantly took a step back.

'Would you prefer to dance then?' he mocked.

Suddenly Sam had had enough. He didn't want to waste a moment more talking to Morcant Pauperhaugh. 'No,' he said, 'I wouldn't. I'm going to wait for Professor Stuckley and then decide what to do.' He turned to Emily. 'Are you coming?'

Emily nodded and with a little contemptuous shake of the head turned on her heel.

'You have it all wrong!' Morcant called after them as they left the room.

Sam didn't look back.

'Where are we going?' enquired Emily.

'We're going out into the garden while we wait for Morcant to leave. Then we're going right back to that Way-curve.'

'Okay.'

They reached the main staircase without pausing and were soon down its steps and back out into the warm sunshine.

* * * * * *

The day was warm and they put together a picnic of fruit and sandwiches and spent the early evening strolling beneath the trees of the Island Walk. Sam told Emily more about the Faerie woman he had met. Somehow he knew that the feeling of ease and security at the hall was because of her.

Inevitably, though, he also wondered about Morcant Pauperhaugh. Why didn't he really like or trust the man, especially when it was clear that Brennus, Drust and Jarl did? Or *was* it clear? But then Morcant had been at the meeting at the Seven Stories and Brennus had sent him here. So what was it?

It wasn't just the way he looked, Sam decided. That wasn't particularly pleasant, but there had to be more to it than that. The confrontation outside his mother's house in Gosforth hadn't helped matters, but to be fair to Morcant, it had been Jarl who had sent him on the errand. Then there was the story surrounding his altercation with Eagan. Of course there were always two sides to every story, and he had only listened to Eagan's. Sam tried hard to be fair, but he had to admit Morcant didn't help himself with his sneering smile and patronising manner. He wondered what sort of relationship he had with Kenrick.

Emily didn't have a good word to say about her cousin. 'I wish we didn't have to go back into the house and risk meeting him again,' she said.

Sam sighed. He wasn't keen on another encounter with Morcant either. 'Let's stay out here a while longer then.' He smiled at Emily. 'That was an easy decision to take.'

Emily smiled back, but her mind was still running on Morcant. 'I bet he's taken root in that reading room,' she muttered. 'How do we know what he's up to?'

Thinking about Morcant led Sam's thoughts back to Eagan. What was *he* up to? Was he still down by the sea trying to salvage the *Celtic Flow*? He felt a little guilty that he hadn't appreciated Eagan's pain, hadn't understood how something made of wood could mean so much. Perhaps instead of walking through the woods, he and Emily should be down on the beach helping him, but would that be what he wanted?

They had walked several miles and were beginning to loop back through the wood towards the daffodil bank when between the turning of the light and the rustling of the fading leaves, there was a flutter.

Sam stood still. He didn't like it.

Emily had seen the change in his face. She stopped too and looked around her. 'What is it?'

'There's something happening.'

'What?' Emily's voice had risen a notch.

Several caws broke out high above them, making them both jump. They took cover under an ash tree, flattening themselves against the hard trunk. High above came answering calls, from what Sam reckoned to be the north.

'Why can't they just leave us alone?' whispered Emily, taking his hand.

'They will never give up until they have answers.'

He felt a stronger fluttering in his mind.

Beside him, Emily was trying to wipe invisible cobwebs from her face. 'I hate this,' she said more loudly. 'What answers are they looking for? Hey, talk to me! You've got your "not at home" face on, Sam.'

There was alarm in her voice. But Sam could no longer hear it. Another voice was calling. It was the voice he had heard the night they had escaped from Alnmouth, a forceful vibration that wanted you to do its bidding. But this time it wasn't speaking to him.

'Emily, show yourself! Come to me!'

It was beguiling, but he could see strands of both light and dark draining the colour out of the wood and he knew instantly that the voice could not be trusted.

He gently raised his hand and the light came to him and he felt a great zest lifting his fatigue until he could feel vitality surging through him. He called to the light with words that seemed nothing more than vibrations flickering in his mind's eye, and then the voice was gone and he could see something else – the figure of a man shimmering in the distance, on a shoreline.

But even as he watched, trying to decipher the scene, he felt a sudden wave of terror as out of nowhere a roiling blackness appeared and seized the man. As he disappeared, a single word escaped the darkness and he heard it: '*Traitor.*'

Then he was back looking at Emily, who was looking at him.

'What just happened?' he asked.

'You raised your hand, and as if by magic the crows fell silent, but so did the entire wood.'

Sam nodded, still a little disorientated. 'And then what?'

'You said the word "traitor".'

As she spoke, Sam felt the wave of terror all over again. That swirling blackness, the shoreline… Almost without thinking, he said, 'The traitor's Eagan.'

The sentence froze the air. In the sudden chill Sam and Emily looked at each other.

Then Emily howled, '*No!*' Anger flashed from her eyes. 'How can you say that?'

'I know he's your cousin—' Sam began.

'He may be many things, but he isn't the traitor. He can't be! How many times has he saved us?'

'I saw a vision of a man on a shoreline. There was a great darkness behind him and it took him.'

'That doesn't mean—'

'Listen, there's more. I heard the Grim-Witch calling your name.'

'*My* name?' Emily looked startled. 'She knows my name now?'

'Don't ask me how. But I can tell you that I could see her vibration in the flow. She's not all darkness – there is some light in her yet. What if she *is* trying to help, just like the Grim-were?'

'Sam, will you stop it?! That Grim-were was a hideous creature!' Emily was almost in tears. 'You're losing your mind! How can you say these things? How can you say Eagan is the traitor when you have *Morcant* walking around the place?'

But Sam wasn't having a word of it. 'I know what I saw. And *you* remember what he was like at the old school house. How volatile he can be.'

'But apart from that, all he's done is help us,' Emily wailed. 'And how do you know Morcant isn't walking around on the beach right now?'

Sam took a deep breath. 'Eagan's a liability,' he said, 'and I think we have to be prepared to listen to what the Grim-Witch has to say.'

'So let me see if I'm following you.' Emily was angry now. 'You think Eagan, who has rescued us over and over, is the traitor, and you're prepared to speak to an evil witch who sent her horde of crow-men to snatch me and kill the Forest Reivers.'

Sam flinched. Put like that, it did sound ridiculous. And yet… 'I know what I saw and heard,' he said stubbornly.

The feeling of security and harmony had gone. Sam was scowling and Emily was glaring at him.

'I'm not going to listen to another word.'

Folding her arms decisively across her chest, she turned on her heel and set off in the direction of the house.

Sam ran after her. 'Emily! Listen!'

'No! You're over-tired and irrational.'

She kept walking and he knew there was no stopping her, but he stood there for long minutes watching her disappear into the gathering gloom.

# THE TROW-HULDA

Under the trees there was very little air. Sweat was dripping off Brennus's nose and his nostrils were burning from the intense humidity. He was now being carried along by Drust, who seemed not to feel the heat. Neither did the creature. It had set a relentless pace. Brennus couldn't be sure, but it seemed they were following some sort of overgrown path up the wooded hillside. It was steep and zig-zagged round trees and bushes. Now and then Brennus would spot a stone that had been placed in the middle of the path, for what reason he could only guess. But the stones were becoming more prominent and before long he realised they were beginning to form jagged steps entwined in a strange dance with the trees, which were now much closer together.

Looking up through the dense foliage, unable to see the afternoon sun, Brennus felt helpless. Here he was, clinging to his brother like a frightened child, while behind him the Faeries had been unable to prevent the Shadow Ruins from crossing the Dead Water and other servants of the Ruin might be crossing this very moment. How had it come to this?

Then he caught sight of something in the trees: a figure clinging to a trunk. As he looked more closely, something moved at the very edge of his peripheral vision, this time on the opposite side of the stone steps, but when he turned, it was gone.

'Drust,' he managed to say through parched lips.

'I have seen them.'

At the thought of danger now encircling them, the last of Brennus's strength seemed to leave him. Exhausted, he buried his face in Drust's dark curls. There was a haze settling across his vision, a sickness in his stomach and a heaviness in his body. He was struggling to stay conscious.

Then a single horn blast split the silence and he felt Drust come to a sudden stop. There were further blasts, perhaps answering calls. Forms were dropping from the trees all around them. They were short and squat, no more than five feet tall, and they had long beards almost to their waists. Each of them carried an axe with an ugly blade which they held before them threateningly. Brennus couldn't tell by their dark faces whether they were friend or foe.

'Ezru!' A voice deeper than any man's called a name he had never heard before. 'Why have you not come alone?' The voice sounded angry.

'Breth,' came the creature's voice in reply, 'you need to close the path. You cannot delay – the Ruin's servants are coming.'

Brennus was struggling to focus on the men, if that's what they were, now forming a tight circle around them. They had thick necks and grizzly faces, painted with brown and green flecks and masked by long beards and eyebrows. They were wearing thick animal hides and looked as though they could have come straight out of the Stone Age. Their arms were muscular and had also been painted with spots of brown and green.

'Why have you brought men here?' The voice boomed through the clearing, followed by what Brennus thought was the rumble of thunder.

The small men seemed disturbed by the sound, looking around and raising their weapons as if an attack was imminent.

'What darkness do you bring with you?' called the voice.

As more rumbles were heard, Brennus realised they were drums filling the wood with an ominous music.

'A horror from the Otherland,' the Grim-were said. 'Close the path.'

The drums rumbled through the wood with renewed vigour, and then axes were being deftly placed behind backs and, with surprising speed, bearded men were clambering up the trunks of trees like apes.

Brennus was hauled roughly from his brother's grasp by arms with skin as rough as bark and carried into the trees almost without effort. With the last of his strength seeping away, he seemed to enter a bizarre dream of rope bridges and tall trees. At one point he was lifted above the canopy of the wood and the afternoon sun dazzled his eyes whilst all around him the trees were alive with the rumble of drums and the sound of horns, then he was back beneath the trees, being carried along lines of rope that were fastened by the most curious knots. He imagined a giant web of interconnected ropes running through the whole forest. Then the man he was clinging to suddenly leaped across a gap, making his stomach flip. He barely had time to worry that he might fall to his death before they were off running again. There were several thuds as the men grabbed the trees behind him, and on and on they went, until Brennus heard the drums beginning to quieten and the horn blasts becoming less frequent. Then his stomach flipped a second time as they slid down a long rope from the very tops of the trees down to the forest floor.

He was dumped unceremoniously on the ground whilst his captor repositioned his axe. Somewhere off to his left, hidden by branches, he could hear the Grim-were's voice warning them not to stop.

The gruff voice he had heard earlier cut across him. 'It is forbidden for men to go beyond this point. Our elders will not permit it.'

'The men are Keepers of the *Druidae*. You must allow them through. The Bodika wishes to speak to them.'

There was a sharp intake of breath from all those who had heard. Even lying half-conscious on the ground, Brennus could tell that several of the men had turned to look at him.

'What mischief is this?' called a voice.

'No mischief, only the truth. You must close the path and take us to your elders.'

'There has been a darkness moving on the edge of our lands this past week, we have seen the crow horde flying east and the Ruad Roshessa has been following his rivers through the Blindburn. The Forest Reivers have called a council at the King's Seat and now you say the Bodika has woken!'

A solitary horn blast silenced the man.

Then another voice said accusingly, 'Whatever darkness you have brought with you, it has reached the stone steps.'

'It took two of my brothers, two Vargr,' explained the Grim-were. 'It may be them.'

'Then let us go!'

There were several grunts and before Brennus could locate Drust amongst the throng, he was thrown over someone's shoulder and they set off again. Whoever these men were, they had supernatural stamina and a strength he had never felt before. He bumped against a cold axe that seemed disproportionate in size to the man carrying it, and wondered how these men could climb trees and run so quickly with such weight strapped to their backs.

The trees ended suddenly and Brennus saw that they were on the very edge of a steep hill that turned into a sheer cliff. Before them was a stunning vista, a dizzying array of colours and contours stretching off in every direction. The afternoon sky was deep blue and marked only by thin white clouds. A gentle breeze was playing over Brennus's tired face, but when it eased, he could still feel the autumn sunlight warming his skin.

He could now see the men more clearly and they were stranger than he had first thought. In all his years of travelling with the Forest Reivers, he had never come across them. Had they been there all along, though? He had realised that the brown and green marks on their faces and arms helped them blend in with their surroundings, serving as camouflage in the gloomy forest as well as perhaps some form of tribal markings. Who were these people? Where did they come from?

He stood slowly, his legs shaking and his vision jumping. He heard guttural grunts around him, and then the man who had been carrying him gently led him past a dozen of the men, their faces looking up at him curiously, to where the Grim-were, now looking more feathered than ever, was standing with a man whose long red beard trailed beneath his waist. He wore a simple cloth shirt which hung loosely around his stout and muscular frame, and when he looked at Brennus, his eyes shone blue. There was still no sign of Drust amongst the company.

'Where is my brother?' Brennus said feebly, almost unable to stand unaided.

'Ezru says you are a Keeper of the *Druidae*. Is that so?'

Brennus was reeling, dizzy, blinking back waves of sickness. 'Tell me where my brother is.'

Behind him he heard angry grunts and then he felt a strong hand on his arm, steadying him.

'Ezru says the Fall is dying. Is this true?'

'Yes,' he managed to reply.

The bearded man shook his head and took a step forwards. 'Then you understand there will be war.'

Brennus nodded.

'Why did you seek Fer Benn at the end of the Druids' Way?'

Brennus took a deep breath. 'The Druids' Way?' he repeated.

'Ezru says you spoke to the Dagda at the Dead Water. What did you hope to find?'

'Hope,' whispered Brennus, his body shaking with the effort to remain standing.

'The only hope is with the *Druidae*. It is in their sacrifice that you will find hope. Is that not the story that your kind has been preaching for a thousand years and more?' The man laughed, and the sound wasn't pleasant. 'But our elders say the Druids perished.'

'No!' Brennus closed his eyes. 'There is still hope in the world.'

A horn blast came from the woods.

'Breth!' called Ezru.

The man nodded and turned to the edge of the hill. Taking a curved horn from beneath his shirt and placing it against his beard, he took a lungful of air then blew a single piercing note out into the wilderness.

Then he turned to Brennus. 'We will take you with us.'

'Where are we going?' Brennus asked.

'We will go across the rope bridges to Kyloe Shin,' Breth replied. 'From its top there is a secret path to our villages.'

'Can you tell me where my brother is?'

The man kept his gaze steady. 'The pale one?' he asked. 'Ezru says there is a magic in him that cannot be trusted. My people are taking him to the Hedgehope. When you have met the elders, you will join him there.'

Brennus felt his heart sink. He too had noticed how pale Drust's skin had become, how the dark rings beneath his eyes had given him a ghostly look. How he had not felt the cold in the forest or the heat as they had climbed the last hill. What was happening to him? What magic was in him? He was beginning to think the unthinkable – that it could be too dangerous to take his own brother back to Sam.

He looked across at Ezru and saw his grey feathered face seemed to be changing as well, appearing to be more bird now than man.

'I will scout back,' the creature said, 'and see where the enemy is.' With that, he leaped over the edge of the cliff.

Breth seemed as surprised as Brennus. He shot out a hand to grab Ezru, but he had already gone. A few seconds later, a magnificent grey bird of prey rose up and swept over the peak. With a few strokes of its giant wings, it disappeared over the trees.

Brennus was stunned. The Forest Reivers had told him about shapeshifters, but to see a creature changing before his very eyes was something else.

Breth disappeared over the edge next. Brennus blinked, until he realised there was a small drop to a ledge before a larger one plunging into the gorge below. He watched several of the bearded men join Breth on the ledge and pull a thick rope from a concealed iron ring.

Brennus could see a single knotted rope stretching across the gorge to a hilltop half a mile east. Through the shimmering heat he could see figures moving around there, but he didn't understand what was about to happen until Breth, who was fastening a second metal ring round his body, called him over, said bluntly, 'Don't look down,' then looped the ring around him and, without giving him chance to answer, swung them both out into nothing.

For a second they both hung upside down whilst the clifftop and the ravine merged into a blur of sickening colour. Brennus felt the bite of the steel ring and, as the blood rushed to his head, thought it might break his back. The breeze, which had been gentle at the top of the hill, whistled through his ears as Breth, his feet wrapped around the rope, pulled them both out further from solid earth. Then the rope began to vibrate as the rest of the bearded men began to follow one by one.

Breth was pulling both his own and Brennus's bodyweight hand over hand and soon Brennus could tell he was beginning to struggle. Every few minutes he would stop, breathing deeply through his mouth as his sweat dropped into the gorge below and Brennus hung there, several hundred feet in the air, upside down in a sickly daze.

The rope was now jumping to the rhythm of the men following behind and oddly this seemed to bring Brennus back to his senses. Breth got them moving again and they reached the barren peak and were met by several more bearded men, some carrying their axes before them. Breth unfastened Brennus and greeted a man with the same red hair and an equally long beard. For a second, Brennus thought hanging upside down had given him double vision.

'This is Kiltrevern,' said Breth as the other man greeted Brennus with a nod. 'He is my brother.'

'Twins,' thought Brennus, as he turned to watch the last man fall exhausted from the rope.

Then a distant horn blast, followed by a second and quickly a third, had the men looking back towards the wooded hill.

Breth turned to another man. 'Kerr, this darkness cannot be allowed to reach our villages. Go back and take our families to the fort at Simonside. Then bring the elders to the stone circle at

Bloodybush Edge. Go by the rivers and the woods. Do not travel across the hills, for they are vulnerable to attack. I will go directly to Bloodybush with Kiltrevern, Ezru and this man, for he has been in the presence of Fer Benn and this cannot be ignored.'

Brennus felt his heart sink. He had nothing to tell these people's elders. He had gone to the Dead Water to seek answers and if possible alliances and to draw the Shadow from Sam. That was all. But he was beginning to like the bearded men. Whoever they were, he could sense some good in them.

He looked round for the Grim-were, but couldn't see him. He was strange and cold, but Brennus had to admit he and Drust might not have got through the bizarre wood with its inanimate army without him and his wolves.

Thinking back to them, Brennus felt helpless once more. They had been so big and strong – how had they perished so easily? What kind of enemy were they dealing with here? One that could apparently not be stopped by Faerie or Grim-wolf. What kind of power did the Druids have to repel such monsters? He had sensed Sam's power in his tutorial room only a week ago, but already it seemed a lifetime away. How could a mere boy stop such relentless hate?

There was also something else troubling him. It was clear Breth knew the Grim-were and had heard about the old man and the Fall. The Forest Reivers must have mixed with these people or at least known about them, and yet they had chosen not to mention them.

Then a call from the sky cut through his thoughts. Ezru was back and he looked more twisted than ever as he started changing back into his feathered Grim-were form. Towering over the bearded men, he looked briefly across at Brennus, and Brennus thought he saw fear, or something close to it, in his misshapen eyes.

'What is happening?' Breth asked.

'The Shadow Ruins have taken your men.'

There was shocked silence.

'All of them?' Breth gasped.

'Including my brother?' cried Brennus.

'I am not certain.'

The creature turned to Breth and Kiltrevern, whose eyes were now red with anger and tears.

'But there is not an army that could stand against them. Your only hope is to protect the *Druidae*. Only their magic can stop this madness.'

The bearded men were shaking their heads.

'We have lived peacefully in these woods and valleys for many years,' Kiltrevern protested. 'We do not venture from these lands, or cause pain to others. *You* know that, Ezru! *And* that there have been no children for several generations and therefore our time will come to an end. We want that end to be peaceful, not to be in battle for a cause that has long left our blood.'

The Grim-were replied bluntly, 'You will be drawn into this war whether you like it or not. When the Fall dies, nowhere will be safe for those who locked the Ruin beyond time. The only option left to us is to defend the Druids with our last breath. The time for hiding has come to an end. The time to stand together has only just begun.'

Brennus stared at him, feeling a sudden warmth for the awkward creature.

Breth wasn't so impressed. 'I hear your sentiment, Ezru,' he said, 'but don't forget what my people and my family have already given. Didn't we stand blindly with you on the shores of the Dead Water? And weren't we betrayed by a Druid?'

Brennus's eyes widened in surprise. Betrayed by whom? He sat down, suddenly exhausted, overwhelmed by his own ignorance. It seemed he barely knew half the story. Breth, Kiltrevern and Ezru were now arguing more fiercely, and almost in a daze, Brennus turned his head away from them and stared back at the tree-lined hilltop they'd come from. Several figures were emerging from the cover of the wood. From this distance he couldn't tell who they were, but they seemed to be moving, and with rising alarm, he realised they had found the rope.

'Look! We have company!' he managed to croak, as the first figures started shimming across the steep gorge.

'Cut the rope!' commanded Breth.

Kiltrevern drew his axe and with one devastating blow cleaved the rope and its metal ring in two.

Brennus watched the rope zig-zag like a headless snake across the chasm. The figures were beginning to fall, but there were no noises, no screams. The black dots fell silently into the shimmering depths below.

'To the rope bridge!' yelled Kiltrevern.

Breth grabbed Brennus and threw him over his shoulder and off they went.

Kyloe Shin was a barren hilltop, a complete contrast to the thick wooded crest they had just come from, and for a second Brennus was disorientated, but the bearded men were equally quick at covering this open ground. As they ran, occasionally Ezru would transform and suddenly launch himself into the air. On wings wider than those of any bird of prey, he would disappear over their heads and return several minutes later, bringing news to the brothers. From what Brennus could see of their faces, it didn't seem that it was good.

After a while he found himself being placed firmly on the ground once more. He looked around him. Ahead was a slender rope bridge that had been pinned with thick iron rings to two blocks of rock. His heart sank.

The Grim-were was also standing looking at the bridge.

'Did you see my brother?' asked Brennus, almost pleading with the creature.

'He was not with those who fell into the valley.'

'Then it was our people who fell,' Breth said sadly.

'Yes.'

Tears flowed freely from the two bearded men. They stood there with their heads bowed and racking sobs coming from beneath their long and thick beards.

Then Breth addressed the Grim-were: 'You have brought great misfortune on my people, Ezru. You should not have brought men to the stone steps, or into our world. But if what you say is true, then we will stand with you.'

The creature acknowledged him with what looked like a nod and then said simply, 'We cannot delay our departure. Cutting the rope will only have delayed them.'

Breth and Kiltrevern gave each other a quick look, then moved towards the rope bridge. Brennus could feel a little of his strength returning, but didn't protest when Breth placed him over his shoulder once more.

This time there was no iron ring attaching them to the bridge. Brennus felt his stomach turn upside down as he stared down into the Usway Valley below. The bridge was already swaying and then began to bounce erratically, making Brennus feel sick. He wondered whether they would ever make it across. Breth shifted his hold and for a terrifying moment Brennus thought he would fall. Then, as Breth tightened his grip, behind and somewhere out of sight he heard the gruff voice of Kiltrevern calling to his brother to steady the bridge.

Swinging precariously from side to side, slung over Breth's shoulder, Brennus reflected that his entire world was now upside down. His brother was perhaps not to be trusted and he was having to rely on a creature whose kind had tried to kill him on the shores of the Dead Water and a pair of bearded men who claimed a Druid had once betrayed their people. And without them, he knew he wouldn't be alive now.

A piercing horn blast shook the thoughts from his head, then the swaying stopped and he was again on firmer ground.

They had reached one of two hilltops named the Castles. Brennus took a deep breath of colder air and realised that the warmth of the sun had left the hill. Standing there, he felt exposed and vulnerable to attack. He was now facing the way they had come and could see two figures standing atop the distant tree-lined hilltop. Even at this distance he knew who they were. Whilst he could not use the flow like his brother, he could feel it recoil at their touch. He felt sick as he realised the Shadow Ruins had been waiting in the trees while Breth's people had been tumbling into the valley below.

'Look!' he managed to shout, unable to take his eyes from the lightless figures standing unmoving on the distant crest. 'They are coming!'

'Cut the bridge!' roared the voice of Breth.

Kiltrevern drew his huge axe and with a single ringing swing sheared the rope in two.

Again Brennus watched a bridge snake downwards into a valley. And though the distance they had placed between them and the wooded hilltop was remarkable, he knew the pursuit had only just begun. It was this that was troubling him most. He needed to get back to Sam and give him the guidance he deserved. He needed to speak to the Keepers and seek their counsel about the Staff of the Druids. And what about Oscar? Where did he fit into this madness?

When he looked back, the figures were gone and the sun was beginning its descent in the west. And he knew that no matter how many bridges they crossed and no matter how hard they ran, nightfall would bring great danger.

Ezru and the bearded men did not stop to chat now, but moved swiftly onward. It was clear to Brennus that they knew the nature of the danger that would not be stopped. This time Breth let Brennus walk between him and Kiltrevern, though every now and then, when the ground steepened, he would feel Kiltrevern's strong arms pushing him up the hillside. But they didn't stop, even when they came breathless to the second Castles summit.

The wind was now cold and the light had faded further still. For the first time, the bearded men seemed to be feeling the pace. Only the Grim-were looked unruffled. It was now covered in grey feathers from head to foot and Brennus couldn't look at its contorted features. But for all that, he found himself feeling reassured by the creature's presence.

Finally they halted and Breth and Ezru looked at each other.

'You must close the path when we reach Bloodybush Edge,' began Ezru, but before he could finish, Kiltrevern swung his axe in a lightning arc and it thudded into the rocky hilltop a foot away from the Grim-were.

'Let it be known that I do not trust you, Ezru!' he shouted. 'Your mistress has brought much misery upon the Three Kingdoms. You bring men into our lands, pursued by the Ruin's servants. And now our people have been killed!'

Breth stepped quickly forwards. 'Let us not argue amongst ourselves. I understand your grief, Kiltrevern, and I share it. Ezru, though we believe that you are not as vile as some of your kind, you have brought darkness at your heels, and Kiltrevern is right to be wary of you. As for this man, if he is a Keeper of the Druids, we must trust him until we are proven wrong. So let us go forwards together.'

'The only way,' continued Ezru, as if nothing had happened, 'to slow the Shadow Ruins is to find the secret paths through the Cheviots and then close them behind us. The Ruin's servants are no longer in shadow. They now walk as the Grim-wolves who slept under the spell of the Dagda in the deep dark places.'

'We will meet our elders at the stone circle, for only they have the power to close the secret ways,' Breth said firmly. 'Let us hope some of our people have got through with the message for them to meet us there.'

'I do not think it likely,' said the Grim-were.

'We will see,' said Breth firmly.

Meat and water were now passed round, and once he had eaten, Brennus felt his strength return.

The evening light was turning grey and there was a sharp wind blowing down from the north as the unlikely companions started their descent from the Castles, with Brennus now walking behind Ezru. They moved quickly, but Brennus knew it would be nightfall by the time they reached Bloodybush Edge. He didn't like the idea of meeting the elders in the open. It wasn't just the Shadow Ruins dressed in the bodies of the Grim-wolves that frightened him, it was Drust and Ezru's words about their ability to bring the dead back to life. The very idea of dead bearded men coming out of the darkness with their axes sent a chill dread across his body…

# 8

# AN UNEXPECTED MEETING

Jarl Reign was tired beyond anything he had known. The last week had taken him to the limits of his endurance. Now he was sitting with the heads of the Reiver families beneath a large oak on the very edge of the orchard, where the wall met Birling Wood. Its leaves were already falling gently around them, signalling the end of summer.

The ghostly company had stayed with the Reivers for a while. The woman with pale skin and grey eyes had told them that a great darkness had brought war to their lands and their queen had sent a company of her own guard to seek the help of the Faeries. On the edge of the Otherland, they had been met by the Shadow and many of them had been killed. Those who had survived the onslaught had found themselves deep in the dead lands. They had come upon a lake there and had come through it. She would say little about this part of their journey, except that they had found an old man waiting for them on the other side. It was he who had sent them to follow the Shadow, saying it had come through the waters and would lead them to the Druids, who would help them.

The Reivers wanted to return to the wood to bury their dead, so Jarl had sent the ghostly company on to Alnmouth. The Reivers had been unable to follow the tracks that he hoped were Sam, Emily and Eagan's, but there was a chance they were heading that way and he knew they would need any protection he could send to them.

The Reivers had then buried their dead. This had taken hours and been a grim business. As the sun had gone down, they had rested and had eaten the rich fruit from the orchard. Now the heads of the Bow, Raeshaw, Dun-Rig and Broadflow families were sitting in a circle. There was grief in their faces, a haunted look in their eyes. Most had wounds and bloodied clothes. They had lost Dwarrow, and Erin Dun-Rig took her uncle's place. Only Ged Broadflow seemed uninjured. He sat there expressionless, a direct descendant of the weapon masters of old.

Braden Bow was pensive, his brown eyes dark, the scar on his cheek aflame. His clothes were ripped and bloodied. His sword was laid across his legs as if he was unable to sheath it. His clan had paid a heavy price and his people's despair was displayed in the shadows beneath his eyes and the deep lines criss-crossing his face.

Jolan Raeshaw sat with his sister Bretta, who was still pale and shivering from the crow-men's poison. She sat with a blanket wrapped around her, even though the sun had not completely set. The Raeshaws were the youngest of those gathered, but they had fought hard in battle. In their eyes Jarl could see an unshakable steadfastness, and yet every so often he could also see a flicker of bewilderment and fear.

Jarl began by speaking of how Brennus and Drust had been protecting Sam in Oxford. Then he spoke of Oscar's message to Sam that the Circle was broken and the Fall was dying.

'He told me that story last night,' Bretta broke in, a frown on her face, 'but I could scarcely believe it. Hasn't Oscar been dead for a while?'

'Yes,' Jarl confirmed. 'We don't yet know how it is possible that he visited Sam.'

With a sigh, he went on to describe how Sam had been pursued by a Shadow in Oxford and Brennus and Drust had brought him north, only to be attacked by the crow-men at the Seven Stories, and how Brennus had decided to seek counsel at the Dead Water and to try and draw the Shadow away from Sam and towards them.

The Forest Reivers were dismayed by the news.

'I can't understand why Brennus or Drust would leave Sam to his own devices!' cried Braden. 'And what counsel would they receive in such a place?'

'I don't know,' said Jarl miserably.

As he continued relating the events of the past few days, he couldn't help wishing Brennus was there to guide them now. He was relieved when Braden told him he had met Eagan high in the Blindburn and was intrigued by their meeting with the old man.

'There may be help coming from more quarters than we know,' he commented.

'But nothing makes sense, Jarl! We have lost friends and family, and for what?' Jolan was wiping angry tears from his eyes.

'Listen,' Braden's voice was low, but he spoke authoritatively, seeming to choose every word with great care. 'Brennus and Drust didn't go to the Dead Water on a fool's errand. Nor did Sam and Emily come to this wood by chance. And it was no coincidence that the old man met me and Eagan in a place inaccessible to old men. The red mare has been seen beneath the Cheviot Hills. Whether we like it or not, war is coming. That much we can be sure about.'

'Look around you,' said Ged, breaking his silence for the first time, 'it's already here.'

The words brought a chill to those gathered.

'That's true enough,' agreed Braden. 'How many of our dead have we just buried?'

'What I want to know,' said Bretta, 'is how we can defend ourselves against a magic that can bring the dead back to life? How can the Druids help us when they are scattered and seeking information? How can the grey company? There are so few of them. There must be another way.'

She sat back against the tree, clearly exhausted.

'Bretta is right.' Jolan, too, looked on the edge of collapse. He seemed to seesaw between anger and tears. 'What are we even facing? I thought these crow-men were fireside tales!'

'I hear you, Jolan,' interrupted Jarl. 'We didn't expect things to deteriorate so quickly. We didn't expect Oscar to bring the Shadow to Oxford, for a start. We still do not fully understand how this could have happened.'

'It would be good to understand how it can move around.' The words came from Erin, who had been silent until now. 'How it can move so quickly.'

'And where it is now,' added Bretta.

All Jarl could do was nod in agreement.

'How can we even be certain that it isn't still *here*?' Ged wondered. 'I'm not a betting man, but I would bet that the Shadow had something to do with those marauding dead. One minute they were fighting, then boom and they dropped where they stood. How is that possible? We don't even understand how they came back to life in the first place.'

'I believe the Shadow has power over the dead,' said Braden. 'I think it followed Jarl to the King's Seat. I think it believed he would lead it to Sam. I am fearful for Brennus and Drust. If they have faced the Shadow, then I don't think we can expect them to come back. I am sorry to say that, but it threw our rangers down as if they were made of hollow wood. It let you live in the Usway Valley, Jarl. If it hadn't wanted you alive, even with the help of the silver company, it would have been too much for you – I'm sure of it.'

'So what can we do?' asked Jolan.

'I don't know,' Jarl admitted. 'All I can think of is that we could stay at the stronghold of the Marcher Lords in Bamburgh. If the Shadow comes again, it won't penetrate those walls quite as easily as the crumbling stones of the orchard.'

'If it's after Sam, it won't go there unless it thinks he's there,' Braden said. 'The question is, how long would he be safe there? Or anywhere? We really need to know why it's pursuing him. We need to know for what purpose our people have perished.'

'Yes, the question that needs answering,' Jarl mused, 'is where Sam and Emily will go next. If Eagan is with them, he may go to my wife's brother in Howick.'

'The *real* question,' said Braden, 'is how we help our people, Jarl. There are seriously wounded amongst them.'

'Right, Braden, then let's make for Howick Hall. It will have the space and staff to attend to them. My brother-in-law is steward there and can organise it. We can take the coastal path that is rarely used these days. We should stay here this evening and push on first thing tomorrow, when we have rested.'

'Shouldn't we press on now, whilst there's still some light left?' asked Erin. 'We've left hundreds of dead crow-men by the wall. If they spring back to life, we'll have little chance of stopping them.'

'We'll have little chance wherever we are,' said Jarl, 'and now Sam and Emily are no longer with us, I think we'll be safe enough.'

'There was a woman amongst the crow-men,' Bretta remembered. 'She was frightening and beautiful all at the same time.' She pulled her blanket even more tightly around her. 'She appeared to be the crow-men's leader. When she questioned me, it was as if she could read my mind. I've never met anyone like her.'

'What did she ask you?' Erin said, leaning forwards.

'Where the girl was. She was hunting the girl. She wasn't interested in the boy. They were fighting us to get to the girl. I'm not sure what she wanted her for, but I do know that nothing will stop her.'

Jarl rose to his feet. 'We must tend to the wounded and make our move to Howick. And if that is not Eagan's plan, I will search the Northumberland wilderness until I find him.'

'I think we have to find them all before this so-called woman and her murdering crows get there first,' added Erin.

'You're right,' agreed Braden. 'But I think the greater danger is this Shadow. What is it that can bring the dead back to life?'

No one had an answer.

As the shadows grew long around them, the Reivers made camp for the night in the orchard.

* * * * * *

The next morning saw Jarl leading them along a slender path that snaked its way down to the sea. Braden followed him and behind them came the Reiver horses bearing the wounded. Next came the walking wounded, many in number, helped by those less injured. Bringing up the rear were Ged Broadflow and Erin Dun-Rig.

Emerging from the winding path, they crossed the Aln in single file. It had taken a while to break camp and the sun was already high in the sky. The going was slow, for the healers amongst the Reivers had to tend to those poisoned by the crow-men. They rested often and every now and then Jarl would send Ged and Jolan scouting ahead. Somewhere in the area was the horde of crow-men, perhaps thousands in number, and with so many wounded amongst them, the Reivers were in no shape to fight. Even those who were uninjured were grief-stricken, and their tears flowed along the path.

As the day wore on and the sun began to set over the Northumberland hills, Jarl realised they would have to make camp once more. He called Ged to him.

'We can't go on like this,' he said in a low voice, anxious not to disturb those around him. 'Can you go out and scout for a place where we could rest safely until dawn?'

Ged nodded.

'Don't take Jolan this time – leave him with Bretta. She's looking very poorly.'

Ged nodded a second time, then moved quickly along the dirt path. To his right he could see the waves rolling in from the sea, smell the salt on the air and feel the chill breeze on his face. He was used to being by the water, as he had spent part of the year on Iona before travelling to Holy Island, where he always spent the summer solstice with the Order of Lindisfarne. He had stayed there for several weeks this time and had seen the comings and goings of the Marcher Lords from Bamburgh and Alnwick. On Holy Island itself, there had been uneasy murmurings, and now, as he moved stealthily through the dimming light, he realised the island had been preparing for an attack. Perhaps news had reached them that the borderland was full of creeping shadows. Or more than shadows. Three days ago he hadn't dreamed he would be fighting crow-men. He hadn't thought he would be watching them come back from the dead either.

The weapons master wondered what else he might have to face. What allies he might have. He couldn't get the woman with the silver hair out of his head. Where was she now with her ghostly company? Her voice and frame had been gentle, but she had fought with a strength and speed that he'd never seen before. He wondered about the land she was from. What sort of lands might lie beyond the Dead Water? There had been men amongst her company, but in the main they had been female. Their weapons had been the bow and arrow, but he couldn't tell what material they were made of. The arrows seemed to obey some unknown physical law. They had again and again struck the dead crow-men in the throat, and this had seemed to finish them. It seemed they knew exactly where to strike, Ged mused. He'd been full of burning fear when he'd come face to face with the dead, but the company had fought them with a courage that was superhuman.

Suddenly he tensed, then dropped to the ground and rolled silently into a hedge in one fluid movement. He lay still, listening. He could see little from his position, but his ears were pricked and his skin crawled with apprehension. He knew that something was out there.

Angry with himself for being preoccupied with his own thoughts and walking into a potentially dangerous situation, he reached for the short swords that were strapped to his back. He could feel the tension building. He slowly rolled onto his side so he could be ready, then froze as a number of low growls broke the silence.

Shadowy figures were moving through the twilight. Ged stayed completely motionless, careful not even to glance in their direction, afraid the slightest movement would give him away. He counted several figures. Some were tall, whilst others walked on all fours. As they moved alongside and then past him, they were close enough for him to make out what they were – or what they looked like. But what were wolves doing in Northumberland? He had heard the Reivers talking about dark wolves in the borders and had heard similar tales on Holy Island, but had dismissed them as rumours. And perhaps these weren't wolves after all – it almost looked as though some of them had feathers. Then, to his amazement, he saw some of the figures that were walking on two legs drop to all fours, and some of those on all fours stand upright. These were wolves that could walk on two legs.

'Stay calm, Ged,' he thought to himself, but his mind was racing. These were beings out of fireside stories. But they were here, now, in physical form, and he was sure they would pick up his scent.

Yet still they filed past and none of them seemed aware of him. Ged was beginning to wonder whether he was actually dreaming when one of those bringing up the rear stopped and turned towards him, its eyes blazing white. It raised its head and began sniffing, growling as it did so. Ged tightened his grip on his swords. He could not hope to defeat so many.

The wolf began to walk back towards his hiding-place, continuing to smell the breeze. Soon it was no more than ten feet away and if it looked down it would surely see him. But instead it looked up.

Out of the sky came a winged shape. From his vantage point in the hedge, Ged couldn't make out what it was. For a second he thought his mind was playing tricks, as it seemed to fold its wings behind its back and approach the wolf on two legs. Growls and barks of greeting rumbled from both throats. What sort of creatures were out there, wondered Ged. He was relieved when these two left together, following the other wolves.

For long moments he lay where he was, trying to understand what he had just seen. Strange creatures were moving through Northumberland freely. Who would stop them? It seemed the Forest Reivers had been broken.

Finally he left his hiding-place, keeping close to the thick hedge and moving in the direction the creatures had taken. He wanted to make sure that the Reivers weren't walking into a trap. Howick Hall was still several miles to the north. He would have preferred to travel directly to Bamburgh, an almost impregnable strong-hold of the Marcher Lords, but he accepted that there were those amongst the wounded who needed help now and would barely make it to Howick, let alone Bamburgh.

Bending down to examine the path, he realised the wolf tracks had crossed over the hedge. He felt wary – he would have to make sure that the wolf-like creatures weren't doubling back on him. Seeing a narrow gap in the hedge, he pushed through, stopping just on the edge of a newly harvested field. He could see the tracks clearly as they headed towards a small copse of trees a few hundred yards away. If he followed them, he would be approaching the trees without cover, a prospect he did not savour. But he couldn't report back to the Reivers without understanding the enemy's position.

With the sound of the sea fading behind him and the sharp wind dropping, Ged set off across the field. He could feel the hair on the back of his neck prickling and fear slipping its grip around his stomach. As the dark trees loomed out of the twilight, his hand clenched his short sword and he felt the first beads of sweat slipping down the sides of his face.

The clawed tracks left the muddy field and entered the trees. Without delay, Ged got under the cover of the first line of trees and stood with his back to an ash's hard trunk, listening to the gentle rise and fall of his own breathing. Then he followed the tracks though the silent wood, moving from trunk to trunk, crouching ever lower, his sword poised.

He arrived at a natural fork in the trees and to his dismay the tracks divided, one set going left onto a faint path and the other going off to the right. Ged didn't like the idea of following one whilst not knowing where the other was going. There was a feeling creeping over him that he couldn't shake. Somewhere in the back of his mind he just knew he was walking into a trap. He was convinced the wolf that had turned had smelled his scent. It couldn't have missed him. And yet he didn't turn or go back. He had a desire to find out what was in the wood – a desire that was smothering the fear that was telling him to stop and the hint, the whisper from a deep part of his mind, that if he went any further there might be no going back.

Night fell as he went deeper into the wood. He had had no idea that it would be so big. Or strange. At one point he thought that the trees were full of unmoving wings. But there was a burning desire to keep going, a yearning that had clouded any alarm. There was also a faint buzzing that could have been the beating of a thousand wings, but he no longer cared, such was his thirst to keep moving deeper into the dark wood. At one point he thought he saw shadows to his left and right, but by now he was running carelessly through the dense undergrowth. At one point he was momentarily startled by his own clumsiness – this was not the way of the weapons masters. Then he was emerging into a clearing where the wolves and the winged creature were waiting.

The wolves were standing on their hind legs, towering above him, whilst the winged thing seemed half-man and half-vulture, its face distorted by a cruel beak. Then the trees erupted and he realised every branch was full of giant crows. Their caws, shrill and loud, filled the wood with horror. He stood in the middle of the clearing, surrounded by a thousand watchful eyes and flapping wings. There would be no way out for him. Not against such numbers. Even if there had been fewer of them, the wolves alone would hunt him down within seconds. He had no time to think how stupid he had been or where he had lost his wits before the crows fell silent and he heard the voice he had been searching for.

'You are not the one I summoned. Why did you come here?'

Ged felt his swords slip from his fingers and drop noiselessly to the ground. The wood was alive with the trembling of wings and he knew the clearing was thick with magic, as his legs and arms were no longer his to command. He was a simple spectator as crows flew in from all directions and seemed to fuse into a figure standing before him.

A woman was before him and both passion and foreboding pulsed through his body. He wanted to touch her, but she had already immobilised him. He could feel her in his mind and in his body, searching for some truth that he did not know. A flicker of frustration rippled through his body and for a second he thought she would strike him down. Then a voice like water surfacing from the deepest places of the earth flowed freely into his mind.

'There is one that travels with her that we do not understand. Who is he?'

Ged could not respond, but he found his thoughts flickering through his conversations at the King's Seat and in the orchard. Round and round his thoughts sped, as if they were on a merry go round, and he could feel her frustration beginning to burn. Then a picture of the ghostly company sent a shudder through him, or was it through her?

'Elves!'

Hatred flowed through his mind like burning liquid, a poison so powerful he dropped to his knees.

In the trees the crows were calling as one, filling the night with their jeering squawks. Even the wolves let out angry growls.

'What are Elves doing in the Mid-land?'

The hot liquid poured through his mind and he had no alternative but to release every thought he'd had about the silver-haired woman and her strange companions.

'The Elves were with my people on the edge of the Sea of Souls two thousand years ago and they left us to rot. They are no better than the Druids or the Faeries.'

He could feel her wrath streaming through him.

'Does this mean anything to you? Would you understand even if I were to tell you part of the truth?'

He could feel her withdrawing from his mind and stepping forwards, drawing closer to him. Still he could not see her clearly. He was unable to focus on her face, no matter how much he squinted in the dark.

'I see you have fragments of the story stitched together by half-truths. So tell me, who is the enemy, Ged Broadflow?'

He wasn't surprised she knew his name. She had laid him bare. She knew his every thought, and somehow he didn't care.

Now she was laughing. 'I have been desired by more than men!'

She was almost within touching distance. He could not tell whether she was a monster or the most beautiful woman he had ever seen. One thing was certain: she had a power he could see, feel and smell. He was both frightened and intrigued. Fearful and excited. He thought she was beautiful and terrible at the same time, and all he wanted to do was touch her, no matter how painful that might be.

'Now listen well,' she continued in a voice both powerful and seductive. 'The Druids are not innocent. Let me tell you something about them. Even now no one knows where they came from, but for a while they reigned supreme. Some turned to the light and others turned to the dark. Those who turned their backs on the light fled to the dark places of the world – places where those who embraced the light could not find them. In the darkness, their magic grew.'

She was now within touching distance of Ged, whose eyes were streaming with the effort of focusing on her face. He thought through the haze of his aching eyes he could see black feathers, and when he looked up into her face, there seemed to be scales there, but he also saw a beauty that took his breath away.

'But in the darkness an unimaginable horror found them. It twisted and broke even their power and filled them with a darkness that kept them alive. They hid in the Otherland until they were powerful enough to march on the Three Lands. Two thousand years ago a great fellowship from the Three Lands journeyed deep into the Otherland, into the Darkhart, and a great battle was fought. The Fall was created then, and the Ruin was locked away behind the gates of the Sea of Souls.'

'How do you know all this?' Hearing his own voice took him by surprise.

'Ha!' He could feel her anger flicker into life, then burn into his mind until he thought he would scream. 'How do you think?! I was there. I witnessed it. Go back to your people, Ged Broadflow. We know where they are. I wish to speak to the Keepers of the

Druids. There is one amongst them who was also there the night the Fall was born. I wish to speak to him.'

'Why are you telling me this?' Ged felt he was slowly regaining control over his senses.

'They will listen to you. And listen they must. The Keepers do not understand the nature of what they face. So, although another Fellowship of *Druidae* may come together, they will be led blindly into the Otherland and slaughtered before they reach the Darkhart. The Ruin's servants will be waiting for them on the other side of the Dead Water. They are there already. I am the Keepers' only hope. Look at me now.'

As she said the words, Ged's vision cleared and he gasped in horror. Before him stood not a woman, but a feathered and scaled creature. In the pit of his stomach he began to feel a crawling, a loathing. What was this monstrosity?

As if in answer, she said, 'I was once the most beautiful of all the Faeries, Ged, but the Ruin's servants caught me. The Druids who hid in the heart of darkness tried to twist and break me. But they could not. So now I am the Bodika, the Grim-Witch of Reiver legend.'

Ged turned away, unable to look upon her a second longer.

'Now you know who I am,' she continued, 'I ask that you take my message back to your leaders. There is only one left amongst the Keepers who can speak to those from the past. If all goes well, he will arrive at Holy Island in five days. Tell him I need to speak to the one they call Oscar Hood.'

Ged found he could move again.

'And of course I need the girl. She is our only hope. Now go, Ged Broadflow, and do not look back.'

Ged couldn't believe he was being allowed to walk away. The wolves were watching him, their eyes blazing in the night. The entire wood was eerily quiet, but he knew a thousand eyes were following him. He left the clearing, unsure what had just happened, but knowing that the woman, if that what she had once been, had only let him live to deliver his message.

As he left the wood, a cold wind soothed his burning face. He would deliver his message, but how could they ever trust a creature whose horde had attacked his people and killed them in cold blood? And if she had been at the creation of the Fall, that would make her two thousand years old…

Questions rolled towards him out of the night as he passed from the field back to the path. There stood a wall of Forest Reivers, their swords drawn, looking out into the darkness.

* * * * * *

Jarl knew something was wrong with Ged the moment he appeared walking down the path. He took the weapons master to a place where they could not be overheard, with Braden only a step behind.

'What happened?'

'I met the Grim-Witch.'

'Are they coming here?' Braden was already drawing his sword.

Ged was shaking his head. 'She asked me to deliver a message. They are searching for the girl. She's caught up in this as much as the boy.'

'Why?' Braden demanded. 'And why are they murdering our people? We haven't got the girl.'

'You haven't got her *now*,' Jarl pointed out.

Braden scowled at him.

'What did she say?' Jarl asked, turning back to Ged.

'She said she was with the Druids the night they created the Fall.'

'That's impossible!' Braden's patience was gone. 'Enough of this nonsense! She bewitched you, Ged.'

'Oh yes, she did,' Ged admitted.

'Well, then.' Braden turned away.

'Wait!' Jarl said. 'Tell me what message she wants you to deliver, Ged. You wouldn't have walked away so freely without it. She must think it's important.'

'She wants to speak to the Keepers – not those from the present, but from the past.'

'From the past?' Jarl seemed to repeat the words to himself.

'How can you speak to people from the past?' Braden was puzzled.

'There's no time to explain that now,' said Jarl, 'but it is possible. More importantly, *why* does she want to talk to them?'

'Does that matter?' broke in Braden. 'We cannot negotiate with a murderer. And we need to get moving. If they were to attack, we wouldn't stand a chance in the open. Not with all these wounded.'

'That's true,' Jarl said. 'Okay, let's—'

'*Jarl*,' Ged's voice seemed a little more urgent, 'she wants to speak to Oscar.'

Jarl paused. 'Do you know why?'

'She says the Keepers don't understand the nature of the enemy. That if we attempt to go through the Dead Water, the enemy will be waiting. It is what they are expecting us to do.'

'Why is an enemy who has killed our people warning us of this danger?' Braden was looking tense. 'What if this a trap? What if they have sent Ged back to lower our defences?'

Jarl could almost feel the strain in Braden's voice. 'We are very much in the dark,' he admitted. 'Go and tell Jolan and Bretta that we are pressing on to Howick Hall. We can't stay out in the open now and we need to get the wounded to safety.'

Braden nodded and left Jarl and Ged staring out into the night, their minds full of unanswered questions.

* * * * * *

The Forest Reivers moved as fast as they could along the coastal path. At this point it was winding its way along cliffs and they could hear the crash of the white waves on the black rocks below. When they reached the place where Ged had left the path and gone into the wood, it was silent. Braden took a dozen Forest Reivers and they spread out across the field, but there was no sign that the wolves had crossed back onto the path.

With the cold sea air keeping him awake, Jarl was thinking about the Grim-Witch's message. Beside him Ged was silent, the same thoughts no doubt going round in his mind.

They came to a place where there was nothing between the path and the cliff edge. The long line of Reiver horses was spooked by the drop and one or two had to be held firm by those walking alongside. One minute the path took them up dark cliffs with sheer drops onto sharp rocks below, then it led them down amongst the sand dunes with the biting sea winds in their faces.

Wherever they were, now and then the caravan would stop so the healers could tend to the wounded and the horses be fed and watered. And every time they stopped, those who could still hold a weapon would fan out into the night and station themselves around the long line of Reiver horses.

Braden occupied himself with sending out riders looking for the Grim-Witch and her crow-men, but they found nothing.

Jarl was also finding nothing – or nothing that made any sense. Was the Grim-Witch's message genuine or had she cast some kind of spell on Ged and sent him back to deceive them? Perhaps Braden was right and it was a trap after all.

Something else was worrying him. The more he thought about the night in Oxford, the more he found Brennus and Drust's version of events impossible to fathom. He knew Sam was special. Drust had told them that the flow never left him alone. It was just waiting for him to find it. Was he the heir of the Druids? Drust had at first thought that Eagan was the one, but later he and Brennus had come to believe that Sam was the one who would eventually learn to control the flow like no other. And so *why* had the Shadow let him live? Had it used him for some purpose?

His thoughts were punctuated by the groans of the wounded Reivers and the anxious whinnying of the horses. They had come to a place where the path took them within feet of a sheer drop. Jarl knew that for the next few miles they would be exposed. If they were attacked, they would be pushed into the sea.

Then Braden came to him. 'The enemy is ahead.' His voice did not betray his fear, but in the faint blue dawn Jarl could see it flickering in his eyes.

'How many?' he asked.

'Three.'

'Crow-men?'

'We couldn't tell. They are waiting where the path narrows.'

'Are they alone?'

'Yes,' replied Braden, his face hard and unmoving. 'Take care – I think it is a trap.'

'I think they wish to speak.' Ged had come upon them unnoticed.

'They are murderers, Ged.' Braden could not hide his distaste.

'It won't do to squabble amongst ourselves,' Jarl said quickly. 'Braden, send one of your men to tell Jolan to take the Reivers down onto the beach and wait for us to return. If we don't, tell him to wait until the sea allows him safe passage to Howick.'

'Jarl, it is *clearly* a trap. We should stay with our people.'

'*They want to speak.*'

This time Braden chose to ignore Ged. 'Jarl, what do you think?'

'They have chosen their place well. So help get your people to the beach. If this is a trap, they will be safer with the dunes at their back. But we will speak to them.'

Braden shook his head. 'Have your way, but there are many things here that make little sense. The Forest Reivers seem to be the ones sacrificing their blood, and for what?'

'To stop a great darkness from creeping across your forefathers' lands, Braden. It will not be in vain.'

Jarl watched Jolan, Erin and Bretta lead the long line of horses down the steep path, their descent protected by the rangers. It seemed to take an age before the last horse was off the path and disappearing onto the dark sands below.

'If it is a trap, Braden, then Ged and I will hold them until you get news back to Jolan. Make for Howick – no harm will come to you there.'

'How can you be certain?' asked Braden.

'My brother-in-law Kenrick will make sure of it.'

Jarl did not wait for Braden's reply. Instead he set off down the path with both fear and determination beginning to rumble through his body. Beside him Ged walked silently with his short swords drawn, whilst Braden took his place on his right.

The path hugged the side of the cliff face here and the sea was alive with slithers of white waves crashing on the beach below.

It wasn't long before it narrowed and Jarl drew his sword as he caught sight of the three figures standing there, blocking their way. He thought he had walked into a nightmare. Just ahead, now clearly visible, were two wolves, their deep growls warning them not to come a step closer. He could feel a cold sweat break out across his body as their glowing eyes settled on him. Standing between them was a feathered creature, an abhorrence that could have once been a man but was now something altogether hideous.

Jarl, Braden and Ged came to a halt and stood staring in disbelief until a voice broke the silence. It was deep and thick with an accent that made its words twist into strange sounds.

'Who is the one that leads you?'

'Why does it matter?' Braden's voice was full of cold venom, his sword poised, his neck muscles flexing.

'There are no leaders here. We speak with one voice. Why do you block our path?' Jarl asked, hoping he didn't sound as apprehensive as he felt.

'My mistress met the Keeper of the Druids at the Dead Water.'

The words rang out in the cold night air.

'He sent a message that he would meet her there.'

Jarl could feel Ged and Braden's eyes on him as his mouth ran dry. 'Why are you telling us this?' he managed to say.

'He is the only one left amongst you who can speak to the past. My mistress sent her most powerful servants to bring him back with a message.'

'What message?' Jarl could feel his trepidation turning into fear – fear not of these strange creatures but of the idea that Brennus had gone to the Dead Water not to speak to the Dagda but the Grim-Witch. It chilled him to the bone.

'They cannot be trusted!' Braden seemed to be filling with rage.

'I think there is some truth in what they say,' contradicted Ged.

'Why did the Keeper want to talk to your mistress?' asked Jarl, his head still swirling.

'Our mistress is the only one who knows the way to the Darkhart. She has been there.'

He had been told the Fall had been created two thousand years ago. It would have been impossible for anyone to have survived that length of time and yet, like Ged, he thought there was truth in the words.

A gentle light was beginning to seep into the landscape, but it only made the being that was speaking look even more grotesque.

'Our brother Ezru travels with the Keeper,' it continued. 'They will arrive in Holy Island in five days' time. She asks you to bring the girl there.'

To Jarl's left Ged was a statue, whilst to his right Braden was rippling with tension, his face grim.

'What has this got to do with the girl?' asked Jarl.

'She is in danger. She needs to be kept safe. She will have to go to the Otherland.'

Jarl found himself dizzy and bewildered. Here he was, facing three creatures he didn't think existed. Three creatures who seemed to know far more of what was going on than he did.

'We do not trust murderers,' Braden growled.

The wolves let out low threatening growls in reply and were quickly back on all fours. Just for a second Jarl thought Braden might rush them. He put out a warning hand.

'We are *not* murderers,' the creature said. 'You attacked us. We were following the girl. We have always been following the girl.'

'You killed my people. I should strike you down this minute!'

Jarl could feel the tension rising.

'You slaughtered my people without thought,' came the creature's cold response. 'Now you will listen to me. As the Fall weakens, the Shadow Ruins will grow stronger. They are coming and you are ill prepared. The Ruin will wage a war and we must stand together. My brother Ezru and his Grim-wolves will bring the Keeper of the Druids to the shores of Holy Island in five days' time. My mistress will be there to speak to him and to speak to the past. Be there and bring the girl.'

'We will be there.'

'*Jarl!*' Braden was incredulous, but Ged's face was impassive. They remained standing as the creatures turned away and vanished into the night.

'It is a trap, Jarl!' Braden's disbelief turned to anger.

'I don't think so. We will meet them at Holy Island and find out.'

## THE CALM BEFORE THE STORM

Eagan Reign was standing on the soft white sands of Howick Bay, watching the sun rise over the sea. The first night he had been at Howick, he had slept for hours, but last night he had tossed and turned. Crow-men had stalked him through his slumber and at one point he had been back in the garden of the old school house, unable to move and rigid with fear. He had awoken, drenched in cold sweat, his bedclothes damp, only to fall asleep again and see the Grim-were looming out of the night. There had been other blurred faces in his dreams, too – his mother, his father, Sam, Emily and even Oscar had all made an appearance. One by one, a great Shadow had come for them, and each time he could do nothing to stop it.

So he had walked down the tree-lined avenue to the quiet beach, to the *Celtic Flow*. The previous day, as a cold breeze had rolled in from the deep blue sea, he had stood beside the broken remains of the boat and wept. Then he had got to work. Over the years, each timber of the *Celtic Flow* had been lovingly fixed or replaced until not a single original piece was left and it was held together only by its name. Now it was being built all over again. Eagan had borrowed a heavy tool box from Kenrick and had spent the rest of the day repairing the internal structure. The boat would not sail again until he had fetched wood from Craster to fix its broken prow, but he had made a start.

Today he would continue. But despite being satisfied with his work so far, he didn't feel relaxed. Even in the early morning calm, with the waves gently lapping the warm sand, he was apprehensive. This was the calm before the storm. The way Sam and Emily had described the Shadow, he knew it would come again. He felt overwhelmed by the responsibility. How long could they stay at Howick? And where could they go from here? The Hoods' home in Bamburgh? As he stroked the boat's broken wood, his mind was wandering through every possibility.

When the line of horses broke from the narrow path that led south, he found himself crouching down and then lying flat against the hull, watching and waiting. There were dozens and dozens of horses, most with riders hunched over their necks or lying over their backs. Beside them he recognised the Forest Reivers, but he did not move. These were people he loved, but he did not move. These were proud and fierce folk. They were rangers, the fiercest of all the Reivers, and yet they looked defeated. As he watched them approach, Eagan's eyes filled with tears once more.

Then he felt a weight lift from his heart and was up and running towards them. The autumn sun flashed from swords drawn in dismay, but then the Reivers recognised him.

'Eagan!'

Jarl seemed to breathe his son's name in. Then they were embracing like only a father and son can. Braden Bow joined them, hugging them both.

Finally Eagan stepped back and stared at his father. He was horrified by how haggard he looked. The lines on his face were deep and ragged and smudged with dirt. There was blood on his clothes and there seemed to be wounds to his leg and shoulder that had only just stopped bleeding.

Braden also seemed to have changed since their chance meeting in the Blindburn. Even though he was now smiling, there was a tenseness about him, almost an inner rage.

Others were approaching too, people Eagan knew but who were now almost unrecognisable to him. Jolan Raeshaw had an angry and confused look about him, whilst Erin Dun-Rig seemed distraught. She squeezed him tightly and he could feel her sobs as he held her.

'What has happened?' he asked, but his father quickly shook his head.

'Let us get the wounded to Howick and we can answer your questions there. I am so glad you are safe and well, Eagan. Are Sam and Emily with you?'

'They are at the hall.'

Eagan could see the relief flooding across his father's face.

'Come along then.'

Eagan placed one arm around his father and the other around Erin, whose tears continued to flow, and left the *Celtic Flow* to the beach.

As they walked along the path under the tree archway, only the sound of the horses' hooves punctuated the silence. It was clear the Reivers had come fresh from battle, and Eagan couldn't help wondering who they had been fighting. All around him, the horses were carrying men and women who weren't moving. There were some, he thought, who must be dead, as their faces were ashen and they didn't stir even when their mounts stumbled. Then he gasped as Bretta's colourless face passed by.

'Bretta!' he called, but his father hugged him close.

'She is overcome by the poison of the crow-men,' he whispered.

Remembering it only too well, Eagan turned pale.

'I'm hopeful that Kenrick can help these people,' Jarl murmured.

'You'll need a stronger magic than that,' Eagan whispered, horrified. 'They are dying.'

* * * * * *

Ged Broadflow was watching the leaves falling. He didn't quite understand it. He would have expected to see trees beginning to shed their foliage at this time of year, but this was different. As the Reivers had moved beneath the trees there had been a light wind, but it had fallen to a whisper as they had proceeded along the winding path. Yet whereas at first there had been just a few leaves gently spinning to the ground, now there were swirls amongst the stillness and murmurs amongst the Forest Reivers as streams of leaves came dancing between them.

Jarl barely noticed it at first, though he did find a comforting warmth easing his aching body as he limped along with Eagan. But beside him, Braden, Ged and Erin were looking up towards the canopy as more and more leaves fell, tumbling and twisting until the archway was filled with them.

'What is this?' Jarl heard Erin say, but he couldn't reply, only marvel at the unfolding spectacle. Eagan was saying something to him, and seemed to be laughing, but he could no longer hear him, as leaves were falling between them. All around him Forest Reivers were placing their weapons on the ground and embracing the swirling leaves, which were dancing around the wounded in ever greater numbers, and seemed, Jarl noticed, to be thickest around the horses carrying the worst affected.

The sound of rustling leaves mingled with the Reivers' happy voices, filling the quiet space with soothing music, and there was a goodness in the warm wind that for a moment flushed the exhaustion from Jarl's body. For the first time since Brennus had returned from Oxford, his fear left him. The sickness he had felt in his stomach dissipated and he was overflowing with a relief that for an instant made him feel weightless.

Braden felt his anger leave him. It simply melted away, leaving him drained and tearful. Looking up, amazed, to the very highest part of the canopy, he thought he could see the wings of giant birds. Perhaps those that had come to their rescue at the King's Seat, he thought. Most were hidden by the leaves that were raining down, so he couldn't tell for sure, but whatever was happening, he didn't want it to stop. He could feel a warm wind and slight crackle of energy as the leaves pirouetted around them, and it almost made him want to dance. He too noticed that the leaves showered the horses carrying the wounded and would not leave them alone.

As the Forest Reivers' astonishment hummed through the tree canopy and the tumbling leaves gathered momentum, Bretta lay draped over a horse, too weak to move. The initial flare of the poison igniting within her body had given way to an awareness of the venom snaking its way into her, numbing and weakening as it went. She had been hot, then cold and shivering. Then there had come a suffocating mist that had scrambled her senses, a darkness that had blinded her, a dizziness that had made her unable to stand. Soon she had found herself unable to keep awake. As if in a dream, she had felt the cold hands of the healers and had heard her brother pleading with her to stay with them, but there had been a heaviness that had softly taken away the pain, a darkness that had rolled away the fear. The fire that had burned through her had been doused by an icy chill. At first she had welcomed it. But as it had taken her further into the cold darkness, there had come a time when she hadn't been able to remember her name.

Now in the blackness there was no pain, only bewilderment. Where was she? Who was she?

'Bretta.'

The woman's voice was lyrical and soothing. But it seemed to pull her back towards the pain. She was tired, and the silence and darkness comforting. She wanted to stay where she was.

'The fellowship needs you, Bretta.'

This time the voice was stronger and Bretta thought there was an urgency to it. But she wanted to rest in this quiet place.

'You must follow me back.'

The voice was insistent and Bretta could no longer ignore it. She opened her eyes and saw darkness with touches of grey. Slowly she could feel the pain returning. She could not understand why the voice wanted her to go back to the pain and hurt.

'The *Druidae* have chosen you.'

The voice was close, almost by her side, but there was now a whisper in the darkness asking her to stay. Bretta hesitated.

'*Druidae*. What do they want?'

'Follow me and you will see.'

When she opened her eyes again, the darkness had turned to grey and the whisper was fading. Leaves were dropping all around her.

Others were also beginning to stir atop their horses, gently sitting up as the leaves continued showering down until the air was empty and the Forest Reivers were standing on an autumn carpet.

* * * * * *

Sam and Emily had been walking on the small hill atop the daffodil bank when they had seen people breaking out of the Silverwood. Long lines of people, and at their head they could see Eagan. But as they went down the hill and approached the horses, their joy turned to dismay as they caught sight of the wounded Reivers. Sam wondered whether these were even the same ones that they'd met in the wood.

Eagan turned to greet them, but then Sam gasped as an unkempt and bloodied figure emerged from behind him.

'Jarl! Can that be you?'

A broad smile spread across Jarl's face as he hugged Sam, and then he was opening his arms and sweeping Emily off her feet and hugging them both until Sam could barely breathe.

When the hugging finally stopped, Sam noticed they were now at the centre of a small throng. He felt uneasy with so many unfamiliar faces around him. He noticed a tall, lean man with blond hair and a young woman whose eyes flashed blue. Another man, with a jet-black beard and shaved head, was standing back quietly observing. There was something about him that made Sam look across at him and meet his piercing green eyes.

Then Kenrick was bursting through the crowd.

'Give the boy and girl some space!' he cried.

'So this is Sam,' said one of the men standing closest to Jarl.

'Yes,' said Kenrick, 'but let us attend to the wounded first and then we will call a council. There is much to be done!'

He was interrupted by the toll of bells that filled the air with their echoes, but it wasn't long before he was busy ordering people about. Gardeners appeared from every direction and quickly helped the wounded from the horses. Most were now conscious and able to walk, although there were those who needed carrying.

The crowd that had gathered around Sam and Emily would not disperse so readily, though, and even Kenrick losing his patience and trying to shoo them away didn't help. It was clear those gathered wanted to understand why they had been forced into battle for people they did not know.

Just like the night in Birling Wood, the Forest Reivers ringed Sam and Emily, but this time Jarl and Eagan stood with them.

'We will answer your questions later,' said Jarl firmly. 'I will be inviting the heads of the families to sit down with Sam and Emily this evening. They will report back once we understand the bigger picture.'

There was a clamour of discord that made the hair on Sam's neck bristle. It seemed those around him were looking for someone to blame.

'Jarl, my people have died defending this boy and girl,' said a thick-set man with dark brown hair and a scar across his left cheek. 'We need to know why! We have a right to understand why my people have sacrificed so much.'

Sam could tell he spoke for the rest of those gathered.

But Jarl replied, 'Braden, this is not the time to discuss such matters.'

'So you say, but what happens when the Grim-Witch and her horde descend on this place? They know we are here. Time is against us, Jarl. How long do we have?'

Sam felt his stomach knot, and when he glanced at Emily, she was looking uncomfortable too. He felt the man Braden probably had a point. The Reivers looked in no shape for another battle. But Jarl and Kenrick were still shaking their heads.

'We have several hundred people to accommodate,' said Kenrick. 'And horses to feed and water. Do come along now.'

He put his arm round Braden's shoulders and led him up the stone steps leading to the front gardens.

The others followed more slowly, still glancing curiously at Sam and Emily as they went. It took several long minutes before the hill had been emptied of Forest Reivers and all the horses led away. Jarl had gone with them, and Sam, Emily and Eagan were left by themselves.

'There are so many wounded!' said Emily, her eyes glistening with tears.

'Yes, they've been in a terrible battle.' Eagan's voice was low.

Emily shivered, despite the warmth of the morning sun. 'Poor Uncle Jarl does look as though he hasn't slept for a week. His trouser leg was covered in blood. I can't bear it, Eagan, and it's not over, is it? You heard what that man Braden said. What if the Grim-Witch and her army attack? What if they are out there right now, waiting for darkness to fall? If you think those poor Forest Reivers can save us this time, then think again!'

Emily's voice was getting louder and Sam could feel his cheeks beginning to burn. 'It's time we saved ourselves,' he said abruptly. 'The Forest Reivers have already paid a heavy price. But listen, the Grim-Witch is not the enemy.'

He looked straight at Eagan.

Emily drew a sharp breath. 'Sam! No!'

'What is it?' Eagan turned to her.

She flushed. 'I just meant … Sam, please don't start all that again.'

'I know you said you thought they were trying to help,' Eagan said, looking back at Sam, 'but her horde has killed our friends.'

Sam moved from one foot to the other, but kept his gaze firmly on Eagan as he replied, 'Do you really believe she is the enemy?'

Eagan's dark eyes narrowed. 'Do you really believe I am the traitor?'

Emily gasped.

'*Should* I think that?' Sam asked suspiciously.

'No, but you do. I know it.'

'How?'

'I can feel the flow just like you. But it affects me differently from either you or Drust. It affects me in ways that you could not possibly believe. And all those who feel the flow are connected.'

Sam looked surprised.

'I am no traitor, Sam.'

Emily looked from one to the other, not knowing what to say.

'When you rescued Emily at Alnmouth,' Eagan continued, 'I saw your blazing resonance in the flow – a fire I had never witnessed before. You have only just started to explore its power and already it's amazing what you can do.'

Sam's mouth had gone dry. He felt more confused than ever. 'You were with the Shadow on the beach yesterday evening. I saw you.'

Eagan shook his head.

'I don't know why you would say that, Sam, but when you talk with the flow it won't always be those from the light that are talking back.' His eyes flashed suddenly. 'If you begin to think your friends are your enemies, then where will that lead you? I told you earlier – we're all caught up in this together, and together we must stand.'

Sam hesitated.

'When the Shadow comes again, Sam, I am going to stand with you.'

Sam felt ice travel through him at the mention of the Shadow. He looked away.

'Don't worry,' Emily said encouragingly. 'You stopped it once and you will stop it again.'

Sam whirled back round to her. 'No! I've said this before and I'll say it again – I *didn't* stop the Shadow! Oscar did.'

'Hang on. We've also been here before. And you don't see flames sprouting from *my* hands!'

'This is getting us nowhere,' Eagan interrupted.

'You're right,' said Sam, recovering himself. 'I'm sorry, Emily. I'll go to the Way-curve in the hall and speak to Oscar. I need to find out more about this child once and for all.'

To his surprise, Eagan was smiling.

'What is it?'

'You say it so casually, and yet it took Brennus several years before he could light up the Way-curve.' Eagan was shaking his head in disbelief. 'And Brennus was taught by the best. Oscar spent years teaching him to speak first across space and then across time.'

Out of the blue he grabbed Sam and gave him a hug.

'You wield the flow like no one since Oscar. I have seen this for myself.'

By this time Sam's face was burning hot and he was feeling a little uncomfortable.

'At the same time it's scary,' he confessed, as Eagan released him. 'It seems to be growing stronger. Every day I can see it more clearly.'

'Well, I'm glad we're back to being friends,' said Emily impatiently. 'Now how are we going to get back to the reading room without running into Morcant?'

Sam shot her a warning look. But it was too late.

'*Who*?' Eagan turned towards Emily, his eyes blazing. 'What is Morcant doing here?'

'Brennus sent him to seek help from Kenrick,' she said. 'At least that's what he told us.'

'How long has he been here?'

'I don't know.'

'Ha!' said Eagan bitterly. 'Obviously Kenrick's trying to avoid trouble. He never even mentioned to me Morcant was here.'

'I think it's best if you just avoid him,' Sam murmured lamely.

'*Avoid* him?' Eagan growled. 'There's nothing I'd like more! I don't know what Brennus is thinking of. I know no one believes me about what happened in Alnmouth, but it's all true. *And* Morcant's a Pauperhaugh and can't be trusted an inch.'

'*I'm* half Pauperhaugh.'

'Don't *you* start.'

Emily was about to open her mouth again, but saw Sam's little shake of the head.

'Let's just speak to Oscar,' he said, 'and then we can set off for Holy Island.'

The bells had fallen silent, but the hall was still busy with people coming and going. Looking back at it, once or twice Sam saw the white hair of Kenrick bobbing about amidst the throng.

'Though I will miss it here,' he added, 'and I do think we're safe here. I don't think the Faerie I met would let anything bad happen to it.'

'That reminds me, something very strange happened earlier on.' Eagan took a deep breath. 'Somehow the poison in the veins of the Forest Reivers was almost completely neutralised. Just like when we arrived, the avenue rained leaves and I could feel the flow close by. Though no one saw her, it must have been the Faerie who showed herself to you.' Eagan's face softened. 'She lit the flow up like nothing I've ever seen. An intense glow that you could almost feel inside.'

Tears welled in Sam's eyes. 'I know,' he said softly. Who had the woman been? Why had she had such an effect on him? What was so special about Howick Hall? So few answers and those unanswered questions creating so many more.

And he was still uneasy about Eagan. What could he trust? The vision that Eagan was the traitor or the fact that he had done nothing but help them? If he was the traitor, then why had the Grim-were's poison almost killed him? Unless he wasn't working for her, but someone else. But who?

* * * * * *

The hall was a hive of activity. The gates of the Walled Garden were now thrown open and gardeners were pushing wheelbarrows full of freshly picked vegetables from there to the kitchens. Smoke was billowing out of the kitchen chimneys, staff were bustling everywhere and orders were being shouted. Where had all the gardeners and helpers come from at such short notice, Sam wondered. How they were going to feed so many mouths was anyone's guess, but they were clearly going to give it a go. Elsewhere, horses were being stabled or led out to the fields, upstairs windows were being thrown open and piles of fresh linen were being carried into the house.

Sam's heart sank. 'We can't get back to the Way-curve with all this going on.'

'Let's go and sit in here and wait,' said Eagan, heading into the Walled Garden.

The others followed.

'So what's the plan?' said Eagan as he seated himself on a bench at the far end of the garden.

'I'm going to speak to Oscar if I can,' Sam answered, 'and then find out more at this council meeting this evening. I hope that will give us more of an understanding of what's going on.'

'It might give Morcant more of an idea as well,' Eagan muttered.

'He does look and act like a villain,' Sam admitted, 'but Brennus and Drust trust him. And Jarl.'

Eagan looked a little perplexed. 'It seems they do, but I don't know why. If I'm right and Morcant is the traitor, then it could jeopardise everything. Or perhaps they're just keeping their eye on him. Have you ever thought that sometimes you have to keep your enemies closer than your friends?'

Emily looked exasperated. 'What's that supposed to mean?'

Her cheeks flushed and Sam again thought how beautiful she was.

'Perhaps Brennus wanted to get a message to the enemy?' Eagan suggested.

Whilst Emily shook her head, this did prick Sam's thoughts. 'It would make a lot of sense,' he said slowly.

'But which enemy?' Emily protested. 'The Shadow, the Grim-Witch or someone else?'

'If the Grim-Witch *is* one…' Sam couldn't help adding. 'Listen, if Brennus wanted to fool everyone apart from Drust and Jarl, then perhaps he would have left the traitor in the camp long enough to tell him that he was travelling to the Dead Water. Then the traitor could get the message back to whoever he's working for.'

'Making sure that they follow him to the Dead Water and leave the way open for you two to escape,' finished Eagan. 'Yes, it's a possibility. So it's not looking good for Morcant, is it?'

He stood up.

Emily and Sam exchanged glances. 'You're not going to look for him, are you?' asked Sam worriedly.

Eagan shook his head. 'You don't need me with you at the Way-curve and you might not even get there. So I'm going to carry on repairing the *Celtic Flow*. All I need is to get some wood from somewhere. There must be some in a shed, or some firewood that I can use. You just never know if we will need the boat. I've got a feeling about it. So remember it's there if you have to make a quick getaway. And remember to take me with you.'

He gave them a brief smile then turned and walked away in the direction of the long line of wheelbarrows heading for the hall.

Emily plonked herself down on the seat that he had just left and looked up at Sam with an impish grin. 'You aren't going to forget to take *me*, are you?'

Sam laughed. 'I don't think I can.'

'Does that mean you would if you could?'

Sam smiled. 'That would be telling, wouldn't it?'

Emily laughed too. Then she became more serious.

'It's all a bit of a mess, isn't it? You need to start trusting people, Sam. It can't be much fun for you.'

'It isn't really,' Sam agreed, sitting down next to her. 'Tell me, is this what it's like in Warkworth all the time? Hoods, Reigns and Pauperhaughs squabbling away? Whatever happened between them all those years ago, what's the point of it now?'

Emily sighed. 'It isn't easy being in the middle of it all,' she admitted.

For a moment she almost thought about telling Sam about her parents' divorce. She had meant to mention it back in the book-shop, but so much had happened since then it had become irrele-vant. Part of another world.

'We must be on our guard,' Sam was saying. 'Eagan might mean well, but he is angry and that will make him blind.'

'He might actually be right about Morcant.'

'Yes, I know.' Sam sighed. 'Wouldn't it be nice to have some answers?! I mean, I'm going to talk to Oscar, but what if *he* doesn't have any? I've been thinking about the Oscar we met in the Garden of Druids. I can't get my head around how he didn't know who I was, even though it had barely been a week since I'd met him in the Fellows' Garden.'

'That *is* strange.' Emily frowned.

'Sam! Emily!'

They were interrupted by the appearance of Kenrick at the garden gates. He marched to where they were sitting, saying hello to the gardeners as he passed them.

'Sorry I couldn't talk earlier,' he said, pushing his hair from his eyes.

He stood there, touched by the autumn sun, whilst the garden remained full of men and women tenderly filling their wheelbarrows with a harvest fit for a king.

'Something incredible has happened to the Forest Reivers! In our beloved walk from the wood to the sea it seems those Forest Reivers who were poisoned were healed.'

Sam and Emily exchanged glances.

'There's certainly a magic to this place that you can almost feel on your skin,' Sam said.

'It doesn't surprise me that you can feel it, Sam.' A warm smile broke across Kenrick's face. 'I have spoken to Jarl and after lunch he would like to speak to you in private before calling the council together. The Forest Reivers have suffered greatly and the head of the Dun-Rigs was lost last night. The anger you saw earlier was from exhaustion. But the heads of the Reiver families do deserve to understand why they have been drawn into this. It is time to put the jigsaw pieces together and make our next move swiftly and with great resolve. Why don't you join us in the great hall for lunch in a few minutes and afterwards you can have your conversation with Jarl?'

'Why is Morcant here?' asked Emily bluntly.

Surprisingly Kenrick took the question in his stride, almost as if he had been expecting it. 'Because, whatever people may think they know about him, he has been a loyal servant of the Keepers.'

'He's just not very pleasant,' Emily commented.

Sam wondered where she was going with this.

Kenrick remained composed. 'If that is a reference to Eagan's misdemeanour concerning Morcant, then we will never know the truth, so I suggest we all just move on.'

'Misdemeanour?' Emily repeated. 'It was a bit more than that, wasn't it? And Eagan claims he *told* the truth. And that he was the innocent party.'

Again Kenrick looked unruffled. 'So does Morcant, and he was the one who ended up in hospital, remember. What we should also remember,' he went on, 'is that we will need the strength and courage of all those who are here today. Let's take each person as we find them and not allow empty words to make them guilty. Now come and join us when you're ready.'

He gave a slight bow, span on his heel and marched off through the throng of gardeners.

Immediately Sam turned on Emily. 'Why do you have to be so argumentative?'

'Why don't you ever say anything?'

She glared at him and his stomach flipped. Even though she looked tired and exasperated, she was back to her beautiful self. Guilt, irritation and desire flooded through him all at once. He turned away, unable to look at her.

'You are a drama queen.'

'Drama queen!' Emily stood, furious. 'Look, I have to ask all these questions because it's important we know who is on our side.'

'Kenrick clearly means well. I just think you like to be difficult.'

'Difficult!' Emily said the word loudly and then laughed.

Sam looked at her in surprise. 'Have you lost the plot?'

'Yes, Sam! You make me laugh. I'm sorry.'

It was so unexpected that Sam found himself smiling too.

'I just find it incredible,' Emily went on, 'that one minute your hands are on fire and the next you can barely ask a question. You throw down some kind of weird terrifying creature outside the orchard and yet you can barely look me in the eye. You speak to Druids and see things in the flow and yet you stumble over your words and constantly apologise for this gift.'

Sam knew Emily was trying to build his confidence, but her words simply made him feel even more awkward.

'Have you finished now?' he asked, blushing.

'No!'

Emily plonked herself back beside him and without warning leaned across and kissed him on the lips. He felt a hot flush spread across his face and down his body. Then he felt her hands on his chest and her lips on his once more. He could hear her breathing and feel the warmth of her body and for a second his fear, troubles and even the voices of the gardeners dropped away and it was just him and Emily in the safety of their embrace.

* * * * * *

They went hand in hand to the hall. Amidst all the hustle and bustle, they walked down several long corridors and finally came to the great hall. Its Georgian windows and sweeping French doors had been thrown open, revealing stone terraces bathed in the early afternoon sun. Running the full length of the hall were four tables that were now crowded with Forest Reivers, and around them a military operation was going on to bring them food and water.

As soon as Sam and Emily entered, a hush spread like wild fire throughout the room and Sam felt himself trying to take his hand from Emily's just in case Jarl thought he was taking liberties. But Emily wasn't having any of it – she gripped his hand with renewed vigour. Then at the far end of one of the tables they could see Jarl waving at them and they were relieved to hear the hum of voices start up again.

Sitting beside Jarl was the man who had seemed so angry that morning. Sam felt his eyes on him, and when he looked, the man gave him a courteous nod. Across from them was the man with the jet-black beard and piercing green eyes. He smiled at them both warmly and continued dipping his bread into a bowl of soup.

Eagan was missing, but on another table Morcant was sitting several places down from Kenrick.

Sam guessed there must have been several hundred Forest Reivers sitting at the long tables. He was glad to feel a fresh wind blowing through the open doors, or the room would have been roasting.

Lunch became a marvel of precision and perfectly timed dishes. Sam particularly enjoyed the lentil soup with crusty bread that was warm to the touch, and couldn't help but cover it from end to end with lashings of butter. In between courses Jarl quietly introduced him to Braden, Jolan, Erin and Ged. They all seemed to be remarkably free of blood and dirt and looking much more relaxed than they had earlier in the day.

There was a murmur of voices that waxed and waned as the courses flooded the tables with their smells and colours. Outside, early afternoon became late afternoon and Sam could feel the breeze from the open doors turning chilly. As he was finishing his pudding, people were beginning to leave the table and heading out into the gardens or wandering down to the Howick Burn. It wasn't long before Jarl was signalling him to follow him outside too. Emily got up from her seat as well, but a little shake of her uncle's head made her sit back down with a thump.

Sam followed Jarl out onto the tiered patio and borders. There were Forest Reivers sitting in every corner talking quietly. They acknowledged Jarl and Sam with little nods and half-smiles as they passed by.

Jarl led Sam into the quietness of Kenrick's private gardens.

'Let's sit, Sam. You've had quite a journey since Oxford. We have decided to hold the council meeting tomorrow afternoon now, when everyone has rested. The Reiver clans are looking for answers and we cannot give them what they are looking for today, but we must show them great respect. What they faced the other night was a nightmare I hope we don't have to face again.'

He sat down with a grimace, clutching his leg.

'We went to the Dead Water with good intentions. Brennus and Drust wanted to seek the help of the Dagda and his daughters. We also wanted to draw the Shadow away from you.'

'I don't know if you did draw it away or not,' said Sam bluntly, 'but it caught up with me in the Garden of Druids.'

For a second they stared at each other.

'*What* did you say?!' asked Jarl.

'Yes, it caught up with me,' admitted Sam.

'And what happened?' breathed Jarl.

Sam took a deep breath. He knew Jarl had brought him here to hear the truth and that was exactly what he was going to give him.

'Do you know,' he began, 'Brennus once told me that Cherwell College was nowhere and everywhere at the same time. I didn't understand what that meant, but now I do. The Garden of Druids is like that – it's wherever you need it to be. And I needed it to be in Birling Wood that night so I could meet Oscar. I created the paradox, not Oscar.' He stopped. 'Then again, it could well have been Oscar, but that's not important. What is important is that we were saved from the Shadow by Oscar.'

Jarl looked pensive. 'I thought—'

'I was saved that time by Oscar,' Sam interrupted him, 'and the reason I survived in Oxford the first time is because the Shadow was never after me. I think it was after Emily. I am not the last Druid – she is.'

'Emily?' Jarl was bewildered. 'Why, Sam?'

'The Grim-Witch is searching for "the girl", not me.'

'Her messengers told us that as well,' Jarl said. 'But how do *you* know?'

'A Grim-were turned up my back garden in Gosforth asking for her. Then one pursued us through Birling Wood and asked again. Eagan took us to Alnmouth, but the crow-men were after us and we had to escape. They grabbed Emily from the boat, but at no point did they attempt to seize me or Eagan. Then earlier today I heard the Grim-Witch calling Emily's name in the flow. Whatever the reason, there is a race to reach her. We just have to make sure that it's not the Shadow who gets there first.'

'But, Sam,' Jarl said, 'Brennus and Drust would have known if the flow had touched Emily and not you.'

'It has touched me,' Sam admitted, 'but the Shadow is looking for Emily.'

'Hmmm,' Jarl was thoughtful. 'The Grim-Witch's servants told us the girl had to go to the Otherland. But with the fading of the Fall, the Otherland will come to us. So I don't know what they meant by it.'

Sam felt a sense of desperation. 'I just need to speak to Oscar,' he said, 'and find out who the child was that he rescued.'

'You know about that as well?'

Suddenly Sam was angry. 'I know a lot things *now*,' he said, 'despite all your best efforts. I know about Oscar and the fellowship. I know I am supposed to go to a garden on Holy Island and find the Staff of the Druids.'

'The Staff of the Druids?' It was clear that Jarl had never heard of it.

'Yes, and I still don't know enough! I want to know whether that child was me or Emily.'

Jarl shifted uncomfortably on the seat. 'I don't want you using the Way-curves. They are no longer safe.'

'Well, how else am I to get any answers?!' Sam exploded.

'Calm down, Sam. When Brennus and Drust get here, they'll be able to—' Jarl stopped as he saw Sam drop his head. 'What? What is it?'

'I don't think they're coming back.'

Jarl turned pale. 'And how do you know that, Sam?'

'It's in the letter that Oscar brought to Oxford.'

'From the Keepers?'

Sam nodded.

'Time and space can be tricky things,' Jarl observed. 'What if it's wrong?'

'I hope it is.'

Jarl sat stroking the craggy lines of his unshaven face. 'On the road here we met servants of the Grim-Witch who said that Brennus and Drust would arrive at Holy Island in five days' time.'

'Let's hope they are right then,' Sam said. 'That's another reason to press on to Holy Island and find this staff. The woman said it would open the Druids' Way. Do you know what that is?'

'The Druids' Way is the path from Holy Island to the Dead Water. No one goes that way now – it passes through the middle of the Underland. I've never heard of the staff before. Who was the woman?'

'I met a Faerie woman in the walk between here and the sea.' Sam smiled at the memory, then became more serious. 'She said war was coming and that I must form a fellowship that could protect the Three. It's clearly the same message that either I delivered to Oscar or he to me.'

He looked away across the gardens as a sprinkler split the water into the colours of the rainbow.

'It's happening all over again.' Jarl's voice was full of disquiet. 'War is coming. I think we are safer here with the Forest Reivers for now.'

'But isn't Holy Island where this is going?'

'Why would you think that?'

'We met Alice in Alnmouth and she said she went there with Oscar and the Keepers. That it was the final stronghold of the Druids. She told us about Oscar's journey into the Otherland.'

Jarl sat up, visibly shaken. 'If you met Alice, then you are lucky indeed! What else did she tell you?'

'Only what we already knew.'

Jarl seemed to settle a little at Sam's words. They were both silent for a while. Jarl ran his hand over his face.

'Have you seen Eagan?' Sam asked casually.

'I think he's intent on fixing his boat. He's been asking Kenrick for wood and tools.'

'Thanks.'

'Sam,' Jarl paused and waited for Sam to look at him, 'I sense an urgency in you, a desire to leave for Holy Island as soon as possible, but if you could wait until the council it would help greatly. I can't and won't stop you from disappearing again, but I am asking you not to take Emily with you. The lands around here are growing more dangerous by the hour and the Grim-Witch is out there somewhere.'

Sam hesitated. He had in fact been planning on leaving Emily at the hall. The Grim-Witch and Shadow were bound to catch up with her eventually. And he didn't want it to be when it was just him and her in the wilderness without the Forest Reivers for protection, or Jarl or Eagan for that matter. He didn't like that thought at all. Above all, he wanted to keep her safe.

He realised Jarl was waiting for his answer.

'All right,' he said quickly, 'if I go, then I'll go by myself.'

'I would really prefer if you waited for the council, and then perhaps we could go to Holy Island together. We could wait there for Brennus and Drust.'

Sam stared at the sprinkler showering the finely cut lawn and shook his head. He had to be honest.

'I can only promise not to take Emily with me.'

Jarl nodded. 'Well, thank you for that.'

He ran his hand over his face again.

'You know, if you'd asked me two weeks ago whether any of this was possible, I would have said you were barking mad,' he confessed. 'We've both witnessed one by one the fireside tales of the Forest Reivers coming true.'

'*This* is where you're hiding!'

Emily came striding across the lawn. She tried to skip past the sprinkler, but came through drenched. She stood in front of them laughing, with dripping wet hair, and Sam felt his stomach beginning to swirl again.

'I hope you aren't planning on escaping and leaving me behind!'

Sam glanced at Jarl, who couldn't help but smile at his niece's cheek.

'Come on – you both look guilty.'

'Emily, that's enough!' But even Jarl's mock sternness could not put her off her stride.

'You *know* I'm not staying here,' she laughed.

'There's a meeting tomorrow, Emily, which will decide on where we go next.'

'*Sam's* going to Holy Island.'

Sam opened his mouth to protest, but he wasn't quick enough.

'He'll try to get there by himself,' Emily continued, 'and he'll come unstuck – I know he will. You've got to stop him. He thinks he'll be doing everyone a favour by sneaking off, but he won't. He'll be risking his life trying to be a hero.'

She pushed her wet hair back from her face and Sam was surprised to see that amongst the water there were tears.

'Emily,' Jarl stood slowly and put his arm around her, but she pushed it away, suddenly really upset.

'Uncle Jarl, you need to stop him!'

'Don't worry, Emily. He's not going anywhere.'

There was an awkward pause.

'Now,' said Jarl, 'I really must see how the Forest Reivers are doing.'

He limped out of the garden.

* * * * * *

Sam and Emily took an evening walk through the wood. It was full of Forest Reivers making camp. When they saw Sam and Emily they would stop and stare, although most would give them a polite nod as they passed by.

'Looks as though there hasn't been enough room in the hall after all,' Emily commented. 'Or maybe they prefer it this way.'

'It reminds me of the night in Birling Wood,' Sam said.

Emily nodded, sending sparkles of water running through her hair. 'I wonder how Bretta is. I think I saw her earlier. She looked terrible.'

Sam suddenly felt sick. A cloud of guilt was settling over him.

'The Forest Reivers saved our lives,' Emily went on. 'I can't bear to think that people have been killed because of us. Did you hear them talking at lunch?'

'I can't think about it.' Sam kept his voice low as they passed a group of Reivers.

'I don't know if you noticed,' Emily continued blithely, 'but they couldn't keep their eyes off you during the meal.'

'They want answers, Emily,' Sam murmured. 'They want to know what they are fighting and why. You heard that man Braden this morning. He's pretty angry. He wants to be sure his people didn't give their lives in vain. And I don't blame him.'

'What *are* we fighting for?' Yet again Emily had asked the awkward question.

Sam found he had no answer.

They walked to the top of the hill by the hall and stood there looking down over the grounds. From here they could see east over the arboretum, which now had a cloak of autumn oranges, golds and touches of brown amongst the green. The sun was beginning to set and its glow was arching across the sky. One or two camp fires were springing up, and now and then a cold breeze lifted the smell of burning wood to their noses.

Sighing deeply, Emily took Sam's hand and leaned into him. 'I do feel safe here,' she admitted. 'Eagan's uncle looks after it, and now Uncle Jarl's back as well, and I don't think these Forest Reivers would let anything bad happen.'

She squeezed his hand.

'Out there are those horrible crow-men. And the Shadow could be anywhere. Do we really have to go to Holy Island? Couldn't we stay here for a while?'

She looked up at Sam and he knew that she was trying to both scare and tempt him. For a second he felt a flicker of fear surface, making his face flushed and his hands clammy.

'I think we do have to go to Holy Island. But I promise to come and get you later on and then we can both listen to what Oscar has to say.'

He felt her tense. 'You still think they're coming after me, don't you?'

'I think it's important to find out.'

'And if they *are* coming after me?' Emily voice rose.

'Then we have to find out how to defeat them.'

For just the fleetest of seconds Sam thought someone else had spoken the words. It didn't sound like him at all.

They stood together whilst below them the noise from the hall quietened down. In the far distance white flashes flickered across a colourful meadow as the last rays of sunlight fell across the sea. They left only when the wood had been thrown into darkness.

## THE BRIDGE OF DRUIDS

With twilight thick around them, they passed through shallow valleys and open fields running alongside a confusing maze of streams that criss-crossed the land in ever more intricate patterns. Before them was the unmistakable outline of Bloodybush Edge. Without saying a word, they began climbing its scarred and barren sides.

Brennus could feel the bearded men's food and water bringing him back to life, but there was an apprehension in the air that he could almost smell. The creatures pursuing them were only two valleys further west and they could follow the Usway Valley north, which would eventually bring them to the foot of Bloodybush Edge.

The Grim-were hadn't eaten or drunk anything and Brennus wondered at his endurance. He himself was moving more easily now, but it still took them a further hour to gain the hill's desolate summit. As he stood on the dry and stale wasteland, even in the near-darkness Brennus could make out the hulking Cheviots to the north, while to the west lay the undulating sea of the Barrow and Blind burns, now in almost complete darkness.

Ezru was looking back the way they had come. 'This is no place to stop. They are coming.'

Brennus felt his stomach clench.

Breth and Kiltrevern's faces were set. 'Only the elders have the authority to open the path through the Underland. We would be expelled from our tribe if we were to show you.'

'You are being hunted. We must help this man reach my mistress, where he must deliver his message to the *Druidae*.'

'Ezru,' Breth said, 'no man has walked through the Underland since Oscar and Culluhin.'

'How do you know of Oscar?' Brennus's voice sounded weary.

'Oscar's story is well known to my people. We travelled with him as part of the old alliance and only very few returned.'

It seemed to Brennus that the wind took Breth's words and scattered them over the top of Bloodybush Edge so that he could no longer grasp their meaning. Just as he could no longer grasp what had happened to Oscar's fellowship.

'Even the Grim people suffer when they trust men,' grunted Kiltrevern.

'The servants of the Bodika have suffered the most out of all of the Three Kingdoms,' said Ezru matter-of-factly. 'But the Ruin's Shadows are only the beginning. If the Fall dies, then its horde will come again until there are only the dead stalking the lands.'

Brennus was listening to his words with horror.

'If the Ruin's servants reach the Sea of Souls, all hope is gone,' Ezru continued. 'You know that, Kiltrevern. Now, we cannot hope to outrun these creatures. Only on the old paths through the hills can we hope to lose them. And we must close those paths behind us.'

Kitrevern was shaking his head, but Brennus could tell Breth was unsure. He watched the twins walk off together so they would not be overheard.

'What are these Three Kingdoms you speak of?' asked Brennus.

Ezru did not answer at first. He was watching the brothers having a fierce argument. Then he said simply, 'Our homelands.'

'Where—?'

But the creature carried on speaking, saying, 'Our forefathers were trapped here. We do not belong here. It is time to go back, but without the *Druidae* all hope is lost.'

'He is still a boy.'

Brennus could barely see the Grim-were, but he could feel his eyes suddenly on him.

'Our hope does not rest with the boy.'

Brennus found himself standing there with his mouth open, shock surging through him. Had Drust been right after all?

A distant horn blast cut through his astonishment and silenced Breth and Kiltrevern's argument. It was followed by a second call, closer than the first. A third call brought the Grim-were to life.

'Those calls seem different,' he commented, looking at the twins.

'Those are not the calls of the Stone Watch,' said Breth, and in the darkness Brennus could hear his apprehension.

'What darkness is this?' called his brother.

'The Shadow Ruins will use the fallen to attack,' Ezru said. 'You cannot kill the dead, or allow yourself to be caught with nowhere to run. This is an enemy that your axes cannot hope to defeat.'

The twins looked at each other.

'The gateway to the Underland is beyond Hedgehope,' said Breth. 'We will take you there, but know it is against our wishes.'

* * * * * *

The brothers set a harsh pace and started to take it in turns to help Brennus, half carrying him across the hard ground. Ezru walked behind them and from time to time would disappear into the darkness.

The night began to be pierced by several horn blasts, each one coming from a different direction and each one sounding just a little closer than before. It was clear to Brennus that little by little they were being outrun. It was impossible to think that the bearded men who had fallen into the gorge had somehow picked themselves up and regained all the ground they had lost, but they had.

Thinking about the dead bearded men sent a tremor down his spine and he tried to distract himself by trying to understand Ezru's earlier words. Of course – the Grim-Witch had asked where the girl was travelling. She had not been interested in Sam. And yet the conversations he'd had with the Keepers came flooding back to him. They had not mentioned Emily once. And it was the boy who could summon the flow. Drust had said the moment Sam could understand how to use it, he would be a formidable opponent. So where did this leave Emily? Where did it leave Sam?

The flat ground of Bloodybush Edge came to an end after they had traversed a final stream whose waters had long since been lost and Hedgehope was rising silently to meet them. The horn blasts were more frequent now and the closest was perhaps less than a mile away. With a final desperate push, they made it up the steep bank and found themselves on a flat plateau.

To the north the brooding Cheviots loomed black in the Northumberland night. Ahead there was a new sound rising up above the wind: the roar of water. Brennus quickly realised that Breth was taking them towards Linhope Spout waterfall, which sat between two rugged hills.

Behind, the horn blasts were closer still, and the Grim-were's agitation was beginning to bubble over. He strode past Brennus, now appearing more scaled than feathered, to ask the bearded brothers whether the gateway was closed. But the question was answered only by grunts as the men pushed themselves forwards.

The open land disappeared as they crashed through a copse of trees. The sound of falling water reverberated through Brennus's ears and the horn blasts fell silent.

Breth seemed to follow a path that opened up through trees and dense undergrowth until they came to a narrow fast-flowing river whose waters were turning white. Brennus was relieved to feel its cold spray against his face. Within minutes he was enveloped in a light drizzle. Then the trees came to a sudden almost dizzying stop on a stone ledge whilst down below the seething waters shone white as they crashed into the dark pool below Linhope Spout.

'We cannot linger here.'

It was the first time Brennus had heard the Grim-were's voice raised in a snarl.

Breth and his brother seemed not to hear the creature above the din of the falling water. They were intent on scrambling down stone steps that were covered in a green haze that made the descent treacherous.

Without waiting a second longer, Brennus followed them into the spray and turmoil. Tremendous fear drove him onwards without thought. His clothes were instantly wet and clung him to him uncomfortably, but he paid no attention. All his efforts were on not slipping from the stone steps into the dark pool below. He was almost immune to the madness around him – and then his feet were gone from under him and he was falling into the rumbling night.

An iron grip caught him almost in midair, but there was no time to turn and thank the Grim-were, for yet again he was slipping and sliding down the stone steps. It was with immense relief that he arrived at the very bottom of the waterfall, where the white waters fell into a deep dark pool before tumbling away into the Northumberland night.

'Where is the gateway?'

Ezru still sounded fierce, and still the brothers did not have time to answer, as several horn blasts announced the chilling arrival of several figures. There was a gasp of despair from the brothers as they realised these strangers were the bearded men who had been meant to guard Drust.

'The waterfall!' shouted Breth, and without warning plunged headlong into the whirlpool, followed by Kiltrevern.

Brennus watched the weight of their axes take them beneath the waters. Then above the roar of the waterfall he heard a new noise that sent a cold blade between his shoulders – a seething roar of inhuman hate rolling down the hillside. Terror made him stagger backwards until once more a powerful clawed hand stopped him from falling.

'Into the water!' came the growling voice of the Grim-were.

Brennus looked down into the shadowy depths and still hesitated. Then an axe came whizzing out of the night and went hissing past him before embedding itself with a terrible thwack into a tree trunk. With a surge of fear, he plunged headlong into the black pool and felt an electric shock of icy water pass over him. He swam deeper, wanting to keep away from the surface and the creatures that had come to kill him, but it wasn't long before he felt swirling currents clutching at him. A second later, the waterfall's maelstrom was taking him down into the cold depths of the pool, where his lungs wanted to burst and he could no longer stop his body from tumbling uncontrollably. A set of claws bit into his arms and he wanted to scream, but there was no time, as he was being pushed through the tornado of waters and back out to the surface.

Coughing hard and with blood running down both arms, he was thrown down on a hard rocky floor. Looking up, he found himself behind the waterfall, in a small cavern that was full of thunder and freezing spray. Breth and Kiltrevern were there, staring at him in shock. But they weren't looking at him, but the creature behind him.

Brennus turned and recoiled in horror. Where feathers had been there were now scales, and Ezru's hands had become hooked and vicious claws.

Standing silhouetted against the white roar of the waterfall, he snarled, 'Open the gateway!'

'What trickery is this?' shouted Breth.

'Is this your game?' bellowed his brother, his face angry and his axe held before him. 'To find a way into our heartlands to slaughter us?'

'He is not your foe!' Brennus found himself shouting above the roar of the falling water. 'Show us the gateway!'

He could see no sign of any doorway – it appeared that they were trapped. And that no one was taking any notice of him. There was now a stand-off. The brothers had their heavy axes held out in front of them and Ezru had assumed a slightly crouched position, as if ready to charge them.

The tension was so great Brennus could almost hear it crackling in the air around them. Then he realised the waterfall itself was beginning to twist. He could feel a magic in the air – a magic that he could not identify. It was beginning to distort the water and had stopped the bearded men's confrontation with the Grim-were dead. Before them there was now an arc of water fifteen feet tall forming a coiling wall that glimmered white in the night.

'What is this?' asked Brennus, turning to Breth.

Breth lowered his axe, a look of wonder etched across his face. 'The power of our elders.'

'It is Fer Benn,' announced Ezru, revealing a mouth full of sharp teeth.

'No – magic does not always revolve around the flow,' stated Kiltrevern, glowering at the Grim-were.

'I do know what it is. It—'

The argument was silenced by a number of loud booms as something shattered against the wall's twisting waters. Brennus thought he saw several axes fall harmlessly into the dark pool.

'Our people are outside,' said Kiltrevern.

'They are no longer your people,' warned Ezru.

Brennus thought it could have been a trick of the shimmering water, but the creature no longer looked as fierce as it had done a moment earlier.

Then a figure hurled itself against the frothing waters and its bloodied body was thrown backwards into the dark pool. A moment later, a second shape thudded against the wall.

Behind him Brennus heard gasps of agony as Breth and Kiltrevern recognised the men now desperately trying to come through the wall, whilst before him, the other side of the wall, murderous wails were coming from shredded faces. He felt as though he had been plunged into a nightmare.

The dead came again, slamming themselves against the frothing wall. This time a single bloody arm found its way through, and Brennus could not help but take a step back. The onslaught intensified and there were several more breaches. At one point they watched in mute horror as a bearded face with milky eyes broke through the wall, one side of it crushed and broken. It snarled and tried to force its way through, but a gentle light flickering through the water forced it back.'

Amidst the assault, Brennus suddenly heard what sounded like singing. Could this be real or was he falling into madness? He wheeled round and saw that Breth and Kiltrevern had gone to the back of the shallow cave and were kneeling before the dark rock humming. The Grim-were was watching them too, his scales now replaced by small feathers, whilst behind them more dead men thudded against the wall of water.

Then the attack stopped, the terrifying wails died away and only Breth and Kiltrevern's humming, accompanied by the sound of the dancing water, could be heard.

Ezru slowly approached the wall of water until he was once more silhouetted against the flickering eddies, and stood there looking out. Curious, Brennus came alongside the awkward-looking creature. The Grim-were did not turn to acknowledge him, but kept his eyes fixed on a point beyond the pool.

A chill gust of wind swept through the cave and for a second Breth and Kiltrevern's voices fell silent. The wall of water seemed to dim just a little and Brennus was acutely aware of his wet clothes against his skin. Through the swirling sheets of water, he could see ice creeping across the dark pool, turning it silver.

'Can you feel it?' The Grim-were's words tumbled into the frosty air.

Brennus could not take his eyes off the pool, now glittering white. The ice had reached the wall of water.

'The Dark Light.'

He watched Ezru's words swirl in the freezing air.

'I don't understand,' he replied.

'It's what brings the dead back to life,' the Grim-were explained. 'Though it is not a life that you would want.'

He looked at Brennus.

'You must allow our mistress to speak to the past. For only the First Light can stop this.'

All Brennus could do was nod.

Out across the deep pool, it looked like deepest winter. The ice was now beginning to creep up the wall, freezing its waters. Slowly they were coming to a standstill.

'If the Trow-Hulda do not open the gateway to the Underland, you must do what you can to escape.'

Brennus nodded again.

Fear was in the bitter air and in the ice that was continuing its relentless creep up the waterfall.

Then it reached the top.

'Move back,' growled Ezru. 'They are here.'

Somewhere in the back of Brennus's mind, he knew the Grim-were's words should have filled him with dread, but all he felt was numb. The last few days had taken so many bites out of his courage that there was nothing left but emptiness.

A hush had fallen over the little cave. The wall of water that had protected them was silent and still. It seemed as if time had come to a stop and everywhere was glistening white with expectation.

Then through the blankness of his mind, Brennus heard a voice. It was Breth telling him to run, but his legs were numb. He stood there as if frozen.

And then the darkness struck, exploding against the wall of ice in a thunderous rumble that shook him to the floor. Ezru was still standing, but there were shards of ice sticking out of his body and black blood weeping from several wounds. The wall of ice still stood too, but there were now gaping holes in it.

When the second black tempest came bellowing out of the darkness, there was a cracking noise that split the night in two as the wall of ice fell into the frozen pool, shattering whatever magic had kept the dead at bay. And out of the middle of the frozen pool they came, with their axes and angry shrieks that rang pain into the ears of those who heard them.

There was a fire in Brennus that made him stand with the Grim-were, even though he had no weapon. The creature had taken the full force of the blast; he would not leave him there alone and be slaughtered by his own fear.

The first of the dead men scrambled over the remnants of the frozen wall, and as he stood upright, Brennus felt a whooshing noise pass by his ear and watched in horror as an axe almost rent the bearded figure in two, propelling him backwards and down into the dark pool. Yet within seconds, or so it seemed, he was already dragging himself from the freezing waters, his milky eyes still looking at them. It seemed that nothing could stop the dead.

This terrifying realisation was sinking into Brennus when without warning he was lifted from his feet by the Grim-were. The second attack had begun. As if in slow motion, he turned his head and watched as Breth slowly raised his axe. For a split-second he thought the bearded man would throw it directly at the Grim-were, but then the giant blade leapt from Breth's hands, spinning as if caught in treacle, and he heard it cut through the freezing air, missing him and Ezru by inches, and then a second later the grisly noise as it struck one of the dead directly in the chest.

The man staggered back, but did not fall or reach for the giant axe embedded in his body. Ezru moved with astonishing speed, dropping Brennus and grabbing the axe handle and propelling the wounded man into the one now coming behind him, and for a second Brennus thought the Grim-were's power and speed would be too much for them. But he was wrong.

From the icy waters two figures were emerging that spiked terror through every fibre of his being. The Grim-wolves had been frightening alive, and now they were dead.

Ezru was falling back into the cave, his hackles raised and his mouth open and snarling.

'This way!'

This time Brennus could hear Breth's voice echoing through the cavern. When he turned, the bearded man was standing with his twin before an opening in the rock face.

'Brennus!'

Brennus whirled around. A figure was dropping out of the dark skies and rolling between him and the Grim-wolves.

'Drust!'

His brother was smiling, but something was wrong – a paleness that made him stand out in the darkness.

Brennus's blood ran cold. 'What—'

Then he was seized and bundled through the rent in the rock face.

'Close the gate,' said the Grim-were.

* * * * *

On either side of Brennus freezing water was running down rocky walls, whilst beneath his feet there was an uneven path.

'Where are we going?' he found himself shouting.

Ahead, the ragged breathing of Breth and Kiltrevern was their only response.

Behind, black fire was coming at them. Ezru screamed as it caught him and sent him crashing to the ground. The grisly smell of burnt flesh filled the narrow corridor. Brennus turned to help, but the creature pushed him on.

'Run! They are behind us!'

To think of the Grim-wolves and Breth's dead companions following them down into the darkness was more than Brennus could bear. He felt as though the tension would suffocate him. And all the time his brother's face was swimming up out of the darkness in front of him.

The descent quickly ended and they were soon jogging through a wider tunnel with a cobbled road beneath their feet. The darkness around them was so thick it was almost as though someone had placed a blanket over Brennus's head. He kept his hands outstretched and every now and then he would bump into one of the side walls. He could hear the steady jog of Breth and Kiltrevern ahead and knew that Ezru was following behind, silent now, but every so often the smell of burnt flesh would make Brennus almost retch.

The cobbled tunnel came to an end and Brennus realised their footsteps were beginning to echo. Though he still couldn't see much, they must have entered a larger space.

He jumped as a hand grabbed his.

'We need to go in single file,' called Breth's voice from ahead.

The hand he was holding must have been Kiltrevern's. He reached behind him and found the claws of the Grim-were.

In the gloom, with their footsteps continuing to echo, they held hands as they moved into what Brennus guessed was a cavern. They had no option but to go forwards. Behind was a nightmare that would never stop. He could not begin to understand its reasoning. He was tired and scared. He stumbled in the darkness and felt Kiltrevern pull him back to his feet. Ezru seemed not to have noticed.

His brother's face came to him once more and he felt tears stinging his eyes. Was he now one of the dead? Or something else? Had the journey to the Dead Water really been in vain?

'Where are we going?' he whispered to Kiltrevern.

'The Bridge of Druids.' The bearded man's gruff voice echoed in the darkness.

Brennus had never heard of the Bridge of Druids, but then again he had never heard of the Trow-Hulda. He had been led to believe the Underland was a mythical place, a dark land of the enemy. Now he seemed to be entering it. Nothing made sense anymore.

There was no light in the cavern and yet a current of cool air kept washing over them. They continued in single file, still holding hands, and after a while a shimmer from far below made Brennus realise they were now on a bridge. An arched bridge, he reasoned, for as they jogged along, he felt the ground beneath him begin to steepen, and this continued for several minutes until he almost stumbled as the ground began to slope downwards into the darkness. But not quite darkness now, as there was that strange flicker from below.

Behind Ezru was beginning to growl, whether in fear or pain Brennus couldn't tell, but the noise came from deep within the Grim-were's wounded body.

'We are across!' called Breth from the murk.

It had taken them several long minutes to cross the bridge. Whatever was below it must have been vast.

'Now we must open a doorway into the Druids' Way,' Breth explained. 'That will take us to Holy Island.'

'There is no time! The Shadow Ruins have found this place.' Ezru seemed to be panting heavily.

'The Bridge of Druids will not let them pass,' snapped Kiltrevern.

'Nothing can stop them. We must find a way out.'

With help from the flickering light, Brennus watched Kiltrevern turn and face the Grim-were.

'Ezru! You have brought darkness into our land. When our elders learn that we have let you into the Druids' Way, we will be expelled from our family. As it is, our cousins have been slaughtered and we are fighting our own dead.'

'Kiltrevern! There is no time for this!' called Breth.

A second later the brothers' humming filled the darkness with strange music.

Brennus turned and approached the Grim-were, who was standing on what must have been the very edge of the chasm.

'I will hold them whilst I can,' Ezru said. 'You must find a way to allow my mistress to speak to the Keepers. You are the one who controls the Way-curves. If you do not survive, then our connection to the past will be lost, and we will need it if we are ever to defeat the enemy.'

Brennus nodded, too exhausted ask how the Grim people proposed to do that. He felt demoralised. Everyone seemed to know more than he did.

Suddenly he felt the temperature around him drop. He knew it was the chill of the dead even before he heard their clamour on the other side of the bridge.

As the Grim-were's growls rumbled around the chasm, momentarily blending with Breth and Kiltrevern's music, Brennus stood waiting for the black flames to engulf them. The same ones that had shattered the waterfall. The same ones that had injured the Grim-were. He hoped the end would be quick. And most of all that it would be the end.

As the seconds lengthened into minutes, the tension grew. The cold swarmed over them all and even the shouts of the dead fell away. And all the while the faint flickering from the depths grew stronger.

With each gleam of light Brennus saw more of the bridge. Within minutes it had been revealed as a huge arched structure that seemed to hang in the air. Whether it had been hewn from the rock or whether giant stones had been rolled there from elsewhere, he could not tell. Had it been built by the Druids themselves? Why had none of the Keepers told him about this place?

The light was no longer flickering. Instead it seemed to be hanging in the middle of what he thought could only be a deep gorge. He couldn't make out the source of the light, but it caressed the bridge, leaving the gorge in darkness. Soon it was shining directly over the stone structure and Brennus noticed the chilly air had been replaced by warmer currents. Then he realised the light had thrown back the darkness at the other end of the bridge, revealing several unmoving figures.

Without warning, the dead leaped onto the bridge, their howls filling the great cavern with a noise like rolling thunder. Ezru also leaped forwards, turning his back on Brennus, who saw his injuries for the first time and wondered how he was still alive. Most of his back was burnt, his scales and feathers blackened. Brennus found himself setting off after him, unable to let him face his end alone.

As he heaved himself up the steep arch, he saw the Grim-were standing on the highest point of the bridge. The creature had come to a complete standstill. Though the dead were coming closer, he was gazing up at the immense curving roof of the cavern.

Looking up, Brennus saw the hazy light was converging there. He also found himself coming to a complete stop, unable to take his eyes from the glistening light.

The dead came over the brow of the bridge with their axes raised above their heads, their wounds gaping and flesh hanging from their ragged torsos.

Brennus heard a crackle and for a moment felt the air being sucked from his body. The light streamed across the bridge, sweeping the dead from it and tossing them effortlessly into the depths of the gorge. He watched them spiralling into the gloom and heard the last of their howls fading into silence.

There was a magic on the bridge that he had never felt before. Was this the last vestiges of druidic power? Had the Druids left their signature on the waterfall? Was their magic in the stone beneath his feet? In the light circling above? Was that why the Shadow Ruins did not attack?

They were waiting at the end of the bridge, and with them, standing side by side with them, was his brother. How was it possible that they had let him live?

The light hanging in the air seemed to have grown dimmer and somehow Brennus knew it was waiting. What would happen if his brother stepped onto the bridge? Would he too be tossed into the darkness below like a piece of straw? Would that be a welcome death?

Wrenching his eyes away from the distant figure of his brother, he looked back at the whirling light. Was this the flow? Was this what his brother could see? Was this the light that Sam had described? Who had created the glow that was now stretching the length of the Bridge of Druids? Was this a reflection of the Druids' true power?

At the exact moment the thought flashed through his mind, the Shadow Ruins moved forwards, and with them came a dark fire that charged over the bridge like monstrous black horses.

Ezru could do nothing more than raise his hands in one final gesture of defiance, whilst Brennus resigned himself to being swept into the chasm below. But the dark flames did not reach them, for the light met the darkness in a thunderous boom that for a second lit up the cavern from end to end.

The blast threw Brennus to the floor. He clung to the cold stone, scrabbling to hold on as the howling winds pushed him towards the edge.

Only Ezru held his ground, standing resolute against the storm that was being unleashed all around them.

Brennus raised his head. Far above them a battle was raging between two unearthly forces. The whole cavern was now alive with booms resounding from the rock and flashes of light and darkness rushing together and then breaking apart in the air.

Slowly Ezru made his way back through the tumult and helped Brennus to his feet. Together they crept back, step by step, across the bridge, whilst above them the onslaught continued unabated. They reached Breth and Kiltrevern, who were rooted to the spot, their eyes wide.

Brennus noticed the open gateway behind them, another impossible rent in the rock face.

'Breth, let's go. We can do no more here.'

Almost reluctantly, the brothers dragged their gaze from the spectacle unfolding above them and led the way into another murky passageway.

As he followed, Brennus couldn't help but look over his shoulder to get just one final glimpse of the battle. The figures were now approaching the highest point of the bridge and it was clear that whatever magic had protected it was beginning to weaken.

'Brennus!' It was his brother's voice.

Brennus froze.

Then he turned.

'No!' The Grim-were was blocking his path.

'Let me just—'

'It is not your brother. He has been touched by the Ruin's servants.'

'*Brennus!*' There was now an urgency in the voice.

'I will not abandon my brother a second time.'

'We cannot wait for you!' called Kiltrevern.

'Ezru is right – it is nothing more than a trap! Come quickly!' shouted Breth.

Brennus pushed past the Grim-were into the fading light of the cavern. A hundred thoughts were swirling through his mind. He was more afraid than he had ever been in his life, but he knew he had to be there.

He quickly understood why the attack had stopped. On the very top of the arch stood what he hoped was his brother.

'Brennus.'

'I am here,' he heard his own voice answer. He sounded weak and frail.

The situation was almost unbearable. He stood there no longer knowing what to say or do.

'They wish to speak to you. There is an old power here that will not let them harm you.'

The voice was still that of his brother.

'If you speak to them, they will let me go.'

Was it true? Brennus looked over at the dark figures further away on the bridge. They did not attempt to rush him or move any closer. Neither did Drust.

Wondering how to answer, he jumped as a figure appeared by his side. Ezru had returned.

The Grim-were's eyes were fixed on the light shimmering above.

'I have seen this before.'

'How can you have seen this before?' questioned Brennus.

'I saw it the night we crossed the Dead Water with my mistress and your father.'

'You were part of the fellowship—!' began Brennus, but he was silenced by his brother's voice.

'They will not let me live a moment longer if you do not speak to them.'

'Yes,' Ezru continued calmly. 'The Ruin's servants were waiting. They killed several of the fellowship, but the strongest pushed on into the Otherland.'

'I am in agony, Brennus! Speak to them.'

His brother's voice was now slow and heavy, as if speaking was almost too much.

'They sent those they had spiked but not killed to pursue the fellowship,' Ezru went on. 'They became husks of their former selves, pleading with the fellowship to turn back from their quest.'

From the bridge a terrible howl broke across the chasm, a sound that shook Brennus to his core. He watched as his brother fell forwards, writhing in agony.

'It is a trap,' repeated the Grim-were.

'Drust! I will speak to them, but they must let you go first!' Brennus cried.

There was a crushing force on his arm as Ezru spun him around. '*No!*'

Brennus thought the Grim-were was going to break his arm. He looked into his feathered face and found his dark eyes impaling him on their intensity.

'I cannot leave here without my brother.'

'If you speak to them, we are all doomed.'

Ezru held Brennus's gaze a moment longer, then the chasm was again filled with Drust's screams, an unbearable noise that made the creature release his grip.

Brennus walked unsteadily back to the end of the bridge, where its dark stone met the black rock of the cavern.

'I will speak to them.'

The moment the words left his mouth, Drust's screaming stopped. He quickly got back to its feet. One minute tortured, the next minute standing silently.

Then slowly he began to walk towards Brennus.

'What madness is this?' Breth was now standing at Brennus's shoulder.

'The Shadow Ruins wish to speak to him,' said the Grim-were.

A second later Kiltrevern joined them, muttering into his long red beard.

Brennus watched as his brother came to meet them. He felt his eyes burn with tears as he saw his pale and frightened face. He was about to step out onto the bridge when he again felt Ezru's hand on his arm.

Then Drust stopped walking and stood still, a slight and lonely figure. When he looked up, Brennus couldn't help but take a step forwards.

'What have they done to you?' he whispered, his voice cracking.

'*Keeper.*'

The word rattled out of Drust and echoed around the chasm. Brennus recoiled in horror. He felt the bearded men take a step back. Only the Grim-were did not move.

'*What have you done to my brother*?!' Somewhere within Brennus a fire was beginning to burn.

'The First Dark seeks the *Druidae.*'

Brennus watched helplessly as the voice grated out its words whilst Drust seemed to hang in the air, his mouth strangely contorted, his eyes wide with fear.

It was the Grim-were who answered first. 'This is the Bridge of Druids. You would do well to remember it.'

There was a snigger followed by a blast of icy air.

'The First Light is dying. The First Dark grows stronger.'

The voice was hollow, full of hate.

'Its servant the Shadow has crossed the Sea of Souls and is amongst the living. The Druids' time is at an end.'

'No!'

'You cannot stop the Shadow.'

The noise that came from Drust was loathsome, as if a giant snake was slithering over loose ground ready to strike. Then there was something that could have been a laugh.

'You don't understand, do you?'

Brennus was frozen by fear.

'It was the Druids who let the unliving into the world. We were on the edge of time – unaware, asleep. If the Fall dies, we go back to our place in the darkness before time.'

The words tumbled over them, leaving a bitter chill in their hearts.

'A war is coming to the Three Kingdoms and where is your fellowship now?'

No one could reply. Even the Grim-were had fallen silent.

'The Otherland is already creeping into this world. The Druids' Way will soon be closed and your connection with the past will be lost.'

Brennus was crushed. He could no longer muster the energy to speak. But it seemed the Grim-were was speaking for him.

'The Ruin failed in the Garden of Druids,' he said calmly.

The figure of Drust was silent for a moment, as if the reply had taken him by surprise.

'It has been stopped before,' Ezru continued, 'and it will be stopped again. What message have you brought the Keeper? Our patience wears thin.'

Brennus couldn't believe the Grim-were's courage, although he guessed the light that permeated the cavern had something to do with it.

'We want the child that was taken from the Otherland.'

'We do not bargain with the dead.'

There was a monstrous roar as the black flames came hurtling across the chasm in answer to the Grim-were. It would have killed them all if the light had not sprung to life. The two met in a deafening explosion, twisting and falling into the chasm and throwing everything into darkness.

'Brennus! Run!' It was his brother's voice.

He could not, for Ezru had already lifted him off his feet and away from the edge of the chasm. But he could twist round in the creature's arms and look behind him. Thunder was rolling across the cavern and the air was heaving with light and black streams. And through all this, he could tell his brother was looking straight at him.

Then he was thrown into a new darkness and being propelled down a new corridor.

'We cannot leave my brother!'

Ahead, the only answer from Breth and Kiltrevern was the pounding of their feet as they ran.

Behind, Ezru snarled impatiently. 'He is no longer your brother! The Shadows have him – do not expect him to return.'

'*No, no, no!*'

In the dark twisting corridor Brennus heard a voice rising in anguish and realised it was his own.

# II

## THE GRIM-WITCH

Sam had returned to his bedroom in the annexe that Kenrick's family had made their home. He lay there looking out of the window and the blackness of the Northumberland night stared back. The room felt safe. The wood, the gardens and even the house felt homely. His stomach knotted at the thought of leaving this place. The road to Holy Island would not be easy, let alone in the dark. He also knew that somewhere beyond the edge of the woods and the burn the Grim-Witch and crow-men would be waiting. Could he really take Emily with him and expose her to being seized by them?

Again, he reflected, it all depended on whether Oscar could throw light on why the Grim-Witch was searching for her. If there was something about Emily that none of the Keepers knew, something that Oscar had kept secret from everyone, then removing her from the safety of Howick could be disastrous. But would Oscar tell him if he had kept it secret?

Then there was the traitor. Did they exist or was this part of the paradox? The same one that stopped him from working out who had delivered the original message… Had it come from Oscar to him or from him to Oscar?

The thoughts kept on coming late into the night, but in a way Sam was glad they were keeping him awake. Eventually he realised he hadn't heard a door creak for some time, signalling the house was finally at rest and it was time to wake Emily. He stood, walked to the big Georgian window that looked out across the wood and leaned against the frame in the dark, watching the fluttering fires that were sprinkled through the wood like fireflies. He would have to be careful not to stumble over a sleeping Reiver.

His nerves suddenly jangled as the heavy bedroom door creaked open. He stood for a second, waiting to see who it was, and was relieved to see Emily enter.

'Just making sure you don't leave without me.'

'I was just coming to get you.'

Emily carefully made her way across the dark room and stood next to Sam. 'Uncle Jarl will be watching your every move. He won't let me go.'

'I know.'

Sam jumped as Emily placed her hand on his arm. 'Why won't you wait for the meeting?' she asked.

'We need to wrong-step the traitor.'

'Won't they be watching too?'

Sam took a deep breath. 'I don't know.' Once again Emily had put her finger on the flaw in the plan.

She was looking worried. 'I can't bring myself to think what might happen if the crow-men catch us miles from anywhere, miles from our friends. And what if Oscar tells you something you don't like?'

That was another awkward question. Sam turned to look back out at the flickering light of the Reivers' fires.

'Let's see what Oscar has to say.'

He turned back to Emily and just for a second they looked at each other and said nothing.

Then Sam felt he had to reassure her.

'Emily,' he said softly, 'you know, before Alnmouth I had only seen whispers of the flow, but that night was different. It was as if I'd woken to a world where there was no colour other than light and darkness.'

Even though he'd spoken quietly, his voice seemed to travel from the room and echo through the hallway.

Emily was standing still, her eyes fixed on him, trying to understand.

'The light and dark were moving,' Sam continued. 'They came in great rivulets and from every direction. Even though you weren't in the boat, I could still see you.'

'See me?' repeated Emily.

'There was an intense white light glowing in the dark water – a light so bright that the strands of darkness could not touch it. That light was coming from you.'

Emily shook her head and stepped back from him. 'You've got it wrong.'

'No, believe me, I saw it. It was brighter even than the light I saw coming from Oscar. I think the Shadow let me live at the gates of Magdalen so it could follow me to you. And of course I led it straight to you. I'm sorry, Emily.'

'But why would it be coming for me?' There was a desperate note in Emily's voice. 'That's what I don't understand.'

'That is why I must speak to Oscar. He owes us the truth.'

* * * * * *

As Sam walked down the hallway of the annexe, his stomach started to knot. The floorboards creaked beneath their feet no matter how much they tiptoed. But it seemed that everyone in Kenrick's living quarters was asleep.

Sam took a deep breath as he reached the outer door and slid the bolts back, stopping several times as the metal began cutting the silence with a rustic squeak. He was glad when the last bolt was back and he was able to pull the door open.

As it clicked shut behind them and they entered Kenrick's private garden, a cold wind enveloped them. The gate between the garden and hall was standing open. They were about to go through when suddenly Sam pulled Emily back.

'What is it?' she whispered.

Sam shook his head.

'I hate it when you do that!' she retorted.

This time Sam put his finger to his lips. High above them came the caw of a single crow.

'Quickly!'

Sam grabbed Emily's hand and led her swiftly through the gate. Several distant caws were answering the first. Things were beginning to move.

'Is that the crow-men?' asked Emily, her voice low and shaky.

Sam shrugged, but he knew there was something wrong. The caws were shrill and far harsher than usual, and he'd had quite a few opportunities in the last week to know the difference.

He and Emily edged around the hall's western wall until they came to the double doors. If they were locked, their plan would be in tatters. At first they didn't budge, but with a little persuasion they yielded.

Sam and Emily entered the hall and carefully closed the doors behind them, leaving the cold breeze and the cawing outside.

In the dark silence a stale smell hit their noses. Sam knew upstairs the wounded Forest Reivers were being cared for and he hoped there would be no one downstairs. He didn't wait long before moving across the circular entrance towards the first set of internal doors. He opened them and found the corridor also in total darkness. He and Emily were quickly down it and through the second set of double doors. They came to the final set. They were now shut.

By now Emily was panicking. 'Oh, Sam, what if Oscar tells us something we really don't want to hear?'

'I still want to hear it,' he said, though he was battling his own fears.

The double doors and the door to the reading room all opened easily enough. Sam stepped inside and drew a breath. High above them the night sky shone black through the domed roof and the room seemed to stare back at them.

Sam took another step into the room, followed by Emily, who suddenly grabbed hold of his arm.

'Can't we do this in the day?' she whispered.

'No.'

'Then at least let's have some light.'

'*No!*' Emily was reaching for the light switch, but Sam grabbed her wrist. 'They'll see it.' His voice sounded shaky.

Already their eyes were beginning to adjust to the gloom and it wasn't difficult to get a feel for the room's layout. They had seen it only the day before and it had been exactly like the room at the Seven Stories. There was a round table in the middle, in complete symmetry with the dome high above, whilst on the far wall Sam knew the tapestry was waiting for him.

He edged forwards into the middle of the room, though he could feel Emily almost pulling him back. Nerves were fluttering around his stomach, his breathing was quick and his thoughts were beginning to whirl. What if he couldn't get the tapestry to work? He still didn't know how it had worked in the Seven Stories and now Eagan had told him it was a difficult thing to do, he felt his confidence spiralling away.

'Sam, please hurry up!' Emily whispered.

Sam looked at the tapestry, trying to recall what he'd actually done at the Seven Stories to make that one flicker into life. He closed his eyes and tried to imagine the light and dark strands he'd seen that night. He tried to focus on the crackling energy that had coursed through the reading room four days before. He could even see the light exploding across its rippling surface. But when he opened his eyes, the room was still dark, the tapestry unmoving.

'Sam, quickly, I don't like any of this!' called Emily urgently. 'Let's go.'

'I can't do it.'

The room swallowed up his words.

'Oh!' Emily jumped. Far above them, claws were landing on the glass. 'Sam,' she said through gritted teeth, 'get moving. This is a bad idea.'

Far above they could hear the pitter-patter of clawed feet on glass. Then came a scratching sound like nails slowly being drawn down a chalk board.

Sam ignored it. He moved closer to the tapestry, searching for the flow in the gloom, but there was nothing.

'Come on,' he said to himself, as he stopped directly in front of it. 'Where are you?'

Frustration and fear were beginning to merge. He was fed up and frightened. He hadn't wanted any of this. First his quiet life in Oxford had been brought to an end, then the haven of his home in Gosforth. He was tired and just wanted to go back to his studies and walk in the Fellows' Garden and spend time with Emily. He felt anger flowing through him and then he saw Emily's frightened eyes in the darkness.

The music was subtle and eloquent and he both feared it and was in awe of it.

'Can you hear it?'

'Hear what?' came Emily's alarmed answer, but Sam had already turned back to the tapestry.

Fireflies erupted all around him, crackling with electricity, leaping from deep within his mind. Just like the night in Oxford, he heard what he had taken to be the Magdalen choir, but this time he thought he could hear their long-forgotten words and he was on the edge of understanding them. The fireflies were joined suddenly by a hundred invisible humming birds that throbbed and whirred around his head until the room was filled with a wild orchestra of vibrating light and darkness that he could see, hear and feel.

He reached out and touched the tapestry, and it came to life, its woven strands unravelling in a blur of movement. In his mind's eye the fireflies and humming birds broke up into a thousand vibrating shades of moving colour exploding against the darkness in a pixelated shower of light and shadow. Just like the night at the Seven Stories, a mesmerising flow of images lit up the Way-curve, and just for a second Sam thought he was back there.

In the writhing streams of light, the castle from the Seven Stories appeared, ebbing and flowing with each turn of the swirling fireflies. Unlike the fuzzy images from the bookshop, this time it was clear. Sam could see the colour of the stone walls sitting atop a daunting cliff face, could even feel their rough texture. But this time the scene continued and there were creatures flying high above the crumbling towers. A long snaking wall glimmered from out of the dark canvas and figures in blazing armour stood there, whilst below, out of the darkness came creatures that made him recoil in horror.

In an instant the colours rippled and for a second he thought he was back in the Fellows' Garden – or was it the Garden of Druids? – because he could see moonlight glinting on a pond. But this time there was an iron gate there, with the symbol of the circle with the unknown tree burning white on the dark metal, preventing him from entering. He felt himself reaching out to touch the gate and instantly a new vibration ran through him, a cold resonance that hummed and flickered in his mind's eye. Fear froze his mind and sent a deep chill into his body.

'You are not strong enough to open that gate alone.'

In the clamour of the kaleidoscopic sea, the voice anchored his feet to the floor and he remembered who and where he was.

'Oscar!' he called.

'Sam, you know the Way-curves are no longer safe. You must be quick.'

The words fizzed and popped in his head. Unlike the Oscar in the Seven Stories, this Oscar was more like Jack, Ronald and Charles the evening in the Eagle and Child. He seemed real, although his form shimmered and his face seemed forever out of focus.

Sam felt a little dazed, but he knew he had to seize his chance. He opened his mouth, but his words were already there in the weaving streams of colour.

'We met you in the Garden of Druids. You could not remember our conversation in Oxford. It appears that I could well have brought the message to you.'

Oscar seemed startled. 'What? How can that be possible? I cannot have met you in the Garden of Druids. It is not for the living. It stands in the Otherland, in the place they call the Darkhart. It stands beyond time and forever captures the moment of the Fall's creation.'

'You fought the Shadow in the Garden.'

'Really?!'

Sam could feel Oscar's shock course through his own body. 'Yes,' he persisted. 'It's how you came to Oxford and gave me the message.'

'But I have not met you yet, Sam. The Keepers said that we would meet when the time was right. In fact I am not entirely sure how I recognise you.'

Sam's frustration was replaced by panic. Would this Oscar be able to tell him anything?

'However, the Keepers came to Alnmouth many years ago,' Oscar continued, 'and gave me two letters. One was for you.'

'Yes, I know, but—' interrupted Sam.

'They said I would know the right time to give it to you.'

'*The right time*?! That letter is *out of time*. It seems to know the future. It changes every time I read it!' cried Sam.

He could no longer look at the fluctuating image of Oscar.

'Listen,' he went on, panic rising, 'I met Alice in Alnmouth and she told me that you had raised a fellowship that had crossed the Dead Water.'

'Sam,' said Oscar quickly, 'you should not be telling me all this. If you tell me too much about the future, it will reach back into the past and that future could be lost. Be careful.'

'But I want to know—'

'*Sam!*' This time Oscar's voice was loud and stern.

'Please listen—'

Suddenly the tapestry seemed to be on fire and Sam's skin was prickling with electricity. A second figure was appearing at Oscar's side. Sam's eyes watered as he tried to bring it into focus. Just like the night at the Eagle and Child, the reading room now seemed split between darkness and light.

'Who is there?' he called out.

'Sam, it's Brennus. This is not Oscar. This is *not Oscar* – run!' called the faint voice of Brennus.

'Sam! *Sam!*'

Someone else was screaming his name. In all of this he had forgotten about Emily.

Suddenly the colour and light drained out of the tapestry and in the blink of an eye it went black. Sam felt the pressure in the room drop. For a moment he didn't know which way was up or down. Darkness swirled around him and he was back in the river Cherwell, cold and afraid. Oscar had gone, but something else was taking shape. A place he did not recognise flickered out of the tapestry weave. A single figure was hunched there in the gloom. It had its back to him, but Sam knew what it was before its image had fully formed. It had heard Brennus's words and was standing slowly, a black-hearted stalker reaching out for him through time and space.

A single word came to him, spilled black against the streaming darkness: '*Druidae.*'

Then the whole reading room was dark, he was lying on the floor drenched in sweat and Emily was standing over him.

Disorientated, sick and terrified, all he could do was close his eyes. But he could still see that dark shape reaching out for him.

'What happened?' Emily's voice was strained.

Opening his eyes, Sam found the room swirling. He grabbed hold of Emily to steady himself.

'The Shadow knows we are here,' he gasped.

'*What*? How? Sam!' Emily was shaking him. 'How do you know? 'Didn't you see *anything*?'

'No!' Emily's eyes were wide with fear. 'You touched the tapestry and then a second later you fell and you were wailing.'

'Oh, Emily, I should never have used the Way-curve!' Sam was frantic. 'I've brought great danger here.'

'Just tell me what you saw!'

'I thought I was speaking to Oscar and then Brennus was there.' Sam swallowed hard, trying to get his thoughts together.

'What did they say? Oh!'

They both jumped as a beak hit the glass dome high above them. They froze, looking up. Just as in the bookshop, crows were gathering on the glass.

'We should go and tell Uncle Jarl.'

'No.' Sam was shaking his head. 'We have to leave.'

'Now?'

'Now. If we stay, the Shadow will bring devastation to everyone here.'

'But where can we go? It will take us more than a day to get to Holy Island, and listen to that.' Beaks were beginning to thud against the glass. 'I really don't think they're friendly at all.'

Sam's thoughts were elsewhere. 'Brennus was using a Way-curve – he must be at Bamburgh. We'll head there first.'

'I thought the letter said Brennus and Drust wouldn't return.'

'*Emily!*' Sam's frustration and fear exploded.

Emily stepped back from him. 'I'm scared – stop shouting!'

Sam put his head in his hands. 'Let's go. Let's just go.'

* * * * * *

They left the reading room and went as quickly as they could through all the double doors until they were outside again. Down below them, the wood was in darkness, although the hot embers from the Reiver fires still winked from between the trees like fairy lights. The sky was a blanket of stars and there was a cold wind blowing in from the sea two miles to the east.

Sam waited a few minutes, listening for the crows, trying to discern any movement amongst the trees and to get his bearings. When he was sure the path was clear, he took Emily to the front terraces. Behind them, the large windows of the hall stared at them in silence. They fled hand in hand down the steep steps past the ponds until they reached the edge of the arboretum, where hundreds of Forest Reivers were camping.

'If anybody asks, we're just enjoying an evening stroll.'

'In the middle of the night?! They didn't believe that the last time! I don't understand why we can't wait for Uncle Jarl.'

'I *told* you – we have to move *now,*' Sam growled. 'There's *no time* to get everyone together. The Shadow is coming.'

Emily could feel the fear emanating from his every fibre.

'Okay, okay.'

'We need to talk to Brennus at Bamburgh and then go on to Holy Island.'

'Yes – *oh*!'

Emily jumped again as a giant crow landed just behind her. Sam turned to face it and his blood ran cold. On either side of its black beak, two milky eyes were watching him.

'It's horrid – get it away from me!' came Emily's petrified cry.

Without a word, Sam turned and half dragged her into the wood. Adrenaline racing through every inch of his body, he crashed through the undergrowth, pulling her after him as he ran. He didn't stop until they were down by Howick Burn and across the little bridge. He finally came to a breathless stop on the tree-lined path, a burning stitch in his side.

Emily bumped into him and stood there panting. 'This feels so wrong,' she managed to say.

'They've let us through,' gasped Sam. 'Think, Emily! These are rangers who make their homes in the woods of the borderland. We were like two elephants back there. If your uncle doesn't already know we're making our escape, he soon will.'

'That crow looked hideous. What was wrong with its eyes?' Emily shuddered.

'Let's not speak about it now,' said Sam. 'We need to get out of here.'

They walked alongside the shallow burn as it meandered through the trees rising high into the night sky, their branches entangled to form an almost perfect archway. Sam was angry with himself. The real Oscar had warned him at the Seven Stories that the Way-curves were no longer safe. How much had he told the imposter? That imposter hadn't seemed to be fishing for information, though. Had he just been holding him there long enough to track his position? How long did they have before the Shadow actually appeared?

Even as that thought crossed his mind, he froze as he caught sight of a figure that was keeping pace with them through the trees. What was it?

He led Emily swiftly down the walk until he reached a place where the trees were bare and the leaves were thick around his feet. The path took a sweeping bend at that point and Sam lost track of the shadowy figure. He pulled Emily closer to him.

'What is it?' she called out.

'We have company – stay close.'

All around them the trees were dark and unmoving. In the distance they could hear waves crashing on the beach.

'I think we're making a mistake,' Emily whispered, but Sam seemed not to hear her. They kept moving.

It wasn't long before they reached the entrance to the walkway. A cold dread was now sweeping through Sam, the result of a new idea: what if Brennus had been the imposter? What if this was an elaborate trap? He could barely listen to his own thoughts as he and Emily emerged on the edge of the sands.

'Sam! Emily! Over here!'

It was a voice they both knew. Morcant was leaning against a large tree, his face in shadow.

The hair on the back of Sam's neck prickled. 'Don't come any closer!' he warned.

'Come on, Sam, I need to take you back to Jarl. It's far too dangerous for you to go out there alone.'

Sam was angry with himself. He had put himself and Emily in this predicament. Here they were, on an empty beach at night with a man he did not trust.

Suddenly a dark shape rushed out of the night. Sam found himself jumping, twisting around in terror.

It was Eagan, his face was a snarling mask of anger. 'Traitor!' he shouted as he ran towards them.

Morcant stood unperturbed, seeming to wait for the inevitable clash.

'No!' Sam ran forwards to put himself between the pair, but Eagan threw him to one side almost without effort. In a terrifying second, long knives were again in his hands.

'*Eagan! No!*'

Instantly recognising the voice, Eagan wheeled round. Other people were breaking from the cover of the trees.

'We do not fight each other!' Jarl shouted.

Eagan came to a stop as he was surrounded by Forest Reivers. 'He is the snake in the camp!' he yelled back. 'Why are you protecting the traitor?'

'He is no traitor,' said Jarl, his eyes blazing with anger.

Sam watched Eagan lower his knives, but his face was still full of fury.

Emily felt sick with shock; she had to look away from the scene. A cold wind was coming off the sea and she shivered and raised her face to the sky. It was pitch black and for a moment she almost thought it was moving. Then it started breaking up and she realised what it was.

'*Sam! Sam!*'

Her screams cut through the shouting match now taking place between Eagan and Jarl, and everyone turned towards her. Barely able to speak, she pointed back towards the sea.

A giant murder of crows was landing just on the edge of the crashing waves, then slowly rising up in the form of dark figures.

'Bretta, take Sam and Emily back to the hall,' shouted Jarl, 'and get help.'

He was trying to remain calm, but he knew he had been foolish. He should have taken them straight on to Bamburgh, where they would have been safe.

Silently the dark figures began to move across the beach. Sam heard the sliding of metal as those around him drew their weapons. A hand rested on his shoulder and when he turned, the woman from Birling Wood was looking at him.

'Sam, Emily, come with me.'

He was already shaking his head and Emily was staring transfixed at the beach. It was difficult to tell precise numbers in the darkness, but there must have been thousands of crowmen making their way along the shoreline. The sands of Howick Bay were teeming with them. With their strange gait, they shuffled along, then stopped a hundred yards from the entrance to the avenue.

There was an eerie silence.

'What are they waiting for?' breathed Bretta.

Sam shook his head again, unable to speak. Staring at the spectacle, he felt overcome with dread. Even when the rest of the rangers joined them, they would be outnumbered ten to one. It would seem the Grim-Witch had finally come for the girl.

She was here already, he was sure of it. Something powerful was out there amongst the hordes on the beach. It was as aware of him as he was aware of it. Of *her*.

Then he heard her.

'They are not here to wage war. I wish to speak to you.'

There was something warm and inviting about the voice. It seemed to come from right beside him, but when he turned, he could see only the craggy features of Jarl and the wide, terrified eyes of Emily.

'Come, we have little time to lose.'

This time the voice reached into his mind and soothed his fears. One by one he felt his anxieties begin to lift and all he wanted to do was step forwards.

All around him, rangers were arriving with their short swords drawn. There were archers amongst them and some carried long deadly spears that they quickly placed in the soil to form a curved defensive wall. Sam could hear Jarl and Braden shouting along the line, and all the while the dark, unmoving crow-men watched silently.

'Come now, step forwards.'

Sam hesitated. He could feel his legs trembling.

'Bring the girl.'

Sam stepped forwards.

Instantly she was towering above him, an unearthly figure dressed in darkness flecked with flickers of light. She was ancient and powerful, beautiful and terrifying, and he could feel her in the flow, just as he had felt the Fall what seemed like a lifetime ago.

'Why do you want the girl?' he whispered.

'She is in danger. The Shadow Ruins are now in the world of men. Even the Druids cannot stop them. Do you know why?'

The words glimmered hot in Sam's mind. Dazed, he tried to comprehend them, but the Grim-Witch did not wait for his reply.

'The Shadow Ruins *are* the Druids. Druids whose power has been twisted by the darkness, by the Ruin. They are filled with a darkness that keeps them alive – the Dark Light.'

Sam gazed up at her, overcome by a strange desire.

Her voice continued to purr within him. 'The Dark Light can reanimate the dead. The Ruin can command whole armies of the unliving.'

She paused.

'It can also sow discord amongst the living. It drew the Elves, men and Trow-Hulda into a civil war in the deepest parts of the Three Kingdoms. The Faeries, the guardians of the Three Kingdoms, called upon those peoples to stop their war and to rise up against the Ruin's servants. Some of them did so.'

Light and darkness seemed to flicker around her as she spoke.

'Two thousand years ago, the Dagda and his three daughters raised an army and marched into the heart of darkness. There they found the Ruin and an army of the unliving waiting for them on the edge of time. A great battle was waged and the Ruin's servants trapped some of the Druids and the Dagda's most powerful daughter and began to twist them beyond recognition. The Ruin itself put its darkness into them.'

She paused.

'They would have been destroyed and the war lost if not for three strangers who appeared in the final hour, bringing a gift from the future, the Fall, who froze the Ruin and its servants in time. The Druids used their magic to create a Circle on the edge of time and lock the Ruin from the world. But now the Fall is dying and the Circle is broken. The Ruin's servants have come forth and they will not be stopped until the last Druid is dead and the cycle is broken. Then the darkness can finally overcome the light.'

The words coiled around Sam, but he was struggling to understand. Standing before her, he could see streams of darkness, but also streams of light. And somewhere in the distance, a lightless tide that was slowly rising.

'Yes,' she continued softly, 'the Shadow Ruins are here now – an army of the unliving is approaching. You cannot defend yourself against them. Quickly, take the girl to Holy Island. My servant Ezru will bring the Keeper of the Druids there. They should be there in four days. Will you do that for me?'

But Sam didn't answer. He was watching her beauty fade. As she turned her attention away from him, she was transforming into a hideous creature with giant black wings, dressed in scales. She was looking to the south and calling to the crow-men in a language he did not want to understand, guttural caws that filled him with dismay.

Like the parting of a black sea, a crack appeared in the distorted bodies of the crow-men. Within seconds, a long narrow corridor had opened up.

The Grim-Witch looked back at him over a scaly winged shoulder, and suddenly he understood.

A savage wail broke across the beach, followed by an icy wind that bit into their faces. Sam felt something slam against him and for a second he staggered under its weight before strong hands caught him. He looked up into the bloodshot eyes of Eagan.

'The Grim-Witch!' Eagan gasped. 'I saw her in the flow.'

Sam nodded, feeling a trickle of blood escape from his nose. 'We have to—'

Then he could say no more, for the sandstorm hit them full on. Behind him he could hear the wall of Forest Reivers being thrown into disarray and Emily screaming, but he couldn't see her through the stinging sand. Next a shuddering blow knocked him to the ground and he lost sight of Eagan too.

Staggering to his feet, he pushed through the ranks of Forest Reivers, looking left and right.

'Emily!'

Still he couldn't see her. Sand filled his mouth and terror gripped his mind. His face and hands were raw from what felt like a thousand tiny cuts. Whirling round, he looked towards the sea.

A figure was running towards the ranks of crow-men with Emily across his shoulders. In an instant, they disappeared down the narrow corridor between them.

'Sam!' Jarl was swinging him around. 'What is happening?'

'What terror is this?' called Braden.

From the coastal path, the night was racing towards them, full of what looked at first glance like stars, but were in fact thousands of milky eyes.

'Jarl,' called Sam, 'get the Reivers back in the hall!'

Jarl looked around him wildly. 'Where are Eagan and Emily?'

'Eagan's taken her,' Sam replied. 'He's not the traitor – I was wrong about that, I'm sorry. Brennus and Drust will arrive in Holy Island in four days' time. Meet me there.'

And then he was gone, running towards the crow-men just as the winged storm was beginning to crash down all around them.

# THE SHADOW RUINS

He approached the lines of crow-men with horror and loathing. In the night a thousand black and twisted feathered bodies watched him approach. He was drenched in sweat, his mouth dry. The moment he entered the corridor they had opened up for him, there was a humming in his ears, and with growing terror he realised it was their beaks grinding together. There was a terrible smell to them that burned his nostrils and turned his stomach. Somehow, he realised, each of them was made of several giant crows cruelly fused together. It seemed they were held together by nothing more than the Grim-Witch's power. If he had reached out to his left or right, he would have touched their feathered bodies – a thought he could not bear.

He almost fell out of the hideous throng to find Eagan and Emily standing on the beach arguing.

When Emily saw him, she turned and tried to kick her cousin before running towards him and flinging herself into his arms.

'Sam! He grabbed me when we were blinded by the sand! He dragged me through all those awful crow-men! He *is* the traitor after all!'

Eagan ran forwards too. 'Emily! You have to believe me. We have to leave now!'

From behind Sam came the terrifying noise they had heard in Birling Wood. The Grim-Witch and her horde were going into battle.

'*Now!*' shouted Eagan.

Sam looked down at Emily. 'Come on. We have to go.'

Further down the beach they found the *Celtic Flow* with its newly fixed prow.

'You need to push!' Eagan shouted as he turned and pressed his shoulder into the boat and dug his heels into the sand.

Just like in Alnmouth, Sam and Emily put their backs to the hard wood and began pushing.

As the *Celtic Flow* inched forwards, the noise of the battle seemed to swell and the throng of dark shapes on the beach began to grow closer. It was hard to make out who the crow-men were fighting, but whoever they were, they were pushing them back towards the sea and back towards Sam, Emily and Eagan.

Then a lone figure broke from their ranks and with terrifying speed made directly for them. They saw gleaming white eyes against a broken and twisted face snarling and bearing down on them.

Emily's scream lit up the night and in a blur Eagan slashed the creature across the face with one of his long knives, opening up a wound that should have killed it instantly, but it did not die, or even drop to the ground, but shook its head and came for them again, with part of its face hanging down.

Emily screamed again and buried her face in Sam's shoulder, unable to look at the nightmare unfolding before them.

There was a tormented madness to the creature's movements as it fought on. Eagan landed blow after blow on its head and body, but only when it had been sliced into what looked like several crow-bodies did the creature stop fighting.

When Eagan turned back to Sam, there was a mania about him. His breathing was ragged, his eyes wild. 'Now we know what the Reivers faced in Birling Wood,' he said with a wry smile.

With renewed vigour, and with the fighting getting closer, they pushed the *Celtic Flow* into the cold waters. As soon as it was moving freely, Eagan pulled himself up into the boat, quickly helping Emily and Sam up behind him.

As he settled himself on the rowing seat, Emily gasped.

'What?'

Wordlessly, Emily pointed to the beach. Several more milky-eyed creatures had broken away from the battle and were heading towards them.

'Sam, take the oars and get us to deeper water.' Eagan got up and made his way to the stern. 'Emily, go and join him.'

He stood there with a knife in each hand and counted five creatures swarming towards them. That was all they needed. The *Celtic Flow* was struggling through the breakers and freezing cold spray was being thrown across the boat, and he wasn't sure whether the work he had done to strengthen the prow would hold. The battle with the first creature had taken all his strength and he didn't think he could hold out against five.

Looking back at the beach, he was overcome by the sheer scale of the contest going on there. The sands were now a rolling sea of shadowy figures locked in deadly combat. There was no going back – the only escape was out to sea.

'Row, Sam!' he shouted, as the *Celtic Flow* hit a large breaker and for a second seemed to be heading back towards the beach.

He could see the milky eyes of the figures as they hurled themselves into the sea, but then he felt the boat begin slipping through the dark waters as Sam found his stroke.

The *Celtic Flow* pulled away from the shore, but Eagan remained standing, keeping his eyes fixed on the dark figures in the water until he saw four of them floating as the sea crashed over them, rolling their helpless bodies back towards the beach. There was one missing – where was it?

'I need more speed!' he called to Sam, looking for any sign of movement in the water, but there was nothing but the rolling waves.

He stayed there, looking back towards Howick Bay, until the sounds of the battle finally began to recede. He thought he saw shapes in the sky and now and then flashes of light, but it was a moonless night and everything had converged into a dark tangle. Finally, without saying a word, he took the oars from Sam and began turning the boat north.

Emily was shivering. 'What were those things? They looked like crow-men, but different somehow. Those eyes…'

'They were the unliving,' Sam said bluntly.

'What?'

'Beings brought back from the dead by a darkness that keeps them alive – the Dark Light. Isn't that what the Grim-Witch said, Eagan?'

Eagan nodded. 'There are Druids, too, filled with that light, Druids whose power has been twisted by the darkness. Shadow Ruins.'

Emily shivered. 'You've both been talking to the Grim-Witch? What else did she say? Sam?'

Without saying another word, Sam was making his way to the stern.

Eagan stopped rowing.

'What is it?' asked Emily her voice full of anxiety.

'I thought I saw something. Perhaps not.' Standing there, Sam could still hear the faint sounds of the battle, although the beach was now lost in the darkness.

They waited.

'It must have been a trick of the light,' Sam said.

Eagan started rowing again.

Emily was frowning. 'So is that what the Shadow is? Sam? Talk to me!'

'I don't want to speak about it now,' Sam said, still looking towards the stern. 'The Grim-Witch told me a lot more and I've got to figure it all out.'

'Eagan?'

'I'm not sure I heard it all, Emily. The main thing she told me was to get you away. Fast.'

'Hmph. Well, you needn't have been so rough about it,' Emily complained. 'You hurt my shoulder.'

'*You* hurt *mine* – have you any idea how heavy you are? I just can't row anymore. Sam?'

Sam took the oars and Eagan sank to the bottom of the boat in a heap.

'Where are we?' asked Emily, feeling slightly guilty.

'We're southwest of Craster,' Eagan muttered.

'I'm sorry. This is my fault,' said Sam, as he rowed grimly on.

'What do you mean?' asked Eagan, sitting up and pushing his hair from his face.

'I used the Way-curve at the hall and the Shadow saw where I was.'

'So that worked out well then,' said Eagan, lying back down. 'We must remember not to try that one again.'

Sam grit his teeth and concentrated on pulling the *Celtic Flow* through a sea that had begun to rise and fall more aggressively.

Suddenly there was a loud snap as a piece of the boat's bow disappeared into the night. Eagan leapt to his feet as freezing water gushed into the boat. '*No!* It hasn't held after all!'

He quickly replaced Sam and swung the boat around in the direction of the shore.

Sam and Emily sat together miserably in the stern, expecting to have to swim for it again, but the tide was with them and soon the dark basaltic coastline of Craster was within reach.

Eagan tried to ground the boat on the rocks, but the waves were too strong, and it slipped back into the water again. They all scrambled out onto the treacherous rocks, leaving the boat spinning and bumping against them.

Emily slipped almost at once and fell to her knees. Sam was putting out a hand to help her back up when he froze.

'What's that?'

Something was clinging to the stern of the boat, looking at them with milky eyes.

Eagan drew a long knife which, at that moment, felt as though it was made out of lead. 'I wondered where that one went,' he said wearily.

Emily was scrabbling away from the boat. 'How long has that been there?'

They stood watching the creature, but it just hung there, making no attempt to leave the boat, even when it was caught between the hull and the jagged rocks.

'Eagan,' said Emily, uncertainly, looking up at him. 'Can you…?' But then the boat was pushed up against the rocks once more and she heard a noise that made her almost sick.

They left the creature clinging to the boat with one arm, the rest of its body clearly shattered. They did not want to know how it could have survived in the water for so long.

* * * * * *

They had come ashore between the village of Craster and Dunstanburgh Castle. Behind them they could just make out the village rooftops whilst ahead Sam could already imagine the ruined towers of Dunstanburgh Castle waiting for them. He had always found this stretch of coastline menacing, even on a clear summer's day. To his right the waves were splintering against rocks that stood like shadowy statues, watchful, unmoving and forever looking out to sea, whilst to his left there was open grassland.

'Why didn't the creature attack us?' asked Emily, sounding thoroughly fed up.

'It wanted to know where we were going,' answered Eagan.

'And where are we going?'

'The Grim-Witch said to take you to Holy Island,' said Sam.

'So she doesn't want me, after all?' Emily sounded relieved.

Sam hesitated. But he had to be honest. 'I think she'll meet us there.'

'I hate this,' said Emily. 'We should have stayed at the hall.'

In the distance the broken and jagged towers of Dunstanburgh Castle rose up, silhouetted against the landscape. The castle stood atop a small hill with its main gate and towers looking south whilst its walls sat on the edge of a cliff face, taking advantage of what had once been an Iron Age fort.

It took several minutes before they were standing before the shattered front towers. At night the castle looked sinister, as if it were waiting to snatch weary travellers who had come too close.

'I'm not sure if I like this place.'

Emily sounded tense and Sam didn't blame her. He didn't like it either. Eagan had said very little, but they both noticed that he had a long knife in each hand.

'The path takes us through the castle,' he said. 'Let's keep going.'

Sam followed him up the short path, feeling both afraid and guilty. He knew now he should never have attempted to use the Way-curve. He had shown himself to the Shadow – how long before it caught up with them? This time there would be no Forest Reivers to help them. He was almost overcome with hopelessness and yet at the same time he could feel a fire burning deep inside him, a reminder that he could touch the fire of the flow.

The gateway sat resolute between two crumbling towers, their tops jagged and broken relics. Sam, Emily and Eagan passed through into what would once have been the bailey, but now was a circular hill with a path forking left and right. In the gloom they could still make out the outer wall.

Eagan went right, skipping down a cobbled causeway, light flashing off his long knives as he ran.

Emily span round, grabbing Sam by the arm. 'Did you hear that?' she asked in a frightened voice.

'What?'

Sam could only hear the wind as it came whistling through the castle's crumbling walls. But as if in answer, there came distant caws.

'Eagan!'

'I hear them. Follow me.'

Quickly Eagan took them up a number of stone steps that brought them to the top of the outer wall. From here they could see where the sea met the land, crashing against the dark rocks. They huddled together, trying to hear the caws above the wind that was rattling through the ancient stones. It seemed the crows were drawing closer.

'What are we going to do?' asked Emily, her voice strained, but Eagan seemed not to hear her. He was looking over the wall in horror.

Sam took a look and spotted what Eagan had already seen. From the direction of Howick, a dark cloud was bearing down on them.

'What is it?' Emily looked over the wall too.

For a moment, no one knew what to say.

Then Eagan spoke. 'I think we should head to the far tower. We cannot hope to defend ourselves in the open against such numbers.'

'We won't make it to the tower,' said Emily, almost sobbing.

Eagan looked at Sam. 'Take Emily and head for the tower. I will give you what time I can.'

'No! You will be killed!' sobbed Emily, her face in her hands.

'We go together or not at all,' Sam cried.

Eagan starred at Sam, shaking his head in wonder, then, without saying another word, they all jumped down from the wall and made for the path that ran diagonally across the hill.

* * * * * *

Braden, Jarl, Ged, Jolan and Bretta could do nothing to stop Sam stepping into the hideous throng of crow-men. Just for a second Jarl could neither move nor shout. He watched in mute horror as Sam was swallowed up by the horde, their feathered bodies closing in all around him.

More Forest Reivers were arriving on the beach, but their battle cries were soon trailing off as they realised something strange was happening. The silent crow-men's bizarre beaked faces were turning south and from the coastal path the night was surging towards them, filled with stars. Then Jarl realised they were in fact thousands of milky eyes.

The Reivers watched, helpless, as a hideous battle erupted along the horde's southern flank. Two ferocious black tides came together in a catastrophic explosion that rippled across the beach like an invisible serpent.

'What terror is this?' Jarl heard himself shouting.

'The dead of the King's Seat!'

Ged's answer brought fear to all those who heard it. The Reivers were stunned to see the horde of the Grim-Witch, the enemy they had fought only days ago, sweeping around to meet this new and terrifying threat. They stood on the beach, holding their swords, fear and bewilderment on their faces.

Then Jarl was calling them back to the trees and burn.

He was met by Erin Dun-Rig and a wall of defenders, their long spears dug into the ground.

'What's going on?'

Jarl shook his head. 'There's no time to explain. Get me our fastest horses!'

Without a word, Erin started back up the tree-lined avenue.

The Reivers were squeezing passed the deadly spears and assembling by the burn. Soon Kenrick was weaving through the throng and finding Jarl and Braden trying to bring order to the chaos.

'Where's Sam?' Kenrick's voice was thick with panic and concern. He swung Jarl round until they were face to face. 'Where's Emily?'

Jarl hung his head. 'The crow-men have them. And Eagan.'

'How is that possible?'

Kenrick turned towards the Howick sands, where the sickening noise of battle had contorted into a thousand caws of hatred.

'We have to get them back before it's too late. Jarl, Braden, Jolan, how have you let this happen?'

'We had no choice,' Braden answered. 'They made their escape in a sandstorm.'

Kenrick's anger turned to the weapons master, who was watching the battle. 'What happened, Ged? How could it have happened?'

'The Grim-Witch allowed Sam, Emily and Eagan to escape.'

'Then what are we waiting for? Let's go after them!'

'I've sent Erin back for our fastest horses,' Jarl told him. 'Eagan will know to take them to Bamburgh.'

'What about the sick at Howick?' asked Jolan.

'They aren't after our sick and wounded,' Jarl said. 'They've come for Sam and Emily.'

Erin was returning with the horses.

'Listen!' shouted Jarl above the tumult. 'Don't follow us. This storm will pass. When you are ready, come and find us at Holy Island.'

Jarl, Braden, Jolan, Ged and Bretta were mounting five graceful Reiver horses.

'You must find them!' yelled Kenrick, his white hair flat against his forehead.

'We will!' called Jarl as he settled himself in the saddle and turned his horse, waiting for the Reivers to let them through the long spears.

Jolan came alongside Bretta. 'Are you well enough to ride?'

'Yes.' Since coming to Howick Hall, his sister had made a remarkable recovery from the poison of the crow-men. It had been the same for all those who had been poisoned. This had come as no surprise to Kenrick, who believed there was an ancient magic in the trees surrounding the hall.

The wood was now thick with Forest Reivers shoring up their defences. Ged could feel their fear. Just ahead he watched Braden and Jarl as they turned their horses towards the beach, the Reivers having now opened a corridor wide enough for them to pass through.

Jarl took a deep breath and a final look at Kenrick, who tried to give him an encouraging nod.

'I will come and find you at Holy Island.'

Jarl felt his mouth run dry at the fear in Kenrick's voice. He could only muster a brief nod in reply before gripping the reins. Beneath his legs, the horse reacted instantly to his command, almost leaping through the spears and out onto the beach.

The others followed, then the Forest Reivers quickly closed their defences and watched the horses disappear into the night.

As they galloped across the beach, the roar of battle rattled their bones and it took the riders every ounce of skill not to be unseated. Ged and Braden took the lead, expertly clearing a path through the carnage and crashing their swords through any creature, alive or dead, that got in their way. Jarl was just behind, with Jolan and Bretta bent over their horses, trying to soothe their terrified steeds.

Once they were across the beach, they quickly made their way up a steep bank leading to a continuation of the coastal path. Though the battle was now behind them, it took some time before they allowed themselves to canter.

'The path takes us through Craster and Newton by the Sea,' explained Jarl.

'What about our people at Howick?' asked Braden. 'I am worried about them.'

'I tell you, those dead crow-men aren't interested in our people,' replied Ged.

'How can you be so certain?' asked Braden, a glint of anger in his eyes.

'You already know the answer to that.'

'Do we?' asked Jolan, glancing at Bretta, whose eyes were fixed on the weapons master.

'Now is not the time for mistrust,' called Jarl. 'We have to reach my son before the dead reach him first.'

High above the sea they climbed, and they came to a place where in the darkness below the soft sand turned to thrusting black rock. The sea churned white against its sharp edges, and as the Reivers moved along the exposed path, no longer sheltered from the raw wind, they could feel the sting of the sea air.

Soon Craster's glimmering harbour lights could be seen, a reassuring sign in the vast Northumberland night.

Jarl had travelled the length of the coastal path many times over the years. It turned west, bypassing the fishing village of Craster and then moving north through Dunstanburgh Castle. The five horses passed along it like wraiths in the night.

They were approaching the long winding path to Dunstanburgh when Ged raised his hand and in one fluid movement dismounted, signalling to the others to follow. He led them into the shelter of several trees that clung to the edge of the path.

'What is it?' asked Bretta.

'Hush. Do you hear that?'

The five gathered in the darkness beneath the trees, listening. In the distance they heard caws carried on the wind. They looked at each other, instinctively drawing their weapons.

'It's them,' said Ged simply.

'The dead from the King's Seat?' asked Jarl.

'Yes.'

'They will catch Eagan, Sam and Emily in the open if we don't do something,' said Jarl.

Even as he spoke, a giant murder of crows filled the night sky, and in the darkness they seemed to be flying through a storm of dancing fireflies. Then, with dread, the Reivers realised it was the crows' eyes shining white against their black bodies. Flattening themselves against the tree trunks, they pulled in the horses, who were whinnying and stamping in fear, and waited until the last of the crows had passed.

'They are landing south of Dunstanburgh.' Ged was squinting off into the night.

'How can you see that? One minute you know the mind of the Grim-Witch and then the next you can see in the dark!'

Ged ignored Braden's words. 'They are marching on the castle,' he said.

Then he was racing into the night, leaving those gathered looking into the gloom that was rolling around them.

Jarl urged his horse after him. Fear surged through his mind as the path opened up, with crashing waves to his right and open land to his left. His steed was big and powerful and it took all his strength to stay mounted, but he hung on. He could not bear to think of Eagan, Emily and Sam facing such horror alone.

Braden's anger swept through him as he followed Jarl. He could think of nothing more than taking his revenge on those who had killed his people.

Jolan could not shake his terror of what he had seen at the orchard. He knew what they were about to face and he feared for his sister, who was riding beside him like the wind.

Bretta rode a horse better than most and quickly caught up with Braden.

Rounding a hill, they could see the outline of Dunstanburgh Castle rising sharply to meet the night sky. A sea of figures was moving towards the castle and the outer walls were already swarming with the unliving. They were clambering over each other to scale the walls just like giant spiders.

'Take their heads off!' called Ged.

In the night the five companions rode alongside one another, their weapons drawn, and came down on the throng like thunder. The mass did not turn to defend themselves, but still drove on towards the castle walls. It was a ghastly business as the five slaughtered all within their reach. They showed no mercy, swinging their weapons like crazed animals themselves, only too aware of the horde's dark and evil intent. Whatever was driving them wanted to get into the castle at any cost.

Jarl felt sick to the core as he tried to force his way through the horde, knowing without doubt that Eagan, Emily and Sam were trapped. Beside him, Ged was sweeping the crow-men from their path, whirling his two swords effortlessly above his head, whilst Braden was letting his anger lead the way as he avenged all those who had lost their lives. Jolan and Bretta were working together as a team and headless crow-men were falling steadily before them.

The five companions pushed on, but still there was no way through. Before them Dunstanburgh Castle stood besieged, the unliving now launching themselves forwards in a tide of madness that threatened to sweep the castle from its rocky perch. Jarl watched in horror as they tore at one another in their frenzied attempt to breach the wall. It seemed they weren't even aware that they were being attacked from the flank. They were being driven on like cattle, crazed and ferocious, paying no attention to the people on horses who kept cutting them down.

Jarl sat back, exhausted and sick from the bloodshed, his horse drenched in sweat.

Ged, too, had stopped fighting. He had slain untold numbers and it had made no difference. Now a new foreboding had arisen in his mind.

He stepped away from the carnage and found himself drawn to the edge of the cliffs. He looked out at the dark sea, its crashing waves churning white, and there they were. At first they rolled with the waves, but as they reached the shore they got to their feet. In the dark and from this distance he could not make out who they were, although he knew they were not crow-men from their walk. They were now free of the swirling sea and something about the lead figure made him step forwards, a chill shiver slipping between his shoulder blades.

Coming up towards the hill towards him were Dwarrow Dun-Rig and a host of Reivers – the Reivers he had watched Braden bury in Birling Wood two days ago.

Jarl heard Ged's voice calling above the clamour of the dead. Swinging his horse around, he saw the weapons master racing from the cliffs, clearly panic-stricken.

'Dwarrow!' panted Ged, as he reached the others. 'Dwarrow is here!'

At that moment Bretta gave a bloodcurdling scream. She was staring at the cliffs, her face a mask of terror.

The rest turned quickly towards the cliffs, where figures were beginning to appear. The first was a giant man in a long black coat. Other figures were appearing to his left and right. In the night their milky eyes were shining.

'I cannot fight my cousin,' gasped Braden.

'He is not your cousin anymore,' said Ged coldly, his sword already in his hand.

'But they are our own people!' said Bretta not taking her eyes from the figures. A dozen were now standing on the cliffs.

'Our own people perished in Birling Wood. These are no longer Reivers,' answered Ged.

'What can be done against such madness?' asked Braden.

The Reivers sat unmoving in the darkness, on horses that were beginning to kick and snort with terror.

'Look,' said Jolan.

A deathly silence was falling all around them. The dead were no longer trying to claw one another's eyes out to get inside the castle. Several hundred were now standing motionless before the castle walls, with a hundred more atop them.

Jarl's stomach clenched. Was this a sign that whoever was in the castle was dead? Had the enemy won? Had they perished – his son Eagan, his niece Emily and the person they had let down at every turn – Sam?

Then the milky-eyed Reivers moved forwards at last. Jarl, Ged, Braden, Jolan and Bretta watched in silent horror as their own people came to kill them.

The arrows came out of the night, their white feathers shimmering through the darkness, striking the dead through their throats and stopping them in their tracks.

Jarl turned to see the ghostly company standing on the hillside, their bows flashing arrows into the night.

* * * * * *

'They're over the wall!' Eagan shouted.

Emily faltered as she ran. The far tower was ahead of them, no more than a hundred yards away, but the possibility of reaching it was draining away.

Sam could hear Emily's sobs and feel her hands grabbing hold of him. Eagan was circling them, his eyes flashing fear and anger, preparing to make a last stand, but Sam knew it would be futile against such numbers. He felt sick to the core, for he knew Eagan was preparing to die for them. This was no traitor.

In the night hundreds of milky eyes were now surging over the walls. It would soon be over. Sam could see their broken and twisted bodies, their unblinking eyes. These were creatures that had no place in the world of the living.

Then their caws died away and silence fell throughout the empty shell of the castle.

Eagan tightened his grip on his knives. 'What's happening? Why have they stopped?'

Moonlight was flooding across the hill and the air was now chill. His breath left his mouth in a swirling maelstrom, curling like smoke rings into the icy night. He paused and glanced at Sam.

Sam had felt it too. A trickle of ice ran down the length of his spine. There was a rawness inside him that he had felt before. The hideous understanding that something wicked was on its way.

'The Shadow is coming.'

His words sent a cold tremor through him, but Emily didn't reply. He turned to see her looking back the way they had come.

'It's so cold. How has autumn turned to winter?' she asked through chattering teeth.

It was eerily quiet and in the peculiar half-light of the moon it felt for a moment as if time itself had been captured in the silence. They looked at each other, their faces pinched and cold.

'How…?'

'I don't know.'

Whether it had been there all the time Sam could never quite recall, but there in the north wall of the castle was a round oak door.

Eagan stared at it. Somehow it was familiar. It reminded him of the solid round doors in the old school house and on the seventh floor of the bookshop. But he was surprised when, without hesitation, Sam took a key from his pocket, placed it in the keyhole, turned it gently and heard the lock click back.

He helped Sam pull the heavy door open and they stepped into a place of absolute stillness. The moonlight was gone, replaced by a serene darkness. But it wasn't just the calmness of the place that stole over them, but also its awareness. It was alive with electricity, with consciousness.

Eagan felt suddenly disorientated. The door should have opened out onto the cliffs and the jagged rocks below, but instead as they passed through it the darkness lifted and he saw they had somehow entered a walled garden. Fluttering around him in the half-light was electricity, like hummingbirds' wings. He shook his head. It was difficult to focus, but the further he went into the garden, the softer the beat of the hummingbirds' wings became and the firmer the ground beneath his feet.

Sam took them up a slight incline and through a ring of ancient trees until they were standing in front of a pond, ringed by wooden benches.

'I never knew Dunstanburgh Castle had a garden. I would have known about the garden,' Eagan said. 'Where are we?'

He looked at Sam and Emily and even as he asked the question, the realisation was flooding through him.

'This is where I met Oscar,' Sam told him. 'He was sitting on that bench, on a night like this. It feels as though I've come full circle. Even the words feel familiar.'

'But that's impossible – the Garden of Druids can't be in Dunstanburgh.'

'Just like it couldn't have been in Birling Wood?' asked Emily.

Eagan felt dumbfounded. This was a reality every bit as disturbing as the one they had left outside. If 'outside' was the right word. When he looked back the way they'd come, there was a wall of darkness that was deeply unsettling.

'So where are we? I'm not sure we're anywhere.'

'You don't need to be anywhere to understand that this is somewhere,' said a voice behind them.

Even before Eagan turned, he knew who it was.

'What place is this?' asked Oscar.

'Oscar!' said Eagan, almost falling to his knees. He had not seen Oscar for over fifteen years. He was surprised to see how young he looked. This was an Oscar in his late forties.

'Who are you?' said Oscar. 'Let me see your face.'

'Eagan Reign,' said Emily, faintly. 'We brought him to you seven days ago. He was poisoned. Your servant took him into the waters and cleansed him of the poison.'

Oscar seemed unsure, looking from Sam to Emily and then settling again on Eagan.

'Was this supposed to happen?' Eagan thought. 'Oscar seems a little befuddled, to say the least.'

'My father is Jarl Reign,' he prompted.

'Jarl Reign!'

At last they had found a common thread. It seemed Jarl's name had jogged a distant memory.

'He is a friend of my sons,' continued Oscar. 'They are very fond of him.'

'Brennus and Drust Hood,' said Emily, faintly.

'That's right. And James. Fine boys, full of good manners. Now, whilst we have some time, come along, all of you – tell me why you have brought me here.'

Oscar tapped the bench, signalling for them to sit down. They sat together. Eagan couldn't help but notice Sam and Emily's dazed expressions. Hadn't Oscar brought *Sam* here, he wondered, and not the other way round? Hadn't he just helped him to escape from the unliving? He shifted uneasily on the bench.

'So tell me,' Oscar repeated, 'why you have called me to this place.'

Eagan watched Sam take a deep breath. 'You brought a message to me when we met in the Fellows' Garden in Oxford. You asked me to deliver it to Brennus and Drust Hood. You gave me two letters. You said the Circle was broken and a Shadow was moving through the Otherland, that the Dead Water was lost and the Fall was dying. You asked the professors to seek the help of the Three.'

A look of profound disbelief crossed Oscar's face. 'That is a message that was delivered to me a long time ago! If you're certain that it was me who delivered it, then we have very little time. You've done well to reach me, for no doubt the Shadow will have come through the Fall. Tell me quickly all that has happened since we met. Come now, speak – you look as confused as I did all those years ago!'

Sam opened his mouth, but then came a noise that stopped him in his tracks, a low thrum that seemed to break across all their thoughts. They watched as a thousand tiny ripples skittered across the surface of the pond.

'Ah. It would appear that you have led the Shadow to me.' Oscar said the words quietly, almost to himself. The heavy thrum cam again. This time it made their vision jump. It seemed to be getting louder, perhaps closer.

'Oscar,' interrupted Eagan, 'I don't know how this is happening, but Sam and Emily met you in the Garden of Druids and you battled the Shadow, trapping it in Oxford. I have a feeling that this is still to happen.'

'There is something else,' Sam interrupted quickly. 'I was told by your wife that you led – I mean will lead – a fellowship into the Otherland. At first—'

He broke off as a shudder passed through their feet and the moonlight flickered as if something had passed through it.

'Stop!' Oscar said. 'It is dangerous to tell me what the future may hold.'

'No, listen,' Sam persisted, 'you will go in search of a child. You will travel through a place called the Dead Water. We need to know—'

'Stop!' Oscar shook his head. 'I can see you are intent on telling me all that you know,' he added, 'but please stop. Bringing the future back to the past is a dangerous thing to do!'

'My father will be killed on those shores!'

'Sam, enough!' Oscar stood, clearly startled by Sam's words.

'But if this is the past, then we can change the future!'

Oscar turned to Sam. 'This place is beyond time. Past, present and future have no meaning here. The moment you enter the garden, every moment that has ever been and every moment that will ever be fade away. I have been coming here since my father brought me, and his father before him. The Hoods have always been coming to this place. How you have found me here I cannot say for certain, but I do know that if the Shadow is coming, then we must prepare.'

He was interrupted by a haunting wail that echoed through the mist. It was a sound to break a man's courage.

'Even now, it seeks a way in. Come along, follow me.'

Oscar rose to his feet and stretched before offering a hand to Sam and Emily. Sam found it warm to the touch, although he could feel a tingling as their hands met. Emily reached out and took Eagan's hand, smiling up into his bewildered face.

No sooner had they stepped away from the pond than they were enveloped in a strange half-light. Static electricity seemed to crackle both inside and outside Eagan's head, an invisible spider's web that was impossible to brush off.

Just ahead, the landscape unravelled so they could no longer tell whether they were walking forwards or whether the ground beneath their feet was coming to meet them. There was a dizzying stillness that in places covered them in a suffocating mist. But every now and then Oscar would squeeze their hands and his voice would pull them back from the emptiness of their thoughts.

They were no longer walking in a garden – it had fallen away to reveal a tree-lined path that formed an avenue through the strange grey twilight. Every now and then it seemed to Sam that the trees and avenue would jump and flicker. Whether the place was Addison's Walk or the avenue at Howick Hall, he couldn't tell. A river meandered beside them, but he couldn't see where the waters started, or where they were going. But he knew where Oscar was taking them.

To his surprise, though, when they reached the brow of the hill where the circle of stone statues had been there was only darkness.

'Where is the Circle?' asked Emily.

'It is waiting for the last Druid.'

'The last Druid?' Sam's mouth was dry and his mind swirling.

'Only the last Druid can make the Circle whole again. It is where the beginning meets the end and the end meets the beginning.'

Just then they heard a deep thrum as if something huge was breaking the surface of the sea and drawing its first breath. The landscape was changing again and Eagan found himself standing before two huge iron gates.

'What are these gates?' he asked, but he already knew, for they were exactly how Sam had described them, and Oscar was already stepping onto the bridge.

A chill wind began to blow and Eagan drew his long knives. Sam and Emily were rooted to the spot, waiting for the Shadow to show itself, just as it had done before.

And yet Oscar had reached the centre of the bridge with only the darkness for company.

'I don't like this,' Emily managed to say through gritted teeth.

Sam suddenly felt her hand take his. When he looked at her, she was white with fear.

'It's different from last time,' she whispered. 'What if it's a trap?' What if we've been led here? What if the Shadow knows of your plan to trap it and send it back to Oxford?'

Sam felt panic rising. What if Emily was right?

'We need to get out of here!' she whispered.

'But *how*?' hissed Sam. 'And where is Culluhin?' Where was the man who had saved Eagan?

'Culluhin…' repeated Oscar slowly. 'Of course! Culluhin!' he called, 'Show yourself! You cannot hide forever. Even the dead cannot hide from me.'

But no answer came.

The tension was so great Sam thought his head would burst and all the while Emily's hand gripped his.

Eagan stepped forwards, his hands stinging from their grip on his long knives.

Then Oscar turned, with a smile that did not extend to his eyes. 'I heard you in the Way-curve, Sam!'

They no longer recognised his voice. It was now guttural and edged with venom.

'It was you who led me to Oscar. It was you who led me to the girl. It is you, like those before you, who will let in the darkness. It is you in whom men will have blind faith, and that will be their downfall.'

Standing in the middle of the bridge, his body suddenly became distorted, twisting grotesquely. Suddenly shadowy torrents were spilling out of his body and where Oscar had been standing there now stood the black-hearted stalker from the Way-curve.

A single word slid out from what could once have been a voice: '*Druidae!*'

Sam stood there frozen. He could feel the sheer weight of its malignancy, he could feel its anger rising like a black tide against them. Yet again he could feel it reaching out to strip him of his senses. It was moving, rising up before him, black and shapeless.

Tears slipped down his cheeks and he was unable to stop himself from sinking first to one knee and then a second, but a hand stopped him from sinking further. When he looked up, he found Emily's tear-stained face pleading with him not to fall.

Everything seemed to slow down. Then Eagan stepped onto the bridge.

For a moment, he was alone, standing directly in front of a vast monstrosity that was contorting itself into a towering Shadow.

Then another figure joined him. Bent, staggering, his armour blackened, Culluhin had clearly been in a terrible battle.

He turned a burnt and shredded face to Sam. 'Run! Don't look back!'

He raised his hands skyward and light seemed to flicker from them and from the edge of Eagan's knives.

When the attack came, it was ferocious. A giant wave of black fire came convulsing towards them, bursting down to crush the life out of them. But Culluhin's voice rose high above the chaos and his hands appeared to catch the wave in mid-air. It shattered into a million twisting sparks, and a terrifying wail burst out of him as they tore through his flesh.

Eagan's clothes were whipping around him; his face was contorted with pain.

The black swirling tempest came again, catching them both and throwing them down at the end of the bridge.

'*Sam!*' Emily screamed. 'Save us!'

The words burst through him, shattering the silence of his mind. Streams of dark and light erupted across his vision and he raised his left hand and it was on fire. He held Emily in one arm, while the heavenly voices of the Magdalen choir filled the night with their light and beauty.

His voice rose again, his flaming hand shielded him from the onslaught, and he threw it back. Stepping onto the bridge, he moved against the black flow, his clothes whirling around him, his voice strong and commanding and flecked with anger. At his feet, Eagan and Culluhin lay like rags in the night, crumpled and unmoving.

But even as he stood there, the light and colour started to leave him and he knew that even the flow could not save him from such an enemy. Tears burned his eyes. He had failed them all and they would pay dearly for such failure.

As the colours dimmed and the last voices drained out of his mind, he thought he heard Emily's voice.

'It cannot hurt you here.'

He had heard this voice before. As he heard it now, he noticed a strange mellifluous haze moving through his mind's eye. It seemed to envelop him in a warmth that drove the fear from his body. He saw a light flowing, drawn by a hidden current, gently pushing the long strands of darkness from his mind. Whether a form took shape in the light he couldn't tell, but when he opened his eyes there was a figure standing beside him, a woman of sublime beauty, with colours radiating from her like a newly formed rainbow after a storm.

'My dear Sam, I am here for you, but you need to listen.'

He felt a tender hand touch his face.

'Who are you?' he whispered.

'I am the Fall.'

# TALENT INSIGHT GROUP
## SPONSORSHIP OF *THE LAST DRUID*

I've known Glen Hall for 20 years now, during which time we've become great friends and very close business colleagues. He is a super guy with a heart of gold. I therefore feel honoured, as a director of the Talent Insight Group, to be sponsoring this book.

Glen has always had a thirst for literature and a burning desire to write. It is wonderful to see the result of that ambition in *The Last Druid* trilogy. I'm also inspired by the fact that a key motivation for Glen is to help those less fortunate in life. Every penny of profit made from this book is to be donated to Cash for Kids, a wonderful charity supporting disadvantaged young people who are suffering from abuse or neglect, who have special needs or who simply need extra care or guidance.

Well done, Glen, I'm really proud of you.

### *Tim Gleave*

I wasn't at all surprised when Glen told me he was going to write a book and I wasn't at all surprised when he did and it was a big success. For the whole time that I've known Glen, if he wants to do something, he invariably does it, and it is always done well.

The first volume in Glen's trilogy, *The Fall,* is about many things. For me, it's primarily about 'light' and 'dark'. We all have light and dark within us and, at various points in our lives, have light and dark thrust upon us when we least expect it.

Glen did a wonderful thing by giving all of the royalties from *The Fall* to Cash for Kids North East, effectively helping children with far too much 'dark' in their lives. Glen has provided plenty of 'light' through his incredible donation.

As a director of the Talent Insight Group, I'm very proud that our business has followed Glen's lead by donating a percentage of our profits to the same charity. As two working-class lads from northern England ourselves, it was the very least that Tim and I could do.

Likewise I'm thrilled that we are sponsoring this book, the second volume of the trilogy. It will no doubt be every bit as successful as the first.

**David Steel**

# About the Author

My love affair with books started with my primary school teacher, who gave me a copy of *Prince Caspian* when I was seven, leading thirty years later to the publication of *The Last Druid* and a continued love affair with fantasy. I was captivated by C.S. Lewis's chronicles of Narnia, I devoured the whole seven books and could have cried when I came to *The Last Battle* and realised it was the final book. You can imagine my joy when by pure chance I came across an old copy of *The Hobbit* in my middle school's rickety library. That one act of kindness from my primary school teacher led me to read English at the University of Leeds.

I have come to realise just how powerful acts of kindness can be and what effect they can have on an individual. I wanted therefore to combine my passion for business with my passion for all things literary. *The Last Druid* is a five-year project that attempts to give something back to all those children who are at risk of never having a family or the loving childhood that every child deserves.

All royalties from *The Shadow Ruins* will go to Cash for Kids.